THE AUGUR'S

ASSASSIN

A Read Between the Vines Mystery

MAISIE FRANKLIN

Printed in the United States.
Wagging Tales Press
First Printing, 2025
ISBN: 978-0-9977602-2-4

CHAPTER ONE

"What's a thirteen-letter word for 'murder'?" Dot mumbled. Though between her dentures and the pencil eraser poised between her wrinkled lips, I could hardly understand her.

The daily crossword in the New London newspaper, *The Day*, was spread out on the service counter in front of her.

"Manslaughter," I retorted. Like what I was planning for Addie, my stock clerk, for being late. Now, I was the one balancing a heavy box of 2013 Verdelho dangerously over the top of my wild chocolate mane.

Not that I didn't appreciate the Verdelho. It was a nice, dry white with a heap of character. Ironically, a lot like Addie.

That didn't mean I would enjoy either dropping on my head.

Normally, Addie's tardiness wouldn't have mattered all that much. Our business rarely picked up until sometime near lunch, but this morning's commute had been insane and we were way behind on the daily checklist.

The box teetered for a scary moment as I rose on size five tippy toes. Finally, I gave it a good shove, and it obligingly slid to the back of the cherry-wood shelf. I stood, flat-footed and relatively safe again, on the top step of the ladder and planted my hands firmly on my hips. I blew an errant lock of hair from my eyes.

"There! That should do it," I declared confidently.

"Mmm, nope!" Dot countered. "That's only twelve. By the way, have you met that handsome new boy at the butcher? Tom Sawyer?"

"As in *The Adventures of*?" I couldn't help but ask.

Dot nodded. "He's available, and he's positively yummy. You should taste his linguiça."

"What?" I asked, puzzled, not sure if the sixty-four-year-old just dropped a risqué euphemism or made a recommendation for our charcuterie plate.

Dot's nose was still buried in her crossword, but her bright blue peepers squinted mischievously over her readers.

Risqué euphemism for the win.

Dot looked innocent enough under her halo of silver-white curls, but now and then, she really made me wonder. I sighed.

"What? He stopped in for a bottle of Pinot Noir the other and we got to chatting," Dot began. "He even helped me clean up the broken bottle when I dropped the first one. Such a gentleman!"

A broken bottle? My heart-shaped face pinched in economic anguish.

"Besides," Dot continued. "If Orson can find true love at his age, certainly there's more than a little hope for you."

She was, of course, referring to Orson Tobit, our wealthy, local, third-generation horse baron who shocked the whole borough when he took Sera Hawking, a British national forty years his junior, as his blushing bride.

"I don't think so, Dot," I muttered, almost under my breath. "Orson is a special case. He got lucky."

Dot harrumphed. "What? Because some 'spiritual advisor' turned over the Queen of Hearts and told him to watch for a beautiful stranger? I'll never understand it. In my day, we went down to the soda shop, ordered an egg cream, and held a face-to-face human conversation with a boy we thought was cute. None of this new-fangled mess. Crystals. Astrology. Tinder."

Queen of Hearts or Two of Cups—I didn't think love was in the cards for me.

Ignoring Dot's tirade about modern relationships, I climbed down the ladder. I checked the temperatures on the coolers, a steady 55° Fahrenheit, wiped down the tables, and re-shelved a few stray titles from last night's book club. Sometimes I felt like I was running the place all by myself.

Wouldn't be the first time in my thirty-six years I'd ever been left holding the bag.

But that is a different story for a different day.

And, admittedly, despite all their would-be matchmaker meddling and chronic tardiness, I truly loved my employees. They had become family to this lonely, city girl turned small-town entrepreneur.

My name is Zoe. Zoe Romano. If you're like me, you love good wine. You love a good story. And you're a sucker for long, moonlit walks on the beach.

So, when my perfect Manhattan life got turned on its ear, it made all the sense in the world for this single Italian American gal to pack it all up and move to the small, coastal town of Mystic, Connecticut, and open Read Between the Wines.

It's my own little corner of heaven. A cozy, little *enoteca* — an Americanized wine and liquor library — where locals and tourists alike can check out the latest and greatest from the vine and chaff and thumb through tried-and-true classics and what's topping the best-seller lists.

We hold regular tastings and book reading events with shamelessly "punny" titles: A Connecticut Yankee in King Arthur's Port; Of Mice and Manischewitz; and The Woman in White Wine.

It was different, and goodness knows I needed something different. I just hoped Twain, Steinbeck, and Collins weren't groaning in their graves too much.

My quirky little shop sat just down Main Street from the Mystic River Bridge. Living and working near the bascule bridge required a deft manipulation of timing. You had to be strategic when you head downtown. Didn't matter if you're coming from Stonington toward Groton or the other way around. Watch the clock or you'll wind up in a line of impatient motorists when the bridge goes up.

Lights flashed. Bells rung. Two minutes up, five to seven minutes for the boats to schlep through, two minutes down — or you took the five-mile detour.

I didn't mind it. It was eleven minutes of hazelnut bliss and a soul-soothing peace to plan the day's tasting menu without Dot trying to set me up with Mystic's latest eligible bachelor or Addie nattering on about Kim Kardashian's latest butt-hugging fashion trend or Taylor's Swift's roller-coaster love life.

I swear, my stock clerk had her gel-tipped, polished talons on the gossip pulse, celebrity or otherwise, and continuously regaled us with the latest scoop on everything and everybody... if we wanted to hear it or not.

This morning, though, my eleven minutes had somehow stretched to an unusual twenty. And the lights and bells that had zipped past my beat-up old Karmann Ghia?

Definitely not from the bridge.

The traffic had remained gnarled for an additional twenty minutes, guaranteeing my late arrival. And, while the bloodhound in me had smelled a story, I had quickly given myself a mental swat on the nose.

That wasn't who I was. Not anymore. Now, I was simply Zoe Romano, owner of a charming New England wine bar and bookshop, and there wasn't anything that could steer me from that road.

As if to drive the point home, I had gripped the steering wheel firmly and pointed my classic coupe down West Main as soon as the traffic finally moved.

Read Between the Wines rested within spitting distance of Mystic Pizza. Yeah. That place the Julia Roberts' movie is named after. Which—I have to admit proudly—is prime real estate when you consider the foot traffic it encourages into my store.

The popular tourist magnet still did a steady business even though a couple of decades separated it from its 1988 romantic comedy namesake. Its comfortable but noisy dining room offered a mean eggplant parm, a decent *'ah-beetz*, and, truth be told, my favorite comfort food—grinders.

Something about the spices and satisfying fattiness of a good Genoa salami. The creamy, almost nutty, and slightly salty bite of layered provolone dolce. And that satisfying crunch of marinated cabbage that just lets you know you've eaten a proper meal.

Every now and again, though, I did miss a greasy slice of Brooklyn pie. Sue me.

I stole a glance at the wall clock. My customers would be missing the noon tasting menu if I didn't put some hustle into it.

"Would you quit fiddling with that crossword and help me?" I verbally nudged Dot. "I need you to prep the 2010 Relentless. You know. The Syrah? I want to pair it with the Maytag Bleu for this afternoon's tasting. I really think the full body will stand up well to the tang and pepper of the cheese. Oh, and do we have any dried apricots left? From the Chenin Blanc showcase last night? I'd love to put those out, too."

I flitted like a rabid hummingbird from shelf to table to cash wrap and back again, pulling glasses, folding napkins, and checking the daily bank.

Dot reluctantly pried herself from her crossword and waddled around the counter. "You know, Zoe, if there's one thing this old lady's learned in sixty-four years, it's that sometimes you need to stop and smell the roses or before you know it, girlie, you're gonna be up to your ears in dirt and daisies instead!"

She picked up a tray of Bordeaux glasses and moseyed her way toward the store's small prep kitchen.

Before I could snap back a witty riposte, the shop's door burst open in a wild flurry of bells, pink, and pointy, loopy, nose jewelry.

"She's dead!" Addie blurted louder than the bubblegum color of her hair.

I winced at the sudden crash of twelve glass Bordeaux stems behind me. Between broken wine bottles and decimated crystal, Dot was going to bankrupt me.

"Mercy!" Dot cried.

Dead? Wait! What?

Confusion at Addie's morose proclamation overrode my dismay. I moved to Mystic because it's a nice, quiet town. Nothing ever happens here.

Not like...

I shook my head, not sure if I heard Addie correctly. "Say that again."

Addie sucked in a deep breath and exploded again in full-on town crier mode. "She's dead! D-E-A-D! As a doornail."

I waved my hands in the air. "Slow down, Addie.

Who's dead?"

A flood of information continued to gush from her mouth. "Madame Zorina. The psychic. You know. She's got the shop next door."

Madame Zorina.

How could I forget my eccentric mall mate? Strange zither music vibrating the crystal stemware through the walls. Overpowering clouds of patchouli wafting through the air, nearly strong enough to quell the unique, malodorous perfume of the Epoisses de Bourgogne cheese we sometimes served at tastings.

And we'd nearly had to cancel our Fifty Shades of Grey Goose Martini night when an argument had erupted so loudly through the thin shop walls, our readers could hardly hear themselves talk.

I guess someone hadn't liked their fortune that night.

Dot's puckered puss announced her opinion before a word dropped from her lips. "That Carly Simon wanna-be with the Birkenstocks and Tarot cards? Pah!" She waved a liver-spotted hand. "What a bunch of hooey."

Addie drew her face into the sternest frown she could muster with a lip ring. "Dot! Just because you don't understand something doesn't mean it's not magical."

"I don't understand the Weight Minder's points system either, but that doesn't make it magical. I just don't think it's very honorable to bilk hard-working folks out of their hard-earned money to make some crazy fortune cookie predictions and reveal some made-up name of some mystery lover. It's positively criminal."

"What happened, Addie?" I intervened before it became a spirited debate over metaphysics.

"Well, you know Madame Zorina is…was my neighbor, right?" Addie began. Her voice hitched a little as she corrected her tense. I nodded somberly. "Not that she was a good neighbor or anything," Addie continued. "She let her garbage cans overflow in the alley. She always took my parking place. Her television was too loud half the time. And her door banged as people came and went at all times of the night."

"And she peddled hokum," Dot added from the peanut gallery. I glared at her. She held her hands up in defense. "Reap what you sow. That's all I'm saying," she muttered.

Addie ignored Dot. "So, there I was, on my way to work. Totally on time." Dot sniggered.

Addie just rolled her eyes. "I was just getting ready to lock my front door when the driveway lights up with a paramedic unit and Chief Cody's squad car."

Pitta-pat.

The skip of my heart caught me off guard when Addie mentioned Derek Cody's name. The handsome police officer had turned many a female head in the borough when he transferred to the Groton Police Department from the NYPD just a few weeks prior.

Mine was one of them.

The big city cop was certainly easy on the eyes with his intense baby blues and jet-black hair. A premature streak of white feathered through the ebony locks, just at the temple. And he always ordered his coffee "black, two sugars" at The Lighthouse when I picked up my morning croissant and hazelnut latté.

Not that I was paying any attention, mind you.

"Lights blazing. Sirens wailing. Didn't you hear it? It was noisier than the Blessing of the Fleet parade!" Addie rambled. My eyes widened a little.

The lights and sirens on the bridge.

My inner bloodhound scratched. Scratched at the story like it was an irritating flea.

Down, boy.

"Mr. Iliev, our creepy stalker landlord, found her. In a heap at the bottom of the stairs. He says he went there to collect the rent. Personally, I think he went there to peek through her windows again, the bug-eyed Peeping Tom. Do you know I caught him once, leering at me while I was doing yoga? There I was, in Happy Baby Pose, Zen as you please, and that weirdo was drooling through my living room window. Seriously! I swear he was actually drooling! Creep had the stones to ask me out. Like, on a date! Like that was ever gonna happen. Thought he was going to pop a vein in that scrawny little neck the way he started yelling at me. Called me a bunch of names in some crazy language. But that was months ago. Anyway... so he says he knocked on Madame Zorina's door, went in, and there she was. Dead. Lying at the bottom of the staircase that leads to the second floor of the townhouse. Says her face was covered with blood and bruises. She was cold, and she didn't have a pulse. He called 911."

"What are the police saying?" I asked.

"Accident. There was no forced entry at the front door, and her Tarot cards were scattered across the floor along with glass under her from a broken picture frame from the foyer table. It was horrible. It looks like she just fell down the stairs, knocked into the accent table, and hit her head on the floor."

"Guess she didn't see that coming," Dot quipped, back at her crossword puzzle behind the counter.

"Dot!" I scolded, but my bloodhound keened.

"Aha!" Dot exclaimed abruptly.

My heart jumped in my chest…again. It had had so much stimulation this morning, I think I could safely skip the cardio circuit at the gym today.

"What, Dot?" I burst, wondering if she had some great insight on the case.

"Assassination!" she answered and tapped her pencil to the crossword. "Thirteen letter word for 'murder'."

My inner bloodhound? He howled.

CHAPTER TWO

I tried to push Madame Zorina's death from my mind and busied myself getting ready for the noon tasting. I lined a dozen or so glasses up on the bar and picked one up to make sure Dot had put the right stemware on the tray.

An inadvertent chuckle burbled to my lips. With her ribald opinions on men and love, she should be an expert. I could almost hear her now.

Size does matter.

I didn't know about men, but with wine glasses, it was certainly true. The glass you served a wine in was pivotal to the overall experience. It didn't matter whether you were pouring a red, white, rosé, sparkling, or fortified. How a wine played on the nose was integral — and the glass you used made all the difference.

Almost every grape varietal had a specifically designed glass fashion to highlight or mellow the particular attributes of the grape type — the fruitiness, the puckery tannins, the stringent alcohol.

Syrahs — like the Relentless I planned to showcase — called for a tall glass, tapered to focus the fruit. The wide bowl allowed you to swirl — aerating and mellowing the tannins properly.

"Perfect." I noted my approval.

Satisfied, I turned to grab the hors d'oeuvres tray — the empty hors d'oeuvres tray.

"Dot!" I bellowed.

My cashier looked up, eyes wide behind her bifocals. She looked like a startled chipmunk storing food for the winter.

I gestured to the empty tray.

"What?" she mumbled through her mouth full of food. She swallowed. "I had a weigh-in this morning. I was starving."

I threw my hands in the air and huffed.

"You're really going to be starving if I have to close the shop because no one has a reason to come in."

Dot waved her hands and rolled her eyes. She reached into her purse and pulled out a twenty-dollar bill. She pressed it into my hand.

"Oh, stop bellyaching. Here. Just take this down to the butcher's and pick up some more." She offered a mischievous grin along with the cash.

I eyeballed her, then pointed a waggling finger. "You did this on purpose — so I'd have to meet this butcher fellow."

Dot crossed her arms over her squat paunch and turned her head. "I have absolutely no idea what you're talking about." A beat passed. She opened one eye and rolled it towards me. "His name is Tom."

"Thanks, Dr. Ruth," I grumbled as I headed out the door onto Main Street, but my analogy fell miles short of the mark. The ninety-some-odd-year-old, world-renowned sex therapist had absolutely nothing on Dorothy Richards.

*****

"What can I do for you?" Tom Sawyer's smooth, rolling baritone interrupted my blatant stare.

Oh, I dunno. A few choice things come to mind.

I blinked, flushed with sudden red-hot embarrassment. I stood like a deer in headlights as he leaned two tanned muscular arms on the counter.

My "Next Customer" ticket went limp in my hand.

Dot hadn't been overselling the butcher employee's good looks. His skin had a swarthy cast, an exotic tone that gave his deep brown eyes an air of haunting mystery.

"I need a piece of meat," I stammered, immediately regretting the words as they tumbled from my lips.

This was going oh so well.

Was it too late to just serve cheese-in-a-can on crackers?

Tom's dark eyebrows shot up but, unlike me, he pulled himself together and mustered a professional response. "Sure. Tenderloin? Chops? Roast?"

He turned to tear a section of wax-lined butcher paper off the cutting roll.

"I like a nice rump, myself," a voice creaked at my elbow. I turned to see Mrs. Potter, the town librarian, and the only other customer in the shop, standing behind me. She stared appreciatively at Tom's backside. "Don't you?"

"Linguiça!" I blurted and wheeled back toward the counter. "I need linguiça."

"Yes, ma'am," Tom replied, apparently oblivious he had a burgeoning fan base in town.

I winced. "Please, it's Zoe. Not ma'am."

Tom smiled a thousand-watt smile, brilliant against his tanned skin. "All right... Zoe. How much?"

"A pound or two should be fine. Thanks."

"Got it." He went about preparing my order. I managed a smug smile.

Well, all right, Zoe.

I gave myself a mental pat on the back. I'd managed a five-second conversation with a man without sticking my foot in my mouth.

Okay. A few toes, maybe...

"Did you hear the news?" Mrs. Potter whispered. "About the psychic?"

One single, unequivocal fact ranked true about small towns. It didn't matter if it smacked of the salt air of the eastern seaboard or was nestled among the pungent pines of the Oregon forests. News — bad or good — traveled faster than a social media trend.

"She's dead," Mrs. Potter pronounced. A loud clatter rattled through the butcher shop as Tom dropped the metal pan of Portuguese sausage and it hit the ground.

A garlic and paprika-scented cloud filled the air as the meat smacked fat against the glazed ceramic tile. I

17

groaned inwardly.

Squeeze-cheese it is.

"I'm so sorry, ma'am," Tom muttered the apology as he scrambled to pick up the fallen links. "I think we have some more in the chiller."

He opened the tall, silver door and carried the tray of mounded, shapeless pork. I noticed the worried, almost frightened look he cast over his shoulder as he disappeared behind it.

I sighed and turned toward the librarian. "Yes, Mrs. Potter. Unfortunately, I heard about Madame Zorina. Terrible stuff."

The librarian nodded. "Certainly is. I knew her, you know." The worry lines between Mrs. Potter's brows deepened. "Not that I was into any of that silly business. Crystal balls might work well as a lawn ornament—I have one or two gazing balls myself—but to think you can divine the future from one question? Well, that's just silly." She stared vacantly into the distance.

I tilt my head. "Then how did you know her?"

"Well, the library was her first stop when she rolled into town. Always warms my heart when folks make signing up for a library card a priority."

"A library card?" I felt that old, familiar twitch.

"Most people get in touch with the gas company or the power company before they do anything else in a new town." Mrs. Potter rolled her shoulders back and lifted her chin. "I suppose the written word still holds value for some people."

"Of course." I lowered my head, chagrined. Mrs. Potter accepted the gesture as my apology. Either that or the urge to gossip was just too strong.

"Of course, the only thing she seemed interested in was the obituaries." A pensive look crossed her features. But then she leaned in conspiratorially. "Do you know her real name isn't even Zorina? It's..."

"I'm afraid I have some bad news," Tom's deep voice interrupted.

I tore myself away from Mrs. Potter's juicy revelation and look at the troubled look on the butcher's face. "Yes?"

"We're all out of linguiça."

"Isn't that a shame?" Mrs. Potter declared. "But you still have some of that delightful rump left, right, Tom?" She practically shoved me out of the way.

I turned and pushed through the door to leave. Well, I thought as I headed back toward the bookshop, my charcuterie tray might be empty at today's tasting, but my fevered brain was full — full of questions about the mysterious death of Madame Zorina...

...or whoever she was.

CHAPTER THREE

The question of why Madame Zorina had made the Mystic and Noank Library her first stop tumbled through my mind as I walked back to the bookshop.

What was so important to warrant its priority?

Before I could formulate any plausible theories, loud voices spilled from my shop into the early afternoon air.

"I don't give a flying fig if you're Queen Elizabeth herself. That fancy accent will not get you a faster answer." The irritated voice belonged to Dot.

The crisp consonants of the responding voice suggested it belonged to Orson Tobit's soon-to-be bride, Sera Hawking. "If you're going to be so terribly rude about it, then I'll be happy to take my business elsewhere."

Over my dead body.

I looked up to see Madame Zorina's sign and cringed.

Figuratively, of course.

I dove into the shop to play referee and instantly felt like the prom queen's nerdy best friend. Sera

Hawking stood at the cash wrap, looking as cool and composed as the Duchess of Cambridge in a baby blue Beulah London belted frock with matching Aldo heels. She tossed her shimmering, impossibly perfect hair. I couldn't believe it was natural. It cascaded over her delicate shoulder.

I took a quick survey of my attire, a clean but generic button-down Oxford, faded blue jeans, and five-year-old Chucks. I shrugged. When you're on your feet all day, you dress for practicality — not *Town and Country*.

I took several determined strides towards Sera. "I assure you, that won't be necessary. Sera Hawking, right?" I flashed her a winning smile and held out a hand, which she accepted after a fleeting hesitation.

She broke into a smile. "Soon to be Sarah Tobit. That is, if I can secure ninety-nine bottles of Dom Perignon for my engagement party this weekend."

"Ninety-nine?!" Addie squawked as she came out onto the sales floor from the stockroom, a green rag clutched in her left hand.

What could she have been dusting in there?

She shoved it into her pocket as she approached. "Are you inviting the whole town?"

Sarah laughed. Even her laugh sounded properly British. "No, no. It's just, well, I've always wanted to have a fairytale engagement and wedding — like Princess Diana — and Orson, prince that he is, is determined to see that I have them."

Diana and Charles. A kindergarten teacher and a prince. A fairy tale match if ever there was one.

I considered the relationship between the beautiful

young woman in my shop with the dowdy, markedly older, horse baron and I was hard-pressed not to draw the parallel.

Hopefully, this fairytale ended in a happy-ever-after.

"Princess Diana," Addie sighed, a dreamy, faraway gleam in her eyes. She rested her elbow on the counter, propping her chin in her hand. "Now, she was a classy lady. Do you know she once walked across a minefield and Angola while visiting children who had lost their limbs to active mines? I hope I can do something that meaningful one day."

"I know what you mean," Sera replied. "I want to be just like her, too. And that's why I'm desperately trying to find someone competent enough to take my order for ninety-nine bottles of 1961 Dom Perignon Brut. That's how many Diana ordered for her wedding, you know."

As a matter of fact, I *did* know. I also knew that today each of those bottles would cost around nine hundred dollars.

It didn't matter what I thought of Miss Hawking's May-December romance with Orson. An order like that could keep the shop afloat for months.

Addie's face puckered, and she stalked away, mumbling to herself. I looked after my stock clerk. She'd get over it... right?

"Can you help me, Miss Romano?" Sera asked. I scratched my head. I had no idea how we'd pull this off—I didn't have that much stock on hand—but I couldn't afford to lose this sale.

"Absolutely. You can count on us."

Dot harrumphed from her station. I shot her a warning glance. Her brows raised along with her hands, and she looked the other way.

"Wonderful!" Sera clapped. I scrambled behind the counter. "Let me just find a purchase order."

"I'm sure you can handle the details. Just bill it to Tobit Breeding Ranch."

"But I need you to sign some things," I began, but Sera was already out the door.

CHAPTER FOUR

Emily Post, the original queen of etiquette, decreed that an invited guest should never show up empty-handed. They should always bring a nominal gift to express gratitude to their host: a bouquet for a casual dinner; a potted plant for a housewarming; and a bottle of wine for a murder investigation.

Okay. Maybe that last one was never exactly mentioned in *Etiquette in Society*. But as I strolled up the sidewalk to the brown brick of the Groton Police Department, I figured it couldn't hurt. Especially when you factored in that I wasn't exactly "invited" either. And Madame Zorina's death hadn't been classified as a murder...yet.

The article in the morning issue of *The Day* described it as an ongoing investigation into a tragic accident. But as I had lain awake all night, counting the divots in the orange-peel texture of the ceiling, that old bloodhound kept circling back to the argument we had heard coming from the psychic's shop just a day before her demise.

Someone hadn't been happy with Madame

Zorina. The question was, had they been incensed enough to commit murder?

So, ignoring the teasing from Dot, I had whipped up a welcome basket, including a nice Pinot Grigio, for our new police chief and was now on my way to deliver it and stick my cold, wet nose somewhere where it probably didn't belong.

"No, Mr. O'Leary, the Groton Police Department does take kidnapping very seriously. Yes, I do understand that they have become like family to you. Yes, I did see them decked out in the golfing tams when the PGA came through. But, Mr. O'Leary, the police department simply doesn't have the personnel right now to track down thirty-six missing flamingo lawn ornaments."

Myrna Lawson massaged the wrinkles deepening on her high forehead and adjusted the black headset over her tightly twisted bun. The desk sergeant shot me a look of exasperation, pointed a finger at the headset, and then twirled her index finger in the universal sign for "crazy".

"Yes, Mr. O'Leary. Even if you received a ransom note. Yes, sir, the Chief received your email with the picture of the ransom note written on the bird. Yes, I am glad Arturo was returned as well and I'm sorry he was defaced. Don't worry, Mr. O'Leary, I assure you. We will look into it further as soon as we have someone available. Yes, sir. Have a good day." She hit the disconnect button and sighed heavily. "If I ever try to purchase a garden gnome or a gazing ball, shoot me. That poor man has a seriously unhealthy attachment to his landscaping decorations."

"You got it, Myrna," I replied.

Myrna eyed the gourmet basket in my arms. She nodded her head. "That for the chief?"

I considered Myrna's suggestive stare and looked down at the basket. Suddenly, I was second-guessing my whole brilliant plan.

"Um, yes. Dot thought it would be a nice gesture to, well, you know, welcome the chief to the Mystic area."

A smile quirked at the edge of Myrna's lips. "Trust me, honey. You're not having any thoughts that the rest of us gals haven't had. Who knows? Maybe you'll have better luck. He's already turned down three date offers and a marriage proposal. In his defense, the marriage proposal was from Gertrude Sayers. She's already proposed to the mailman, the butcher, and a barbershop pole…and that's just this week! She sure keeps them hopping at the home."

A dry, embarrassed chuckle escaped my lips. She jerked her head toward the corridor. "He's in his office. Down the hall. To the left."

I schlepped the basket through the lobby, past the familiar blue and yellow logo of the police department. As I gazed at the tall lighthouse in its background, I reminded myself that was all I was here to do—shine a light on what happened to Madame Zorina.

Not get a date.

I passed a few closed doors before I got to the one standing ajar near the end of the hall. The brass plate on the door read "Derek Cody—Chief of Police," but the office stood empty. I shook my head.

This was a ridiculous idea. What was I thinking?

I simply didn't do this kind of thing anymore. I would just leave the basket on the chief's desk and haul my tuches back to Read Between the Wines and leave the investigations to the investigators.

Who did I think I was?

"Zoe Romano." The deep, syrupy baritone behind me elicited a squeal of fright, and I nearly dropped the basket. A pair of shirt-sleeved, well-muscled arms reached out and deftly snagged the basket from certain gravity.

A pair of intense azure eyes caught my own hazel ones with an intent gaze. "Careful, now. I wouldn't want to have to charge you with alcohol abuse. That happens to be a very good Pinot Grigio in there."

Pitta-pat.

Chief Cody handed the basket back to me. The chief had forgone the crisp, creased blue uniform shirt of the department and had opted, instead, for a pale pink, collared golf shirt.

The cuff of the sleeve hugged snugly over the swell of his pronounced biceps. The tail of the shirt veed in dramatically at his trim waist, neatly tucking into the slim beltline of his slim, tailored khakis. Boat shoes peeked out from under the pressed hem of each leg.

The only thing that prevented me from picturing him on the deck of some trim sloop instead of running the police station was the serious black harness that fitted over his muscled shoulders and the even more serious sidearm tucked discreetly into its holster.

Luckily, I found my voice before the drool slid

south down my chin. "No, no, no," I foisted the basket back into his tan arms. I wiped my moist palms on the front of my jeans.

Attempt to look cool, Zoe. For crying out loud!

"The, uh, girls at the shop just whipped this up to welcome you to Mystic. Somebody had to deliver it and, well, I guess I drew the short straw."

Short straw? Seriously?

Mental facepalm.

I wasn't sure, but I thought I saw a hint of disappointment settle into the chief's square jaw. A momentary look of confusion passed over his face.

"Um, thank you?" He graciously accepted the basket and walked it over to his desk. He leaned against the side. His long legs stretched out in front of him as he crossed his arms over his muscled chest. "Please extend my thanks to the ladies for the thoughtful gift. It was very kind."

"Certainly, Chief," I managed.

He rubbed a contemplative hand across the five o'clock shadow gathering on his cleft chin. "Zoe Romano. You know, there used to be an investigative reporter named Romano. Worked for the *Times*. I always read her articles. Good stuff. Solid research." He paused and contemplated me. "Any relation?"

I managed a weak smile. "Guess that cat's out of the bag. Guilty as charged."

Chief Cody stood tall and pulled himself up to his full six-foot-three height. He strode toward me. "Please?" He pulled a chair from the front of his desk and gestured for me to sit.

Okay, so we're doing this.

I obliged. He rounded the corner of his oak desk and sat behind it.

I rapped a sharp-knuckled fist on the hard surface. "Good and hard."

The chief's brows shot high.

I whiffled my hands. "No, no, no. I was talking about the desk. Solid choice for Mystic. Tough as nails."

My unintentional double entendre drew a modest smile from the chief.

Maybe I hadn't completely botched this after all.

The chief leaned forward, elbows on the desk, and tented the tips of his fingers together. He sucked in a deep breath, and that syrupy voice melted into easy conversation. "Miss Romano."

"Zoe, please," I insisted.

Another smile. "Zoe. You did some in-depth coverage on New York psychics a few years back. Their networks. How they worked. Tools of the trade."

I nodded and, honestly, squirmed just a little. The memories threatening to surface pinched like the gripping adhesive of a protective bandage over a deep cut. I winced. Sometimes it was just better to suck it up and just rip the bandage off.

A heavy sigh escaped the drawn bow of my lips. "Yes. A three-part series, actually. It was, uh, the last piece I did for the *Times*, before…before," I stammered in hesitation. I sucked in a huge breath. "Before I moved to Mystic."

The chief cocked his head. He must have sensed there was more to the story but chose discretion over curiosity.

"Well, Zoe," he continued. My stomach did a little flip at the gentle emphasis he put on my name. "I'm hoping I can impose and maybe ask for a little help."

"I'll do whatever I can, Chief."

"Thank you for that." His sincerity was nearly as heart-warming as his wide, genuine grin. "I assume you've heard about Noreen Cox's death." He saw the question on my furrowed brow. "You may know her better as Madame Zorina."

"Yes," I replied. I wasn't too surprised that "Madame Zorina" was not her real name. In my experience, very few psychics used their legal names. I guess "Mary Smith" doesn't exactly invoke the requisite air of mysticism. "It's kind of the talk of the town at the moment."

The chief nodded. "No kidding. And the gossip's about to get a lot juicier when I announce that the M.E. is going to declare her death a homicide."

My eyes opened wide as two steamed clams at Abbott's in Noank. "Excuse me?"

Chief Cody leaned back in his leather chair, exhaustion settling into his features. "It's true. Noreen Cox, Madame Zorina, was murdered."

CHAPTER FIVE

"Murdered," I repeated, though with less astonishment in my voice than the chief apparently expected. He raised one perfect, dark eyebrow over his blue eyes.

"You're not surprised," he stated rather matter-of-factly.

"I have a confession to make, Chief," I began.

A look of genuine concern passed over his handsome features.

"No, no, no! Not that kind of confession!"

Way to bury the lead, Zoe.

Relief flooded his chiseled face. I rushed to explain myself. "I didn't come here just to give you the welcome basket. I have some information. Information about Madame Zorina. I wasn't certain if it was relevant, but considering what you've just shared, I think it just may be."

Curious, the chief leaned forward. "I'm listening."

"Last week, I heard some pretty intense voices coming from Madame Zorina's shop."

"An argument?" Chief Cody asked.

"The tenor of the conversation was definitely heated," I replied.

The chief grabbed a pen from his desk and reached for the small notebook in his back pocket. "Did you recognize the voices, by chance?"

I shook my head. "Only Madame Zorina's. We had a lively book club discussion going on in the shop. Twenty-five old ladies giggling about S&M isn't exactly conducive to eavesdropping."

Both of the chief's eyebrows rose. And I wasn't certain, but I thought I detected a hint of pink at the tips of his ears. He cleared his throat loudly, regaining some composure. "When was this argument?" he gruffed.

I thought about it for a second. "Tuesday last. Around seven-thirty in the evening."

He scratched a note on the pad and looked up. "And you didn't see anyone leaving her shop, right?"

"Sorry. No," came my disappointed reply. "I was up to my ears in blue-hairs and bondage."

The chief nearly sprayed his coffee across the desk.

Composure? Yeah. Blown.

I groaned internally. At the rate of mental face palms I was generating in this conversation, my face was going to have a permanent handprint.

Fortunately, the chief graciously refrained from any awkward comments and busied himself daubing at the spewed coffee with a handful of napkins.

"I wish I had more to offer," I muttered.

Chief Cody set down his pencil. "That's okay. I appreciate what you could tell me. There's something else, though."

"Oh?"

"Something I always appreciated about your work, Zoe? You always backed up your facts with good, solid research. Unlike a lot of reporters these days, who rush to put misinformation out on the front stoop of world news, you? You knew your stuff. And it showed."

I mentally willed the flush threatening to blush my cheeks back down and resisted the urge to toe the floor like a sheepish schoolgirl. I delivered a polite and professional response instead. "Thank you, Chief. It's always nice when someone appreciates your work."

"It's more than just appreciation." He paused for a moment. It looked like he was mentally wrestling with something but came to a decision and pressed on. "A good cop, no matter how good he thinks he is... he can't do it alone. He needs to build, well, relationships." That awkward flush crept its way back to my cheeks.

"Sometimes it's with fellow cops. Sometimes it's with CI's. Sometimes it's with folks who have specialized information or expertise in a particular field," he continued.

The flush cooled. My brows knit together. Maybe I wasn't quite ready for this.

I did a verbal backpedal. "I run a specialty food and bookstore, Chief. If you want to know what wine to pair with puttanesca or which vodka makes Tolstoy titillating, I'm your gal."

Chief Cody broke into another ingratiating grin. "I'd rather pick your brain about these so-called 'psychics' and all the bunk and rubbish they push."

I let loose a snigger. "Careful, Chief. If Dot hears you talking, you may get another marriage proposal."

"Pardon?"

"Never mind," I quickly responded. I considered the Chief's offer for just a moment. The blip of my pulse quickened a few ticks.

The rabbit hole was an awfully slippery slope. If I followed the chief down into Wonderland, Cheshire Cat smile and all, I wasn't at all certain I could find my way back this time.

But it's just this one case, I reasoned. And all I had to do was answer a few simple questions. I gripped the arms of the chair.

Yeah. And I've sometimes believed as many as six impossible things before breakfast.

CHAPTER SIX

The sun hung low. It spilled warm light through the shop's front window. Shadows stretched across the wooden floorboards. They wavered with the motion of the nearby harbor breeze that brought the scent of salt and brine in through the open windows.

Bottles of wine lined up along the counter, their labels simple and inviting, ready for the evening crowd. The familiar blend of old books and wine lingered in the air. Vanilla undertones added a softer edge, a detail I never tired of.

An unbidden thought occurred to me. Books aged like wine—they just got better with time. A tiny snort escaped me.

Maybe better, given the price of some first editions.

My meeting with Chief Cody had fanned the embers of curiosity into a tiny, flickering flame. I hadn't felt that way in a while and I wasn't certain what to do with it.

We didn't get into the nitty gritty of the case because an anonymous tip came in on Arthur's missing flamingos and the chief rolled out, but we planned to meet the next day. For now, I felt safer keeping that light under a basket.

I hovered near the counter and adjusted wine glasses with the precision of a jeweler. I stepped back and tilted my head one way, then the other.

"Perfect," I declared and gave a last nudge to a glass that had dared to misalign itself.

"Are we hosting royalty, or just the usual suspects?" Dot asked. She slid a chair into place at the closest table as we prepped for the evening's book club.

"Presentation matters, Dot. You can't just plop glasses down and hope for the best."

I was lucky I even had any glasses left!

No thanks to you, Mrs. Richards.

Dot bit back a grin. "And here I thought wine was the star of the show."

"It is," I sniffed, "but it deserves a proper stage."

The book club tumbled in with all the grace of a stampede. Mrs. Potter led the charge, clutching her annotated copy of *The Count of Monte Cristo*, sticky notes bristling like a hedgehog. "Dumas is a master, of course, but some of these translations butcher the nuances," she declared to no one in particular. Her spectacles glinted under the warm glow of the shop lights.

"Youse guys," Deidre, the hairdresser from three doors down, drawled, her Jersey Shore showing. She breezed in, her leopard-print blouse a spectacle all its own. She paused dramatically near the counter and tossed her scarf over one shoulder. "If someone doesn't figure out how to stop gawking at the damned bridge and actually drive, I'm going to string lights on my chest just to give them something real to stare at."

Dot snorted at that.

Howard Trent lingered by the door. His sharp eyes scanned the wine display like a hawk searching for prey. He sniffed and pointed at the bottle on the counter. "Champagne? Bold choice. Hopefully not too dry."

Their chatter rose like birdsong in the snug space—more like a flock of chattering seagulls. Snippets floated past me—Mrs. Potter's granddaughter landed a lead role in a school play, Deidre's endless battle against split ends, and, inevitably, the disappearance of Mr. O'Leary's flamingos. Arthur looked quite put out.

I tried not to smirk, though the mental image of pink plastic birds in a covert heist was hard to shake.

Dot raised a glass. "Ladies and gentlemen, the wine awaits!"

"Can we please start with the book this time?" Mrs. Potter asked. She scooted forward eagerly in her chair. "I'm really excited to get everyone's take on Dumas' theme of revenge. I mean, can revenge really ever stand in for justice?"

"I'd consider it," Arthur muttered under his breath as he plopped down on the chair next to her. "If I find the turkeys that absconded my flamingos..."

Dot clapped her hands and commanded the attention of the room. "All right, everyone, settle down! Toni, put a cork in it. Literally. You know the rules— libations before literature!" She pointed to the centerpiece bottle on the counter. "Tonight's feature? The Count of Monte Cristal!"

Deidre squealed, her leopard-print-clad arms flapping. "Ooh! Cristal! You really pulled out the stops, Zoe!" Her long, glittery nails clicked together as she clapped.

I pulled a face. "Not quite. This shop, unfortunately, has a meager budget, so we're cheating a little." I grabbed a bottle of Prosecco from the counter and held it aloft like a trophy. "Tonight, we're embracing the sparkly life on a budget."

"Who cares? Bubbles are bougée!" Deidre beamed.

Howard squinted suspiciously at the label. "It's not a Norton, is it? The Glera grapes make my lips pucker," he sniffed. He adjusted his tie like he was about to host a master class in oenology.

Dot raised an eyebrow. Her retort cut through the room. "Hate to break it to you, Howard, but it's not the grapes doing that."

Deidre let out a bray of laughter that startled Mr. O'Leary. Mrs. Potter snickered into her hand.

Howard straightened, offended, his signature puckered scowl wrinkling his lips. "Some of us appreciate a subtle sweetness."

Deidre leaned in toward Dot and whispered. "The amount of sugar that man needs to be sweet? Good thing I carry my insulin pen."

Ritual sparring out of the way, the members of the club seemed like they were ready to fill their glasses and settle in for the evening's book discussion.

Suddenly, the bell above the door jangled wildly. Bernie Russo, Mystic's part-time medical examiner and full-time source of quirky charm, burst in like an over-eager prom date.

"Oh, joy," Dot grumbled. "Doctor Death."

Bernie clutched a bouquet of daisies, their sunny centers practically glowing under the shop's warm lights. His tweed jacket looked freshly pressed, though his bowtie was slightly askew, like it couldn't quite keep up with his enthusiasm.

"Dot, my love!" he began, his voice carrying the theatrical weight of a man used to delivering bad news, but with style. "These are for you."

Dot stopped her glass of Prosecco halfway to her lips. "For me? What's the occasion? Did I finally kick the bucket, and you're here to deliver the eulogy?"

"Not at all," Bernie insisted. He held the flowers out like a peace offering. "Just a token of my... admiration."

The room quieted for a beat before Deidre leaned over, her leopard-print sleeve brushing Dot's arm. "Looks like you've got yourself a secret admirer." She grinned slyly, then surveyed the room of bug-eyed voyeurs and cleared her throat. "Or not so secret."

Dot's wrinkled lips twitched. I sipped my wine and hid a smile as Dot shook her head. She grabbed the flowers and tucked them into the crook of her arm. "Yeah, well, don't get too comfortable, Doc. I hear this town's still got a murder to solve, you know."

"You're not wrong. Ever seen what a Ten of Swords tarot card can do to a throat?"

A Tarot card?

The room fell silent, save for the hum of the wine fridge. Mrs. Potter lowered her book and adjusted her glasses. Deidre froze mid-sip. Her eyes darted to Dot like she expected a punchline.

"What in the world, Bernie?" Dot finally asked, her voice tinged with equal parts exasperation and suspicion. "Are you trying to ruin Prosecco night, or is this some kind of warped icebreaker?"

Bernie raised his hands. "Just saying, these cases stick with you. More exciting than fly-fishing at any rate. I need something to keep the old gray cells…" he cast a suggestive look in Dot's direction, "…titillated." Dot rolled her eyes. Bernie pressed on. "And Zorina's death? Freaky doesn't begin to cover it. But that's all I can say."

"Gracious heavens," Mrs. Potter murmured. Her hand flew to her pearls.

Deidre let out a nervous laugh, though it was clear she wasn't sure if Bernie was joking or dead serious. "Dot, I think your suitor has a flair for the macabre."

I glanced at Bernie with sparked curiosity. Chief Cody hadn't filled me in on all the details yet. "Zorina? As in Madame Zorina? What's that got to do with Tarot cards?"

Bernie met my gaze, a flicker of something unreadable crossing his face before he shrugged. "Let's just say… whatever you think happened to Zorina?" He paused, letting the weight settle. "It's worse."

He shifted his focus back to Dot, but my mind raced. The gears in my brain worked frantically, trying to piece together the scraps of what he had revealed.

Whatever Bernie knew about Zorina's death, it was far more than Chief Cody let on. That little flickering flame I was keeping under a basket…

Yeah, it was turning into a five-alarm fire.

CHAPTER SEVEN

Tarot cards have not always been tools of divination. When these playing cards originally arrived on the European scene some six centuries ago, they were not even called "tarot" cards. They were known, instead, as *trionfi* and were used to play any number of trick-taking card games called *tarocchini*, originally in the Bologna area of Italy.

It was not until the late 18th century when the cards came into use as a divinatory tool, and not until even later, into the 20th century, when the now eminent Rider-Waite tarot deck would first come into use.

Regardless of whether the deck is the traditional, symbolic Rider-Waite, the brooding and foreboding Thoth deck, designed and favored by infamous occultist, Aleister Crowley, or the quirky and playfully erotic images of The Tarot of the Silicon Dawn, the decks are largely or wholly comprised of seventy-eight traditional arcana cards.

When any of the twenty-two Major Arcana cards turn up in a reading, like The Fool, The Lovers, or The Hanged Man, the supposition exists that events are transpiring that will pull us toward a given path or destiny.

Conversely, the Minor Arcana cards symbolize mundane life and all its daily trials and tribulations. They're meant to guide simple, daily decisions—like whether to drop $350 on that Michael Kors bag or buy groceries.

If anyone had ever bothered to ask me, it was a no-brainer.

Pasta over purses. Every time.

And it certainly didn't require divination through some mysterious Tetraktys Spread or an enigmatic Celtic Cross reading.

As if Tarot interpretation wasn't convoluted enough between the Major and Minor Arcana cards, the various spreads and decks, things really got confusing when you considered a card's position.

What was to the left or right? What was above or below? Upright or reversed?

But there was no spread I had ever researched in my work as a reporter that explained the position of the card I was looking at right then. "Where did you say you found this card?" I asked Chief Cody, as I turn the sealed evidence bag back and forth, trying to get a detailed look at the creased and moisture-warped card.

The Ten of Swords was already an unsettling card—its crimson-cloaked figure, sprawled on the ground, pierced by ten long blades against a bleak, storm-dark sky. But when you added the real blood staining this one… it was downright chilling.

43

"Next to the body. However, Bernie Russo, the medical examiner — he mentioned he knows you — believes at some point, it was in Noreen Cox's throat. We got her saliva and DNA, along with esophageal epithelial cells," the chief replied. "Pretty obvious it was put there intentionally. I was hoping to draw on your expertise to determine what special significance it might have."

"The significance? The significance is somebody really didn't like Noreen very much," I quipped. Chief Cody pursed his lips.

Okay. So, maybe not the time for gallows humor.

I pondered the card for a few moments, rifling through the Rolodex of information in my head. I took a deep breath and settled in to explain the convoluted topic.

"Most of these cards can have multiple meanings. And even the really ominous ones, like the Ten of Swords, don't always mean something bad."

"It was pretty bad for Noreen Cox," the chief pointed out. I couldn't help but nod in agreement.

"True. I suppose, when you consider the circumstances in which it was found, it could be a warning."

"A warning? To whom? If it was for Noreen, I think it came a little too late."

"It's not necessarily a warning of danger. It can be. But it can also be a warning about a person who wants control or is exercising control over someone or something else. Likely for their own personal gain."

"So, did the murderer put it there?"

I set the evidence back on the chief's desk and stood. "That, Chief Cody, is your job. I really need to get back to the shop. I left Dot in charge. She probably has five eligible bachelors lined up and waiting for me and is probably leading Addie around by her lip ring."

The chief winced. "That sounds painful."

I grinned wryly. "Which part?"

*****

It turned out Dot *did* have Addie by the lip ring, though nothing my imagination could muster could explain the awkward position I found my two employees in when I got back to the shop.

Dot was twisting around like a curly-haired poodle chasing its tail. Only it wasn't her tail she was chasing. It was Addie.

For every revolution the sexagenarian made, my howling stock clerk paced her in an endless round. Somehow, Addie's lip ring had gotten hooked on a loop of Dot's signature sweater.

Addie spied me first and gave Dot's fanny a quick rat-a-tat. "Zoe, Zoe, Zoe! Oh, thank God, you're here! You got to help me!" Addie begged. Only, because of her awkward positioning, it came out sounding more like, "Zobey, Zobey, Zobey! Oh, dank God, ooh ear! Ooh gobba heb me!"

"Help *you*?!" Dot squawked. "You're not the one who's been dragging an extra hundred and twenty-five pounds on her rear! I haven't been able to sit for an hour! My corns are killing me!"

"Whab ah ooh cumblayning fuh? Mah poor nodes wud filtering duh red beans ooh ad duh lunch duh whole time!"

"Red beans are an excellent source of protein. And I can't very well help it if they gave me gas. I was all out of Beano. You see, Zoe? This is exactly the reason I keep telling you we need to have a dress code."

I couldn't see how *any* dress code could've anticipated a lip-derrière entanglement, but I rushed forward anyway to disengage Addie from Dot's backside. I was reminded of the adage my editor used to preach: "Be careful whose feet you step on today, single 'cause they might be carrying the butt you have to kiss tomorrow."

In this case, it was literal.

"There!" I declared and freed the two women.

"Oh, thank you, Zoe! You're a godsend!" Dot replied and waddled right back to her roost on the stool behind the counter. She was like a homing pigeon in Cobbie Cuddlers.

I sighed. "Do I even want to know?" I muttered to Addie.

"I was bending down to restock the bags in the cash wrap. Dot was sitting, as usual..."

"It was my lunch break," Dot defended.

Addie steam rolled forward. "... working on her crossword. When I tried to stand up, my hoop got caught up in her sweater."

"Like catching scup off a party boat," Dot mumbled. "Speaking of getting caught..." Dot's eyes twinkled. Freedom had obviously rejuvenated her mischief. "Second date with the chief today. Looks like the basket worked!"

"Dot!" I exclaimed. "It wasn't a date, and the basket wasn't a lure. Chief Cody isn't a bluefin. I was merely trying to be hospitable and, maybe, drum up a little business for the shop." I tried to dodge Dot's meddling and alphabetized the Sue Grafton alphabet novels on one of the nearby shelves.

"Mmmhmm," Dot hummed innocently.

"Did you find anything out about Madame Zorina?" Addie queried about her recently deceased neighbor.

"You mean Noreen Cox," I corrected and move *C is for Corpse.*

"Noreen Cox?" Addie's voice was riddled with confusion.

"Yup," I confirmed. Another book shift. *O is for Outlaw.* "Turns out 'Madame Zorina' was just her stage name."

"Ohhhh," Addie drew out in protracted comprehension. She laid a purple—painted nail alongside her cheek. "Like Lady Gaga."

I sighed. Everything was a pop culture reference for Addie.

D is for Deadbeat.

"But Lady Gaga's real name is Stefani Joanne Angelina Germanotta. She just probably shortened it because it was way too long to say. Noreen Cox isn't very long though, is it? And she probably doesn't have half as many Insta followers as Lady Gaga, I'll bet."

Followers.

A thought occurred to me—about the yelling we heard coming from Zorina's shop and something Addie had mentioned when she first told us about the murder.

"But she had at least one," I mused.

I decided a quick trip to Addie's duplex was in order. But first, I scoured the shelves, looking for a last title. My hazel eyes roved over the bindings, but I couldn't seem to find it.

So intent was I on my search, I didn't even notice Dot until she whispered in my ear. "*Y is for Yesterday.*" She handed me the book and shuffled back to her roost.

"Huh?" I mumbled and glanced down. Then I froze. I hadn't been alphabetizing at all. My subconscious had been spelling out Chief Cody's name!

Dot clucked her tongue as she settled back into her spot. "Yup. Just like scup."

CHAPTER EIGHT

Native Americans consider the weasel to be a bad omen. A harbinger of death to those foolhardy enough to cross its path. Ancient Japanese folklore depicts them as supernatural monsters, their cries a portent of misfortune. In fact, the *kanji* script for weasel loosely translates to "calamitous apparition."

Germanic culture is full of superstitious magic, calling for weasel bits and pieces to manipulate destiny and circumvent fate, like eating a live weasel's heart to foresee the future. My face twinged a little green at that last.

Like Dot, I have never been a believer in fortune, fate, or anything bordering on the mystical or magical. But as I looked at the weaselly, beady-eyed, narrowly pinched face of Miroslav Iliev, I had to consider the validity of some of those dire beliefs.

The small, thin man peered at me from the open edge of his door. His long neck craned from the dark recesses of his apartment. There was a nasty lump, high on his oily forehead, which had just started to purple.

Unkempt nails, cracked, long, and chipped, clicked the wood of the doorjamb.

A callous "APARTMENT FOR RENT" sign hung on the exterior wall already. No one cared much for Madame Zorina, but seriously? Her body was barely even cold yet.

"Vat is it you vant?" he rasped in Slavic irritation.

"Are you Miroslav Iliev?" I asked, though from Addie's perfectly smarmy description of her lecherous landlord, I wasn't harboring even a shred of doubt. His bulbous eyes slithered over every nook and cranny of my petite five-foot-frame.

Was that a lip smack?

I tried not to cringe.

"Da. I am Iliev." Iliev snorted a plug of mucus loose and his Adam's apple bobbed in his skinny throat as he swallowed the mucus down. I quelled a surge of stomach acid. "But if you want apartment," he jabbed a thumb to the sign, "you must wait for *policija* to release to rent."

His eyes slid south of my border once again. "Of course, if you need place right away, I would consider renting extra room in my home. To right person, of course."

His crooked smile, stretched over nicotine-stained teeth, looked more like an invitation to ritual sacrifice than a welcome mat for promising rental property.

I politely cleared my throat. "I already have an apartment."

His smile twisted into a disappointed frown. I surreptitiously slid my foot into doorstop position, fully expecting to have the panel portal slammed in my face.

"Mr. Iliev," I began. "Miroslav." I wasn't sure if it was the sultry tone I let slide into my voice, or the calculated use of his first name. But whichever, it saved my Chucks from a painful door slamming.

"Da?" he asked cautiously.

"I think you misunderstand," I breathed. "I *do* have a place, but I'm not at all happy with it. My landlord, you see, doesn't give me much... attention." Iliev straightened a little. "You see, sometimes a girl needs help with things. Broken pipes. Spiders."

His lips curled. Damn. I was losing him again.
Time to pull out the big guns.
"Keeping warm."

A wildly inappropriate grin cracked his face in two.

And... he's hooked.

"Keeping warm?" His hairy eyebrow arched high.

"Oh, yes. These New England winters can get so brutal. The cold just seeps into the place I have right now. So, you see, I am very interested in this apartment."

It was a half-truth. But the best lies always had an element of truth in them. And while I was perfectly content with my cozy little apartment, I was also *very* interested in the former domicile of the recently departed Madame Zorina née Noreen Cox. More specifically? I was interested in what happened in it and just how much her ex-landlord knew about it.

"But what is this about the police?" I asked innocently and dropped my lashes a tad — enough to keep him on the line. "Surely you could tell me all about it. You look like a man in the know." I laid on the charm, hoping to draw him into confessing some telling detail.

"Is true," he agreed and pulled himself up a little taller. "I know much American police procedure. I watch *True Crime*."

"Really?" I gushed. He nodded. "Do you know I was one what found her?"

"Oh, my goodness! Found her? Who? Was someone hurt?" I feigned ignorance.

"No hurt." He shook his head. "Dead."

"Dead?" I gulped.

"Da. I had not heard from Madame Zorina for many days. I was concerned. I watch over all my residents."

Watch. Stalk. It's a fine line.

"When she was many days late with rent, I began to think something was very wrong. She always pay by first of month with check. I do not think Madame Zorina was her real name. Her initials were 'T. B. R.'. They were always on her check."

T.B.R.?

"Anyway, I go to her apartment. I knock. When there was no answer, I use my key to enter. I see Madame Zorina right away. On floor, near stairs. Is blood everywhere."

I wasn't sure, but I thought I saw his knees give a little. His eyes started an involuntary roll into the back of his head. But whatever I thought I saw passed fleetingly.

Iliev gripped the door frame tightly and dug in with his cracked nails.

He pulled himself together and continued. "I rush to her for aid. I check for pulse but cannot find. I called for ambulance, but it is too late. She is gone." He shifted from foot to foot. The awkward movement drew my attention to his suede boots. The light tan nap of the chukkas was neat and unblemished. Something niggled at the back of my brain.

"Your boots are nice," I mentioned casually. "I've been thinking about getting a pair for my brother. It's his birthday next week. Did you purchase them recently?"

His heavy lids dropped as he looked down at his footwear. "No. Have had for long time. The sole is good for climbing ladder when I must fix things in the apartments."

"Where are you wearing them the night you found Madame Zorina?" I asked.

His brow furrowed at the unusual question. He winced as the wrinkle in his forehead aggravated the nasty contusion there. He smoothed some stringy hair over the tender spot. "Yes. I wear all the time, but what kind of question this is?"

I quickly countered with a distracting, girlish giggle. "Silly curiosity. I was just wondering if you dressed this well all the time."

He looked down at his ripped, stained flannel shirt and wrinkled khakis. By far, his boots were the neatest, trendiest bit of his wardrobe, but he accepted my dubious compliment, nonetheless. He even ran a hand over his length, greasy hair.

"Hvala vam, dragi." He leaned suggestively against the doorjamb—oozing Serbian machismo. Unless he was asking for the time, I wanted no part of whatever he had just said—but I couldn't let *him* know that.

Okay, Brooklyn Community Theater...don't let me down now.

I laid it on—thick. "Such a handsome fella as you—I could see if Madame Zorina thought of you as more than just her landlord. Were you two ever... An item?"

"I offer much opportunities to Madame Zorina. But she is, how you say, already spoken for?"

My eyebrows shot up this time. "Oh! Really?"

"Da. She had been seeing many men. Always to come at odd hours."

"Can you describe some of these men?" I resisted the urge to pull out my old reporter's notebook.

"Why?" Iliev's eyes narrowed to slits. "Why do you want to know?"

"Because I'm a nervous, single woman, of course." I overstressed the "single". It seemed to work. Iliev relaxed. "I mean, what if one of these men did her in? What if they come back around this way? I would certainly want to know what they look like, so I might call the police... or you. For protection."

Iliev seemed to be considering himself in the role of shining white knight to my dramatic damsel in distress. The casting seemed to suit him.

"There is one man. He comes frequently. Large. Heavy. I see him come almost every day. In the evenings. After ten."

"Did you see him the night Madame Zorina was killed?" "Da. They were yelling. And, at first, I thought he came back, too."

"Why is that?"

"I heard the door open after he had already left. But when I check on Madame, I see taller, younger man enter. He is carrying a bottle of wine, so I think to myself he is reason for big man's argument. Madame Zorina was drawing from two decks." Iliev grinned lecherously.

Two men in a struggle for Madame Zorina's affections and a stalker landlord who seemed to know her every move?

The suspect list was growing.

I handed him my business card. "You'll call me when the police release the apartment, yes?"

He eagerly accepted the card and looked at the name. "But of course... Zoe."

As I stepped off the front stoop, I could feel his eyes following me down the walk. I may as well have been wearing the emperor's new clothes for as naked as the little man made me feel.

Note to self. Help Addie find a new apartment.

CHAPTER NINE

As the door closed behind me, I could almost feel Iliev's eyes boring through the peephole, following my backside. I suppressed a shudder.

I walked back to my Karmann Ghia and resisted the urge to break into a dead run. I casually rounded the front end of the small coupe and, as soon as I was clear of the peephole's line of sight, I ducked beneath the side-view mirror.

It was clear Iliev had no intention of letting me inside Madame Zorina's apartment, and any other intentions he might have had, I wanted no part of, anyway. Didn't mean I couldn't do a little investigating on the D.L., though.

I stayed hunched, hidden behind the vehicles parked in the long driveway that butted along the length of the complex. The driveway was filled with crushed oyster shells—not entirely uncommon in a seaport town like Mystic.

Not entirely conducive to sneaking around, either.

Every step elicited a loud crunch and made me regret the two extra teaspoons of calories I dumped in my cappuccino this morning.

Just think skinny.

I grimaced. I slowly slinked from behind my car and squatted behind a rusted-out Chevy. Empty beer cans littered the bed of the truck.

Iliev's.

Tossed among the recyclables were a coil of rope, a length of galvanized pipe with a curious dark stain near one end, and a few assorted rolls of duct tape.

"Regular serial killer kit you've got there, Iliev," I muttered as I continued down the alley alongside the house.

At least Ted Bundy had looks going for him.

The passageway narrowed. The next vehicle parked in the drive took up a much larger footprint than the others. A Hummer. And not one of the downsized H3 models. No, it was an H2.

Nearly as massive as the original Humvee, the H2 clocked in at nearly a whopping seven feet wide—and the fuel bill to match. Arnold Schwarzenegger, along with the rest of the Hollywood set, led to a surge in the impractical vehicle's popularity a while ago. Heck, in the late 90s and early 2000s, you couldn't even go to an action movie without seeing one of the great beasts lumbering across the screen. Noreen Cox's car.

When I thought about it, the H2 was the perfect car for a fake psychic to drive. Fake airlift lift hooks, fake central tire inflation system covers on the wheels, and phony plastic air vents on either side of the rear windshield. The car ran well. It was just nearly as phony as the fortune-teller herself.

I learned a lot about the make when researching an article about GM's plans to release an electric version of the vehicle. The model in front of me, however, hadn't been made since 2010.

Even so, I thought, it came with a hefty price tag. "Madame Zorina" must have been running scams for a while to scrape together the dough for a monster like that.

I shimmied past the behemoth to reach a window just beyond the facade of the building. "Time for a dose of your own medicine, Iliev."

I just prayed he wasn't in Happy Baby pose.

My fingers gripped the base of the window frame, and I pushed up high on the balls of my feet. I wobbled uncertainly as my toes dug for more stability.

Damn my mother's short genes.

It was a delicate balance, but my chin just cleared the sill. I could almost see the entirety of the smarmy landlord's apartment, an endeavor I almost immediately regretted.

Iliev slouched into the room. He yawned and scratched a hairy, pasty belly poking from beneath his tank top as he stretched. He grabbed a half-empty pack of cigarettes from a rickety coffee table and tugged a lighter from his pants pocket. Dry, chapped lips puckered over the filter of the cigarette as the opposite end glowed to life. Iliev tossed the lighter back to the table and slumped onto a low-slung couch in front of the television.

He flicked through a few half-hearted channel choices before deciding and kicked up his feet. The soles of the chukkas were probably the cleanest thing in the entire apartment. I surveyed the grease-stained, empty pizza boxes, a pile of dirty laundry, and the sink of unwashed dishes.

The squalor seemed to have no effect on Iliev as he cracked open a fresh beer and chugged it in one long guzzle. He let out a *basso profundo* belch that practically rattled the thin windowpane in front of me.

"Somebody really ought to let that guy know that just because beer is made from grain does not make it one of the four basic food groups," I mumbled and looked around at the stacks of discarded empties.

A sudden crack-pop echoed between the house and the parked cars as my toe slid into a patch of uncertain oyster shells. Iliev's beady little eyes immediately ratcheted in my direction.

"Dang it," I whispered tersely as I ducked down. My heart slammed against my ribs as I froze beneath the window. I didn't think he saw me, but what if he had?

I thought of the stained pipe in the back of Iliev's truck. I suppose that dark stain could've been rust.

Or it could've been something else entirely.

The acidic bite of fear welled in my throat. I swallowed hard. What was I thinking, snooping around the house of a potential murder suspect?

Answer's easy, Zoe. You were hunting for a story.

You know, mental health experts suggest internal monologues can help you work through problem-solving. Mine was more like having my mother living in my head, saying, "I told you so."

On infinite repeat.

I heard Iliev's footsteps moving through the apartment. They drew closer.

That was just great. Now, instead of being the hunter, I had just quite possibly become the hunted.

I pressed my back as far as I could against the siding of the house as I heard the scrape and squeak of the window opening. My breath caught in a silent bubble as I imagined Iliev's beady eyes scanning the length of the long drive.

Just please don't look down.

"Pah!" Iliev's voice rattled over my head. "Stupid cats." The acrid smell of cigarette smoke wafted under my nose. A tickle in my nostrils threatened to erupt in a sneeze. I pinched my nose.

Damn allergies.

I willed the sneeze away.

Iliev's voice grated and carried down the alley. "I catch you in the trash bins again, and I make sure Madame Zorina will not be the only dead body around here!"

My eyes widened.

I heard the snort of Iliev hocking a wad of phlegm, followed by the distinct sound of spitting. As a fat, wet gob of mucus landed inches from the toe of my shoe, my sneeze erupted, masked only by the slam of Iliev's window on the sash.

I froze in a quasi-runner's squat for nearly five minutes after the sneeze, every muscle in my lower body bunched, ready to spring into a sprint if Iliev came around the corner of the house. My eyes ping-ponged between the front of the alley and the backside as I poised to launch in whichever direction promised escape.

When the opening notes of the "Bad Boys Theme" from *Cops* pounded through the walls and I could hear Iliev warbling along stridently, I let loose a grateful sigh of relief and slowly sank beneath the window.

"Vatcha a gonna dooooo… "

I cringed. Jesus. Even if he didn't kill Madame Zorina with a pipe, his singing might have just done the trick.

The landlord's guttural threat to the neighborhood felines wasn't exactly a confession. At least, not one that would hold up in any court of law that I knew, but it left me with a lot more questions than answers.

It also left me with an idea of where to get some of those answers.

The trash cans.

In 1988, in a little case called *California vs. Greenwood*, the U.S. Supreme Court ruled that there was no expectation of privacy in the trash you put out to the curb. Other subsequent rulings by higher courts have upheld the court standing on fourth amendment issues. Granted, the initial ruling pertained to illegal search and seizures by legitimate law enforcement with probable cause, but, hey… Chief Cody had asked for my help. That meant I was practically deputized, right? And I didn't know what was more "probable cause" than suspicion of murder.

That was the story I was sticking to, anyway, if any nosy neighbors caught me poking around in the refuse.

The Greenwood ruling excluded any bins or other trash receptacles contained within the curtilage surrounding your home, but if it was out to the street for pickup, it was fair game. Lucky for me, it looked like Noreen Cox's bins were parked at the curb for the regular trash schedule.

Garbage is like a mini time capsule. You can glean a lot about a person's daily culture just by sifting through the detritus of their life. I picked my way carefully down the shell drive, avoiding the loose shells, fervently hoping I might garner some clue or insight into Noreen's murder. Or, at least, to the identity of the two men who visited her on the eve of her death.

Three bins sat on the curb. One must be the landlord's, another Addie's, and — if my math was right — the third must be Noreen's.

Gingerly, I lifted the lid on one bin. Energy drink cans, veggie burger wrappers, cotton balls stained with smears of Gothic black polish, and back issues of People magazine.

Addie's.

I carefully replaced the lid and moved on to the second bin. The lid echoed hollowly as it fell gently against the exterior. It was completely empty. My brows knit together, a furrow of confusion deepening between them. I rolled my eyes at my stupidity.

Of course!

The police had probably already confiscated Noreen's trash. Chief Cody hadn't gotten his badge from a cereal box. His forensics team was probably sifting through the cast of bits and bobs of Noreen's life, doing exactly what I was trying to do.

Look like an idiot?

Shut it, Mom.

My inner voice wasn't wrong, though. I really had no business snooping around the Cox murder. I had a tasting menu to plan, books to choose. I turned smartly on my heel and started back toward my car when I heard the distinct crunch of broken glass. I lifted my foot and saw a glass shard wedged in the tread. I gently wiggled it free and held it up to the light.

Dead leaf green.

I had scores of Chardonnay and Pinot Noirs in the shop bottled in glass this exact same color. It was a piece of a wine bottle.

Wine. Not exactly Iliev's flavor. I thought about all the beer cans tossed carelessly in the bed of his truck. Then, I remembered Iliev's comment.

A young man had visited Noreen's apartment the evening of her death. Iliev said he had been carrying a bottle of wine. I turned the glass over in my hand. Maybe the police missed a vital scrap of Noreen's trash.

Before I finished pondering the rationale for its existence here — after all, lots of people drank wine, and I was not the only supplier in town — something else distracted me.

A sound.

Buzzing.

Almost droning.

I glanced around the small yard but didn't see a thing. No movement. No activity.

I stole a glance back at the manager's door, but it remained tightly closed. Still, the noise was disturbing. Familiar in an unsettling way.

I absentmindedly slipped the piece of glass into my pocket and backed up. I bumped into the last bin, and the buzzing ratcheted into a sudden frenzy.

I took steps toward the bin.

Leave it alone, Zoe Marie. You have no business looking in that can.

Yeah? Well, Eleanor Roosevelt said life must be lived and curiosity kept alive.

I took another cautious step forward and reached out a tentative hand.

An abnormally large cloud of blue-green bottle flies swarmed from the bin as soon as I lifted the lid. My arms flailed as I waved the buzzing insects away from my face.

I braved a look down into the bin. Definitely more flies than one would expect from just from a pile of greasy cardboard and abandoned beer cans.

I reached down to the ground and picked up a dried stick, a broken twig from a nearby paperbark maple, and carefully lifted some of the pizza boxes, disturbing a few of the more stubborn flies.

As the cardboard shifted, my face blanched, and I was grateful the stoic maple was the only witness to my sudden and violent retching.

I suddenly remembered the other thing they say about curiosity.

CHAPTER TEN

The second I stepped into the police station, the air crackled with barely contained chaos.

I had a bombshell — a dead cat in Iliev's trash, a clue so disturbing even Chief Cody couldn't ignore it.

But the moment the door shut behind me, I knew I'd be lucky to get a word in edgewise.

Orson Tobit was already at the front desk, boiling over like a pot left too long on the stove. His voice — rich, commanding, a tone that usually made people listen — was frantic, frayed at the edges.

"You call this an investigation?" He slammed a thick, well-manicured hand against the counter, his face flushed with barely restrained fury. "She was murdered, and you're all standing around eating doughnuts!"

Myrna froze at the switchboard, apple fritter halfway to her mouth. Orson's fiancée, Sera, clung to his arm, murmuring something low, something meant to calm him.

It wasn't working.

Behind them, Albert — Mystic's self-appointed Lawn Flamingo Preservationist — was mid-rant about his stolen birds. Chief Cody looked about two seconds from ordering a full station lockdown.

Yeah. No one was in a listening mood.

Orson Tobit was really coming apart at the seams. I'd only ever seen him as the composed, self-assured type — the kind of man who glided through charity galas, handshakes firm, smiles practiced, voice measured. But today, he was anything but polished.

His broad, thickset frame loomed over the front desk. His presence was as heavy as the weight of his family name. His tailored jacket strained against his shoulders, his flushed face slick with sweat. The careful mask of small-town aristocracy had slipped, replaced by something raw, something desperate.

"She was murdered," he roared, his voice swallowing the room whole. "And what do I see? A bunch of bureaucratic feet-dragging!" His palm slammed the counter again — harder this time, sharp enough to make Myrna flinch. The fritter plopped into her coffee. She fished it out, grumbling, and slowly walked over to pour a fresh cup.

Orson's chest rose and fell in ragged heaves. Sera's delicate fingers dug into his arm. "Orson, please — "

He shook her off, his eyes wild. "She deserved better than this." His breath hitched. "She told me — she told me something was coming." His hand curled into a fist. A powerful man with no control left to wield.

Sera's voice was low, urgent, threading between Orson's outbursts like a thin wire pulled too tight.

"Orson, you're making a scene," she murmured, her tone honeyed but brittle at the edges. Her fingers clutched his sleeve, knuckles bone-white against the fine fabric. Not a soothing touch. A vice grip. She wasn't just trying to calm him.

She was trying to shut him up.

Orson barely noticed. His rage spooled out unchecked, battering the room like a Nor'easter storm.

But Sera? She was painfully aware of every set of eyes watching. Her gaze flicked to Chief Cody, to me, to the officers milling behind the desk. Calculating. Measuring. Assessing how much damage Orson was doing with every word that spilled from his lips.

"This isn't helping," she insisted, voice still velvet, but her nails curled in tighter. "We should go."

Orson wrenched his arm free. "I'm not going anywhere until I get some answers!"

Sera exhaled sharply, her composure cracking just for a second. Then, as quickly as it slipped, she smoothed it over. But I saw it. The flicker of frustration. Maybe even fear.

"Chief, if I don't get my flamingos back, I'm taking this straight to the mayor!" The room turned as a unit to Mr. O'Leary, who stood just behind Orson, arms crossed over his plaid suspenders, looking thoroughly put out. His bushy eyebrows twitched with indignation.

Chief Cody pinched the bridge of his nose, exhaling slowly. I could almost hear him counting to ten. "Mr. O'Leary," he sighed, voice strained, "as I told you this morning, we're looking into it."

Orson turned on him, incredulous. "You've got time for lawn ornaments, but not a murder?" His voice practically vibrated off the walls, making Sera's grip tighten once more.

"They're not just ornaments," O'Leary huffed, planting his feet like a man prepared to die on this hill. "They're investments. Limited edition. Signed by the artist. And now? Gone! Poof! Like they vanished into the Bermuda Triangle of crime!"

I barely stifled a laugh, but even through the absurdity, I saw it—Orson's rage now looked even more unhinged, a man furious that he was being lumped in with a flamingo conspiracy.

Chief Cody stared heavenward, muttering something under his breath. Probably a prayer.

Or a resignation letter.

"You're wasting time on kitsch while Zorina's killer walks free?" Orson's voice thundered through the station, but I didn't miss the flicker in his eyes—the quick scan of the room, gauging reactions. Grief, yes. But was there something else?

"She was a good woman," he continued, his chest rising and falling in heavy bursts. "She was helping people. She didn't deserve this." His palm slammed against the counter again. This time, the assault spilled the fresh cup of coffee Myrna had just filled for herself. She clunked the ceramic "Have a Nice Day" mug on the coffee station and stalked off.

She was having a day, all right... but it was anything but nice.

Orson's anger, the outrage—it was all perfectly on cue. But I had seen enough of Shepherd Falls' elite to know when someone was performing. His voice caught, just slightly, on his last words. The break in his tone, the way his lips pressed into a firm, wounded line—it looked real. Felt real.

But then why did it feel... rehearsed? Why did it feel like he wanted the room to believe it?

My eyes flicked to Sera, expecting concern. Instead, Sera's grip on his sleeve remained iron-tight, her fingers rigid against the fabric. Not comforting him. Containing him.

And that's when I knew. Orson wasn't just mad.

He was covering for something.

Sera leaned in toward Orson. Her voice was smooth—too smooth. "Orson, people are going to start thinking you had something to do with this." A nervous chuckle bubbled from her lips, like she was trying to lighten the mood.

But the second the words left her lips, I saw it—a flicker of panic in Orson's eyes, so quick that most people would have missed it.

But I wasn't most people.

Orson's head snapped toward Sera, his jaw tightening. "Don't be ridiculous."

Too sharp. Too defensive. Sera had hit a nerve.

A silence stretched between them, thick enough to cut. The type of silence where unspoken words loomed just beneath the surface. I watched, fascinated.

That wasn't how an innocent man reacted.

If Orson had nothing to hide, he would've scoffed, rolled his eyes, brushed it off. Instead, his whole body stiffened like a man caught in a trap.

Sera recovered quickly, smoothing a hand down his arm like she could erase what she'd just said. "I just mean… getting this upset, making a scene — it won't help."

Orson's nostrils flared. "The only thing that won't help is sitting around while the cops do nothing."

I wasn't sure who was more desperate — Orson, trying to control the room, or Sera, trying to control Orson. But one thing was clear.

At least one of them was lying.

"Mr. Tobit, I get it. I really do. But you shouting at me isn't getting us any closer to answers," Chief Cody said, his voice a strained attempt at reason. He stood firm, arms crossed, his patience clearly hanging by a thread.

Orson wasn't having it. He leaned in, jabbing a thick finger in the Chief's direction. "You want answers? Try looking at the people who hated her." His breath came heavy, uneven. "She told me she was in danger. She knew something was coming."

That got my attention.

I straightened, the dead cat in Iliev's trash momentarily forgotten. Had Zorina actually sensed something? Or had she been playing Orson the way she played everyone else? Because let's be real — psychics made their money off of reading people, their fears, their needs, their tells.

Was Zorina genuinely afraid, or had she planted that idea in Orson's head, knowing he'd cling to it, use it as proof she was the real deal?

I studied Orson carefully. His face was flushed. Sweat beaded along his hairline. His breathing was ragged, but his words were controlled. Calculated. A distraction? A misdirection?

I glanced at Sera. Her fingers were still curled around his sleeve. Her lips pressed into a thin line. She didn't like what he was saying. And that made me wonder.

Why not?

Meanwhile, Orson's jaw tightened, his fists curling like he was ready to drive them straight through the chief's desk. His ruddy complexion deepened to an almost alarming shade of red, and for a second, I thought he might actually explode.

"This is ridiculous," he growled, voice low and dangerous. "Zorina wasn't some… some—" He stopped short, chest heaving.

But Sera wasn't looking at him. She was looking at *me.*

Her lips were slightly parted, her expression frozen somewhere between shock and calculation. I could practically hear the wheels turning in her head, trying to decide how much damage had just been done.

"Orson, just—calm down," she said, but her voice was off. Too light. Too careful. Like she didn't actually care about his temper, just about where it might lead.

"I am calm," he snapped, making it clear he was anything but. They weren't on the same page—not even reading from the same book. Sera was worried. Orson was angry. And neither of them was mourning Zorina the way you'd expect from people who wanted justice.

No, they were protecting something—but not each other. I decided to jump on the grenade.

Stepping forward, I kept my voice casual, but I

made sure every word landed like a well-placed card in a high-stakes game. Let them wonder what I knew. Let them sweat a little.

"That's interesting, Mr. Tobit," I said, tilting my head just enough to feign mild curiosity. "Because I've been hearing that Madame Zorina had plenty of visitors. Late-night ones. More than one."

Orson went still. His gaze darted but it was Sera who made the real mistake.

"That's not true," she blurted, her voice slicing through the air too fast, too sharp.

Orson snapped his head toward her, his expression unreadable—but the shift in his stance was telling. I crossed my arms, watching the little drama unfold in real time. Sera's fingers, which had been digging into his sleeve, suddenly loosened. She blinked like she was realizing, a second too late, that she'd just given herself away.

I turned toward her, my eyes narrowing. "How would you know that?"

She blinked, and in that split second, I caught it— that flicker of panic before she smoothed her features. "I wouldn't, of course." She let out a soft, breathy laugh, shaking her head. "I'm just saying… people like her—"

Orson shot her another sharp look, but she pressed on, tone suddenly gentler, coaxing. "Sometimes they take advantage of good, unsuspecting people. Like my Orson." She wrapped an arm around him. "I just meant she probably had loads of people who wanted to do her harm."

The words came out so smoothly—so

reasonable—but I wasn't buying it. Neither, it seemed, was Chief Cody. His jaw twitched—his broad shoulders suddenly rigid.

"Why can't we just concentrate on the wedding, darling?" Sera pouted at Orson. But I caught her side-eye with her next words. "Some things are better left alone," Sera murmured, her voice low, deliberate.

That wasn't a plea. It wasn't concern.

It was a threat.

A slow, uneasy chill crept up my spine, but I didn't let it show. Instead, I held her gaze, my expression carefully blank. She wasn't just warning me off—she was testing me, waiting to see if I'd fold. Sera's grip on Orson relaxed just enough to look natural, but not before she gave his sleeve a pointed squeeze. She was controlling the damage. And then she smiled. Cool. Polished. Dangerous.

"Speaking of which… you have a big shipment arriving soon, don't you, Zoe?" Sera asked lightly, as if we were discussing the weather. "That huge order? The one I personally placed? It's going to be such an important night. I'd hate for something to… disrupt it."

And just like that, the stakes changed.

Orson muttered something about "his tax dollars going to waste" under his breath as he stormed toward the door, Sera on his arm. His steps were heavy, his fury palpable. But I wasn't watching him. I was watching her.

Sera moved with a fluid grace, her posture impeccable, her expression carefully blank. But the way she steered Orson by the elbow just before they hit the door—that wasn't affection. That was control.

The second they were gone, I let out the breath I hadn't realized I was holding.

Chief Cody exhaled sharply beside me, shaking his head. "Well. That was a circus."

I turned to him, my mind already picking through the debris of the argument, searching for patterns. "Orson was all over the place," I murmured, thinking out loud. "Throwing blame at anyone, hoping something would stick." I chewed my lip. "That kind of desperation—it's almost like he was trying to shift suspicion off himself."

The chief grunted. "Wouldn't be the first time a guilty conscience made a lot of noise." I nodded, but my thoughts snagged on something else.

Sera.

She wasn't just playing defense. She was playing the long game. And I needed to figure out why.

I was mid-thought when Chief Cody's voice cut through. "You wanna get dinner?"

I froze. My head snapped up. "What?"

He shrugged, all casual, like he hadn't just completely derailed my train of thought. "Dinner. I was gonna grab something later. Wondered if you might want to join me."

My mouth opened. Closed.

Was I hallucinating? Or had Chief Cody just asked me out?

My brain scrambled for a response, for clarity, but all I could come up with was the way his broad shoulders filled out that uniform, the way his voice always carried that rough edge of authority. I needed to say something before he realized I'd short-circuited.

"Uh. Yeah." I cleared my throat. "Yeah. Sure. Dinner."

He beamed, his wide smile white against his tanned skin. "Great! What do you say we meet up at seven? Any suggestions for a place? I'm still trying to get my bearings around here."

"Yeah, uh..." I reached for my bag, unfocused, hand swiping at empty air. "How about Abbott's?"

"Sounds good. See you there." He snatched up a file and headed toward his office.

I hardly noticed Myrna chuckling as I walked out of the building, dazed. Instead, I kept replaying the moment in my head.

You wanna get dinner?

The investigation could wait.

I had a date.

CHAPTER ELEVEN

"You or that wine going to breathe anytime soon?" Dot's quip shook me from my apparent reverie before I turned purple.

"Of course," I burst. I shook the cobwebs from my head and uncorked the bottle. Today's pairing? Lacryma Christi del Vesuvio with Pizza Margherita Crostini.

The bouquet of cherries and red fruit tickled the nose in the garnet-colored wine. Its forward notes of juicy raspberries and plums danced with the woody, piney sharpness of black pepper. It would stand up well to the robust tomato sauce of the hors d'oeuvres.

The name of the wine, Italian for "tears of Christ," had its origins in a story. Legend holds that when God discovered a corner of heaven had been stolen by Lucifer, he wept. Piedirosso grapes, the grapes used to create the wine, sprung from the tears that fell.

It was a good story. And the reporter in me just couldn't resist a good story.

Like the Noreen Cox murder.

The chief had flipped the lid on my personal Pandora's box. I didn't want to be, but I was incredibly curious about Madame Zorina's murder and the mysterious tarot card that had been forced down her throat. The uniqueness of the item screamed that the crime was intensely personal.

People usually killed for one of four reasons. There were always variations on the themes, but, ultimately, it always boiled down to the same four. The Horsemen of Homicide, as I like to call them. Love, lust, lucre, and loathing. Answer that, and you had your why.

Right now, I'd be happy with the who.

"Chief called," Dot continued. I clunked the bottle into the lip of the glass carafe.

"Who?" I squeaked. I swiftly wiped up the wine I dribbled on the counter. "Did he say what he wanted?"

Dot grinned. "After a fashion. Though I gave him a few of my own suggestions first."

"Dot Richards!" I tossed the towel at her. "You did not!"

She caught the terrycloth missile and chuckled. "What? You're an attractive young woman. He's an attractive young man. Who says you can't mix a little pleasure with your business?"

I stationed my hands firmly on my hips. "Everybody, Dot. It's like a tenet of the universe."

"Oh, posh. That's even bigger hooey than Madame Zorina and her crystal balls." She grabbed a pad next to the register and squinted through her readers. "Wants to know if Abbott's has a dress code." She eyeballed me over her glasses. "Sounds like somebody's got a date."

I squared my shoulders. "No, I have a meal."

"A meal?"

"Traditionally, that's what they serve at Abbott's," I retorted.

"Hmph," Dot scoffed. "Well, if hunky-stud isn't on the menu, I'd go with the lobster. Only five more weeks till the season's up."

"I think it's nice, Zoe," Addie interrupted from the other side of the room. I hadn't even realized she was listening. She practically lived with her earbuds in. Her head had been bopping along to a silent concert in her head as she shelved some bottles of wine. "You deserve a night off. And I can handle tonight's reading. I'll lock up afterwards."

She cringed a little. "Not exactly in a rush to get home after, well, you know."

I couldn't say that I blamed her one bit. Between Zorina's death and her creepy landlord, I don't know that I would be in a rush myself.

I took a deep breath. "You could always bunk at my place for a few days, Addie, if it would make you more comfortable. Till things blow over? I've got plenty of room and there's leftover pizza in the fridge."

She rushed up to me in a blur of pink and purples. She grabbed my hands and started kissing them. "Do you mean it, Zoe? I could stay with you for a little while?"

"Why, sure, kiddo! Why not? It will be like we're having a slumber party. Just don't put my bra in the freezer or shading cream on my face," I warned.

"Oh, no worries. I don't even have shaving cream. Don't shave!" She grinned, holding up a pale arm to reveal a hairy pit. *"Au naturel* for me." I winced.

Sometimes Addie could be a bit too forthcoming. *Forthcoming.*

I thought back to my conversation with Miroslav Iliev. While he had been willing to share how he had found the victim, I couldn't help but feel like he hadn't been entirely truthful about the exact way events had transpired the evening of Madame Zorina's death.

And what was that nasty bump on his head?

He admitted he put the moves on Zorina on more than one occasion but had been shot down. He had a reputation, according to Addie, of ogling the tenants through the windows. Perhaps he had gotten tired of just watching. Maybe he used his key to let himself into Zorina's apartment and forced himself on her. She fought back, cracked him in the noggin, and he killed her for it, unable to handle the rejection again.

But what about the two men Iliev had mentioned? An older, heavyset man and the younger, taller one. If they existed, what part did they play, if any, in Zorina's demise? Did either of them have anything to do with the shouting match my employees and I had overheard coming from Zorina's shop?

Sigh. For someone who didn't want to be an investigative reporter anymore, I was sure asking myself a whole lot of questions.

All the questions floating around in my head were worrisome. Until they were answered, it meant that somewhere, on the historic streets of Mystic, a killer wandered. But as much as that frightened me, there was an even bigger question in my head that terrified me to the tips of my toes.

What on earth was I going to wear to dinner?

*****

"Bibs?" Chief Cody drew his head back like a perplexed turtle.

I held two white plastic coverings aloft, each embossed with a red claw crustacean like the ones steaming on the platters before us. "Suit up, Guy Fieri," I chuckled.

The reference to the Food Network star came well earned. The chief had pulled up to the Riverside restaurant in a candy apple red 1968 Camaro convertible that probably would've made the grub guru drool.

"Fair enough," he admitted. "But when you're a single guy with no other responsibilities, what else are you going to spend money on?"

"You could always give some to charity," I suggested.

He paused, smiled, and gazed intently into my eyes. "Where have you been all my life, Zoe Romano?"

A warm flush flooded through my chest and up my neck. The chemistry between us was getting hard to deny.

"See?" Cody continued. "I need someone to remind me of things like that. Like a personal assistant."

And the would-be flush receded almost instantaneously.

So much for chemistry.

I turned my attention back to the food. "The

81

lobster looks amazing," I offered, maybe a little too enthusiastically.

At least one of us does.

I straightened out the strapless sundress I had donned for no apparent reason. The lobster did look pretty good, though.

Well, the evening's not a total loss.

Abbott's was one of my favorite dining destinations in the area. Tucked in the Groton suburb of Noank, it was a bit off the beaten path, but well worth the track. It sat cozily beside the Mystic River. Seabirds squawked in cadence to the tenor ding of the buoy bells in the marina. A late summer breeze brought the salty smack of the sea into the dining area, a collection of assorted picnic tables next to the single-story cook shack with its white picket fence.

The place itself had been around for over seventy years. Originally, the establishment served as a cannery. About thirteen years later, Ernie Abbott, the initial owner, added the restaurant. Generations of Groton area teens grew up working the eatery's season—from the first Friday in May until Columbus Day.

Guests could start a satisfying meal with a hardy chowder, either a classic, creamy version or a brothy "Noank" style. You could follow it up with a bag of steamers, clams, and muscles, with drawn butter, and broth, before you dove in for the main course... lobster.

Pick your version. On a famous lobster roll—small, medium, or O-M-G. Over a bed of hot, al dente cavatappi. Or steamed to perfection with a side of coleslaw and Abbott's own potato chips. You could be just as particular as you please.

The seagulls, on the other hand, weren't. The loud "aw uck, aw uck" filled the air as they voiced cantankerous complaints over the near invisible netting that separated them from a king's feast. I held up the bib and gave it a little shake. Hell if I was going to be the only one embarrassed tonight.

"All right. All right." The chief threw his hands up in mock surrender before he accepted the protective dining gear and tied it around his neck. He picked up his lobster shell.

"I wouldn't have thought to bring a tablecloth," the chief mentioned. "Or a bottle of wine, for that matter." He gestured to the bottle of Chardonnay I snagged from the shop before Dot and Addie gave me too hard a time.

I tucked the loose strings of my bib into the back of my collar. "Abbott's is a 'bring your own' kind of place, Chief."

He took hold of my hand before it was covered in lobster juice. "Please, call me Derek. When you call me 'Chief', I feel like I need to gain twenty pounds and eat more of those donuts Orson was screaming about."

"Okay." I smiled. "Derek."

Pitta-pat. There's hope.

"Anyway, you'll see a lot of regulars who bring a thing or two to dress out the picnic tables. Take that guy over there." I pointed to an older man in a dress shirt and tie. "That's Boston Bob. He drives in from Massachusetts twice a season. Once on his anniversary, and once on his wife's birthday. Now, she passed away a few years back, but he still makes the drive. Puts out a white tablecloth, candles, and flowers and orders the biggest lobster they have in the tanks."

Derek frowned. "That seems kind of sad."

I cracked into my lobster. "Not really. They met here. She was just a kid working her way through school. He came with his parents to eat, and he ordered the biggest lobster they had. When she tried to get it out of the tank, she lost her grip and the darn thing hit the deck and scrabbled across the deck. The two of them chased it together, got tangled up, and both fell into the river. Then they fell in love. Not sure what happened to the lobster, though."

"So, he comes here to remember her?"

"Regular as clockwork." I nodded. I rested my lobster fork on the edge of the platter. "Speaking of regulars, have you gotten a list of Madame Zorina's clients? It might help identify someone who had a reason to kill her."

"It hasn't been easy. Fortunetellers don't exactly keep accurate records."

"You're not wrong," I agreed. "When I was doing my investigating in the city, it was totally chaotic. That's how they operate. A lot of their cons are based on the amount of obfuscation they can create. Like a good magician."

"Gotcha. Cause a big distraction over here," Derek began and wiggled a hand.

"While the real trick is happening over here," I finished and wiggled my hand. I wiped my mouth with a napkin. "Which reminds me… I spoke to Miroslav Iliev yesterday."

Derek paused. "The smarmy landlord?"

I nodded. "He mentioned seeing two men the night of Zorina's death."

"Yes. You said that at the station. Iliev mentioned it to us at the scene. Did he also mention we found his blood at the scene?"

My eyes popped wide. "That creepy peeping Tom?! So, why haven't you picked him up?"

"Wait," Derek's tone turned intently serious. "Peeping Tom?"

"Yeah. Apparently, he has a nasty habit of peering in his tenants' windows. And as the landlord, he has a key to all the apartments."

"That would definitely explain why there was no forced entry. He could've let himself in."

I nodded so hard my molars rattled. "What if he decided to take things a step further than just looking? My clerk lives in that apartment complex, you know?" I was squawking louder than the seagulls. It was drawing some curious stares.

Derek patted my hand and held a cautious finger to his lips. "Calm down. Calm down. Let's take a second to think this through," he suggested.

I took a couple of deep breaths. "Miroslav Iliev is definitely a person of interest, but just because he's a Peeping Tom, it doesn't make him a murderer."

"Just a creep."

"Yes. Definitely a creep."

"Where did you find the blood?" I asked.

"On the exterior door jamb," he responded.

85

I thought back to the lump on Iliev's head. "Did you find it anywhere else? On a pipe? A wrench? A candlestick?"

"What are we playing? Clue?"

I grinned sheepishly. "I've been thinking. What if Iliev had tried something, and Zorina fought back? When I talked to him, he kept smoothing his hair over a cut on his head."

"We saw that, too. That's why we asked him for a DNA sample. He claims it happened when he was fixing the porch light. Says he slipped off the ladder and hit his head."

My bloodhound keened. Again, I thought about the stained pipe I had seen in the back of Iliev's truck. "You know there's a length of pipe in the bed of his truck. It's got a suspicious stain on one end."

Derek frowned. "Did a little bit more than just talk to the landlord, huh?"

I grimaced and shrugged. "You didn't touch it, did you?"

My grimace dissolved into a scowl. "Of course not."

"Good." Derek tossed the napkin onto the table and tugged off the plastic bib. The evening's mood had shifted. He took a deep breath and set his jaw. "You know, Zoe, when I asked for your help on this case, it never came with the expectation that you would knowingly put yourself in danger."

"I guess I just have a nose for trouble," I retorted. "It's the one thing my mother and my editor would agree on."

"Well, if your nose smells anything fishier than lobster shells from now on, you call me first. Meanwhile, I'll have my people check out the pipe. We haven't ruled anything, or anyone yet, but we're still analyzing the evidence. So far, the blood on the doorjamb is the only thing we have that links Iliev to the crime. All that gives us is opportunity. But I'll look into this Peeping Tom thing. See if he has a record. Maybe that will give us motive. And do me a favor. Don't interview any other suspects without me."

"No problem there… *Chief.* I wouldn't even know them if they walked into my shop."

CHAPTER TWELVE

"Tom!" Dot cried. "Tom Sawyer! How are you?"

I looked up from my inventory as the young man strode into the shop on his long, lanky legs.

He ambled to the counter where Dot maintained her usual perch and leaned over to give her a quick peck on the cheek. "I'm fine, Mrs. Dot. I finished that book you recommended last week. It was killer."

Dot patted his hand. "Didn't I tell you? That P. D. James could really spin a yarn for an old biddy."

"Not old, Mrs. Dot. Experienced." Dot shot a "see-how-you-should-treat-your-elders" look in Addie's general direction. Addie responded with a sneer towards her that turned into a genuine beam for Tom.

"There's something to be said for experience." Tom smiled a crooked but flirtatious grin my way.

His forward gesture caught me off guard. After my botched dinner with the chief, I was feeling more than a little gun shy with men. And with my track record, I'm probably better off flying solo, anyway.

The thought didn't stop me from doing a proverbial double take at Tom's attention, though. I glanced over my shoulder to see Addie waving enthusiastically.

My shoulders sagged.

Of course.

My clerk batted her dark, mascaraed lashes like crazy. It looked like two daddy long legs twerking on her face.

I stifled a chuckle and went back to counting corkscrews.

Tom continued his dialogue with Dot. "But experience is one thing I'm definitely lacking when it comes to wine selection. I'm hoping one of you lovely ladies can help me out. Like you did the other night, Mrs. Dot?"

Addie vaulted over a case of Syrah, closing the gap between her and Tom in a hot New York minute. "I'm sure Dot's terribly busy right now." Addie looked at Dot's characteristic crossword like it was the Declaration of Freaking Independence and pushed it at the older woman. "I would be happy to help you out, though, Mr. Sawyer."

"Oh, wow. Yeah. I'd say Mr. Sawyer was my dad, but I'm not really sure since he was never 'in the picture'. Please, just call me Tom."

Addie rested a gentle hand on his arm. "I completely understand. Well, Tom, what's the occasion? Is this for a gift? A birthday? A... date?" She blinked those two lash-heavy eyes up at him. Tom shied at the concentrated attention.

Dot pushed the paper away and levered herself from her stool. She waddled to the front side of the counter. "Oh, come on, now. Leave the boy alone."

She hooked a sweatered arm into Tom's and drew him away from my cloying clerk. I'm surprised Addie didn't trip over her bottom lip as she stalked back to her post. Tom glanced at me over his shoulder. I shrugged.

You're on your own, pal.

"So, what's this wine for?" Dot asked, picking up a nice Malbec from the shelf. "It's for a celebration of sorts," he replied.

"Tell me it's not an engagement!" Addie cried plaintively from the other side of the store. I rewarded her with a flying cork to the head.

Tom laughed. "No. Not an engagement. I've just gotten some great news. You probably know I work at the butcher shop."

"Best meat in Mystic!" Addie swooned.

Says the vegan.

I rolled my eyes.

"Well, it's not like I ever intended to make that my career. Fact is, I've always wanted to start my own fishing charter. But out in Phoenix, that really wasn't an option. That's why I packed it all in and moved out here."

"Traded the sand for snow?" I chortled from the corner.

"Hey, when your life isn't going the way you planned, sometimes it takes something a little drastic." A slightly somber tone seeped into his voice. His words struck a chord.

Preaching to the choir, sir.

"Anyway, I just found out the financing came

through. I've got the down payment to buy Captain Talley's boat. He's retiring. And I've got enough money left over for a crew and supplies."

"That's fabulous!" Dot exclaimed. "Oh, but you don't want this old swill, then."

I tried not to grimace as Dot clunked the Malbec back on the shelf. She shuffled back toward the locked cases. "No, siree, Bob. What you want is Dom! Nothing but the finest for news this good!"

"Wait! Dot... that's for..." I wanted to remind her the bottle she was grabbing was for Sera's wedding—the shipment had just arrived that morning after I cashed in my 401K from *The Times*—a move I sincerely hoped I wouldn't come to regret. Especially since I was hoping to use that money to bail out my mortgage issues.But then I thought better of it. Oh, well. I may not always agree with Dot's methods, but if they result in a $200 upsell? Grin and bear it, I guess.

I picked up a box of nice, economy red and headed for the cash wrap. Ugh! If I've told Annie once, I've told her a thousand times. Put the cheap stuff where the customers check out. They're more likely to grab it as an impulse there.

I sighed. Some folks would agree that there are four time zones in the continental United States. I argue that there are five. Pacific, Mountain, Central, Eastern... and Addie.

It's not that my pink-haired employee completely ignored instruction. She just got around to things in her own sweet time.

"Oof!" I lost my grip on the heavy box. Tom

swooped in and saved me from a messy cleanup and a guaranteed tongue-wagging from Dot.

Okay, so maybe Addie wasn't the only accident-prone human at Read Between the Vines.

"Whoa, there!" Tom chuckled as his large hands reached beneath the tilting box and covered mine. "Let me get that for you." His hands were warm. I was almost hesitant to pull away but decided I had better. You know. Before it got awkward?

I brushed a lock of curly hair from my embarrassed face as he deftly lifted the box from my arms.

"Thanks," I mumbled, appreciating his flexing muscles. I allowed myself a momentary daydream.

"No worries." Tom shrugged. "Happy to help. Where do you want it?"

Where do I want it? Hell! On the counter... on the floor...

He stared at me intently.

Crud. Please, if there's a God, tell me Tom wasn't a mind reader.

An unexpected blush crept up my chest and into my cheeks. "Where do I want it? I, uh...," I stammered.

"The wine?" Tom urged.

"The wine!" I exclaimed. "Of course! The wine. I mean, what else would you be talking about?" I covered my faux pas with a nervous chuckle.

Dot ambled past and whispered. "Just like scup." I threw my hands up in exasperation.

A gal has one illicit thought...

Okay. Maybe two.

I pointed stiffly at the cash wrap. "On the floor over there is fine." I threw a warning glance toward both my employees, daring them to make a comment.

Frustrated, in more ways than one, I jammed my hands into my pockets. A sharp, sudden pain shot through my hand and radiated up my arm. I cry out loud. "Yow! What the heck?"

"Zoe? Zoe, honey, what's wrong?" Dot called from across the shop. Concern deepened the wrinkles in her forehead.

Tom abandoned the box of Merlot and rushed to my side, followed by my waddling assistant manager and Addie both. I pulled my hands from my pockets.

The vague imagery of Christmas bloomed in my brain as I stared at the bright cherry stream of blood trickling down from the fleshy bit of my left hand where the chunk of green glass had wedged itself.

Addie's hands flew to cover her mouth. The glass wasn't the only thing that's looking a little green.

"I'll call 911!" she burst, though the sound was garbled by the sound of a heaving wretch as she whirled away.

"Posh, you'll do no such thing," Dot rebuked. "Go grab the first aid kit from the kitchen."

Addie's plentiful jewelry jingled as she nodded her pink head. She darted off toward the kitchen and exploded through the swinging door. A massive crash of metal meeting tile resounded through the small shop. "I'm okay!" Addie's voice echoed.

"Oh, dear," I mumbled. My legs got a little wobbly beneath me.

Just as gravity was doing its thing, Tom reached out and hooked my falling body under the arms.

He gently lowered me to a sitting position on the nearby stack of wine crates. "Seriously, are you okay?" A genuine tone of concern edged his deep voice.

I offered a faltering smile of gratitude and feebly waved my injured hand. An unexpected giggle bubbled up as I watched the shard of colored glass wiggle in my wound.

Tom studied the wound with intensity. A deep furrow knit between his dark brows. "What exactly happened?"

Dot's voice warbled with concern. "Is it serious?"

Tom gently turned my hand this way and that. "A piece of glass. Here," he said to me. "Elevate your hand above your heart if you can." He turned back to Dot. "She's likely going to need a few stitches."

Dot clucked behind him. "Oh, Zoe!"

"That's what I get for noodling around in Noreen Cox's trash, I suppose," I mumbled. I laughed half-heartedly. "Ouch!" Tom squeezed my hand.

"Sorry. I just… wanted a better look." He immediately loosened his grip and his features softened.

Addie returned with the first aid kit. "Here. I got the kit."

"Noreen Cox?" Tom continued as he fumbled through the kit. I thought I caught the flicker of something in his expression. Recognition? Worry? Guilt? But it was gone before I could put my finger on it. "You mean Madame Zorina? The psychic that got killed?"

I nodded.

"What were you looking for?" he asked. Our eyes connected.

Ah, there it was.

I recognized the familiar intensity. I felt it a million times myself working at the paper. Curiosity.

"I honestly don't know," I answered and shook my head.

"I'll tell you what you were looking for," Dot fussed. "Trouble. With a capital T. You've got no business making it your personal business to go snooping around in a dead woman's business."

"That's a lot of business," Addie muttered.

Dot sniffed. "Like you would have the first idea, girlie."

"I just thought I might find something out about the men who visited her the night she died," I countered. "Ouch!"

"Sorry," Tom apologized as he wrapped the bandages Addie proffered around the protruding glass.

"Shouldn't you take that out?" Addie asked. Her scarlet lips puckered in confusion as her eyes reeled toward the back of her head. Artichoke was definitely not her color.

Tom shook his head. "You should never remove a foreign object from a wound. You could wind up causing more harm than good. Just wrap the wound to stabilize until you can get proper medical attention."

"Get a lot of cuts at the butcher shop, do you?" I smiled weakly. He returned the smile in kind. "Have to be certified in CPR and first aid to get your captain's license. Guess the course material is still fresh in my mind."

"And you, Zoe, are fresh out of yours!" Dot barked.

Realizing I was not in mortal danger, she had waddled back to her perch and wagged her pencil in the air. "You say two men visited Noreen Cox that night. I'll bet my bingo money one of them is the one that did her in!"

She adjusted her bulk on the stool and planted her palms on either side of her crossword. "What if they'd come back while you were playing Nancy Drew? What is it they say — the criminal always returns to the scene of the crime? You could have very well been next!" Her tone was scolding, but I couldn't help but hear the current of motherly concern running underneath. My head dipped in shame.

"She's right, you know," Tom agreed. "The murderer could be anybody."

"Yeah," Addie chimed. "Like my creepozoid landlord, for one."

"You're lucky," Tom mentioned.

"I know. I know. No more rummaging and trash cans for me. I promise."

Tom stood to his full six-foot-two height. "There. That will hold you temporarily, but you really should get to the hospital. If you'd like, I can take you."

"Take her where?" The sudden interjection turned all our heads towards the front of the store. Chief Cody — Derek — scowled when he spied the flowering red stain on the gauze wrapped around my hand.

"What happened?" he continued, easily closing

the gap between the store entrance and my pathetic self in nothing flat. Tom edged closer to me, resting a strong hand on my shoulder—a move Derek noticed as he gently grasped my hand and examined Tom's handiwork.

"It's nothing," I grumbled sheepishly. "Nothing doesn't come in Pinot red," Derek countered.

"Yeah, well, remember that snooping you advised me against repeating?"

A scowl twisted his full mouth. "Yes?"

"While I was doing it, I may have picked up a random piece of trash and stuck it in my pocket. Honestly, I had forgotten all about it until I stupidly jammed my hand in there and, well, this." I lifted my bandage hand in the air and weakly waved.

"How bad is it?" Derek asked.

"I was just about to take her to the hospital and get it looked at," Tom answered for me.

A strange, silent little parry went on between the two men. Derek's blue eyes developed a frigid sheen as Tom gave my shoulder a little squeeze.

My gaze pulled to the younger man. Tom's deep brown eyes looked into mine. He offered a warm smile that comforted me in a way I haven't felt in a while. The welcome gesture elicited a stupid grin and an awkward giggle—a reaction I almost immediately regretted.

Derek took a step forward. "I'll take her," he insisted, but almost immediately, he frowned. "Dammit, I can't."

"Is something wrong, Chief Cody?" Dot asked.

I'd almost forgotten she and Addie were here.

Come to think of it, I was almost a little surprised that Dot hadn't popped some popcorn to watch me flounder, under the attention of not one, but two attractive men.

Derek turned toward Dot and jabbed his thumb toward the door. "I'm on duty. Deidre's beauty salon called in a robbery."

"Oh, goodness gracious me!" Dot clutched her ample bosom. "Was anyone hurt?"

"No, no." Derek kept his voice steady. "But Deidre reported some of her inventory missing."

"What's there to steal from a beauty parlor?" Addie let the question float as we all stared at her bright, pink hair, painted nails, and copious eye make up.

Derek sighed before responding. "Believe it or not, a shipment of hair dye went missing. A whopping forty bottles, to be precise. Bunch of odd colors, too. Oh, and some developer."

"Sounds like somebody's trying to open their own shop," I offered.

The chief just shrugged. "You'll be certain to get her to the emergency room now, right?" he asked Tom.

Tom nodded vigorously. "You bet, Chief. Swear to Saint Sarah."

"Good, she means a lot."

My eyes weren't the only ones that widened at that last.

Derek cleared his throat. "To the Noreen Cox investigation," he verbally backpedaled. "She's been very informative. And, as a small business owner, of course she's incredibly important... to the community."

"Heavens to Betsy. What's this town coming to?"

Dot clucked her tongue as she shook her ringleted head. "Used to be you could leave your front door unlocked and sleep peaceful because there was nary a thought of your neighbor doing anything untoward. Today? Today we've got beautician burglars, flamingo felons, and dead diviners!" She gave one final harrumph and crossed her arms.

Tom cringed.

Who wouldn't after that much alliteration?

"She knows about the flamingos?" Derek leaned in with a whisper.

Blood flooded the capillaries in my neck where his breath fell.

"She... knows... everything," Addie rasped dramatically. Her green eyes shifted back-and-forth as she wedged her way between me and the chief. She threw her arms over our shoulders, leaning in conspiratorially. She abruptly clapped us both on the back and straightened.

"At least, she thinks she does," she called as she turned on the heel of her black combat boot and strutted back toward her task. She stuck her earbuds back in her pierced ears, oblivious to Dot's plump, pink tongue giving her a hearty raspberry.

"Forget the stitches," I grumbled. "Do you think the hospital has a pill for snarkiness?"

"If they do," Derek commented and looked between my two employees, "you might want to get the economy bottle."

CHAPTER THIRTEEN

"So," Tom started with a hint of hesitation in his voice. "You and the chief?"

My face pinched, though I wasn't sure if it was prompted by the pain in my hand or by complete confusion. "Pardon?"

Tom stretched his long, lanky legs out in front of him, but was forced to draw them back almost immediately as an orderly in green scrubs barreled past us, piloting a gurney occupied by a groaning man.

"Coming through!" the orderly barked. Tom nearly lost a couple of toes.

As my gaze swept over the bustling ER waiting room, I made a mental note to check if there was a full moon. Under the harsh glare of buzzing fluorescent bulbs, a sort of anarchy persisted. Lawrence Memorial Hospital in New London was hopping.

I heard the automatic shush of the doors as another poor soul fed into the already crowded waiting room. A teenage boy — football player, judging from his build and the illustrated harpoon sticking through the brilliant yellow and green logo of his mud-stained jersey—hopped along, the bulk of his weight supported on the shoulder of his teammate.

Tom gestured. "New London High Whalers." I nodded. "I think that's their quarterback," he continued.

"Guess their season just fumbled." I smiled weakly at the attempted pun.

The repetitive thrill of the phone at the nurses' station rat-a-tat-tatted like an electronic woodpecker. A crying baby across the way squalled in counterpoint. Yellow-green snot smeared across the baby's ruddy cheeks as he dragged a chubby little fist over his runny nose. His mother tried to comfort him, exasperation clear on her face.

The momentary thought flitted through my head. If someone like Madame Zorina had predicted there would be days like these, would the young woman still have chosen motherhood? For that matter, if any of us knew what the future held, how would it color our decisions?

I would have moved from New York ages ago.

The wet cough of the older gentleman seated beside me interrupted my reverie. Spittle flew from his dry, cracked lips as he doubled over with the force of his hacking. I leaned into Tom a little. A surprised smile played at the corner of his lips.

I immediately straightened and tugged at the gauze on my hand. "Are you really sure I need stitches?"

"I would definitely recommend it," he answered.

"Come on. It's just a little scratch," I whined.

He took my hands in his and leveled a no-nonsense stare into my eyes. "Zoe, that is a serious cut.

Not to mention, you picked up that piece of glass from the trash. Who knows what sort of dirt and germs you've introduced to your system? If you don't get it taken care of properly, you could develop a serious infection."

"I know. I know," I grudgingly agreed. "It's just, well—I hate hospitals."

There. I said it.

"Why?"

"Paging Doctor Ginsberg to oncology. Paging Dr. Ginsberg." A sterile, tired voice called over the hospital's intercom system. A dry chuckle escaped my lips.

Matched the antiseptic smell permeating my nostrils.

Somewhere, a monitor beeped steadily—a technological metronome—keeping time in the discord.

"Germs?" I offered a weak answer.

Tom raised an eyebrow. "Really?"

I tried to hold his gaze, but my pulse did a nervous tango in my wrist. I winced before my hand even bumped the chair's armrest. "Okay, maybe that's not it."

His finger brushed the top of my uninjured hand. Tingles electrified my arm. Tom made a quick reconnoiter for any speeding gurneys and, satisfied there was no immediate danger of a trans-metatarsal amputation, he leaned back and stretched his legs out once more. "So, you never answered my other question."

I busied myself picking at the loose strings on my bandage, grateful to change the subject. "What question is that?"

"About you and the chief."

"What about us?"

"Well," he hesitated. He pulled in his legs and leaned forward and clasped his hands together. He looked at the ground. "Are you two a thing?"

"What?!" I squawked loudly enough to be heard above the ER din. Several heads turned. I bowed my head. "What do you mean 'are we a thing'?"

Tom sat straight. "I saw the way he looked at you back at the shop." He snorted. "More importantly, I saw the way he looked at me. Not sure which one of us he would rather have put in cuffs. Though I'm pretty certain it would be for wholly different reasons."

I could feel the bright cherry splotches breaking out across my chest, like they did every time I was absolutely mortified. I tried to ignore them as I scrambled to put together a coherent answer. "Me and the chief? Don't be ridiculous. We are not not now, nor have we ever been a 'thing'. In fact, I haven't had a 'thing' in quite some time."

Oh, yeah. Now the splotch was crimson. Like Roll Tide Alabama crimson.

Why had I offered that last little tidbit of info?

Tom held his hands in the air in a gesture of submission. "Sorry. I just thought maybe you two—"

"Yeah, well, no," I quipped.

The silence that fell between us was louder than the hullabaloo of the ER. I laid my good hand across the top of Tom's. "I'm sorry. It's just that I haven't let myself get close to anybody in, well, a really long time. It's not that I don't want to. It's just been so long." I hesitated. "I think I've forgotten how."

His gaze met mine. "Zoe—"

"Miss Romano? Zoe Romano?" A nurse's voice interrupted. We both looked up.

"Yes?" I replied.

The nurse gave a weary smile. "The doctor is ready to see you now. Right this way." She gestured toward the double doors that led back to the treatment area. She cast a quick glance at my bandage. "Hm. Excellent triage. Someone knew what they were doing."

I passed Tom an appreciative smile as stood to follow me through the double doors.

The nurse held up a warning hand. "I'm sorry. Are you family, sir?"

"Uh, no. Just a friend."

"Then I'm afraid I'll have to ask you to remain out here."

Another explosive bout of phlegm-filled coughing erupted from the old man. Tom gave the nurse a dubious look. "But what if she needs me?"

"I'll be fine, Tom," I assured.

He looked over at the coughing, sneezing, wailing conglomeration of bodies gathered in the waiting room and looked back at me. "Sure. You'll be fine." He gulped. "But what about me?"

*****

"You're a lucky lady." The doctor blinked two enormous blurry blue eyes behind soda-bottle-thick lenses. He held the wedge of green glass up to the light and tilted it back-and-forth with the tweezers. "An eighth of an inch more, and this little puppy could've nicked

104

your radial artery."

"And that's a bad thing?"

"Oh, yes! A perforation of the radial artery would likely result in unconsciousness in fifteen seconds and death in ninety from the resultant blood loss."

I looked up at the glass from my position on the gurney, mostly to avoid looking at the deep, angry, red gash now clearly visible in my hand. The translucent green was stained with my blood, of course, but peeking from beneath the crimson, I thought I spied several smudges across the surface of the glass.

Was that a fingerprint?

According to Edmond Locard, the preeminent, forensic, pioneer's exchange principal, whenever two objects come into contact with each other, a transfer of material occurs. This can be fiber, blood, hair — and fingerprints.

Now, while many fingerprints are latent, meaning they are only visible after processing with powder or chemicals, patent fingerprints, such as those made by grease, blood, or dirt, were visible to the naked eye.

A little woozy from the wound — I hoped I wasn't going into shock — I wasn't entirely certain the smudges I saw were even a fingerprint at all, but my bloodhound instincts howled all the same. If the smudge was a fingerprint, it might just lead to the identity of one of the male visitors who had been at Madame Zorina's the night of her death!

The glass jangled against the stainless steel kidney dish on the roller cart as the doctor dropped it in with the tweezers. "Yup. If you didn't have such a pronounced thenar eminence, your goose could've been cooked."

My heart hammered. That piece of glass could very well be the evidence needed to cook someone else's goose!

I needed to get it to Chief Cody as soon as possible. "Do you think I can keep that?" I gestured to the glass.

The doctor blinked behind his lenses. He volleyed a bewildered look between my eager expression and the stained wedge in the basin. "You want to keep it?" His bushy eyebrows peaked over the rims of his spectacles.

I grinned sheepishly. "Souvenir?"

"Okay. I suppose so. Just don't go sticking it back into your pocket."

I chuckled and held up my uninjured hand in a three-fingered Girl Scout salute. "Promise. Now, can we hurry this along, Doc?"

"Absolutely, my dear. A little anesthetic, a little needlepoint, and bingo, boingo, boffo — you're right as rain."

Right as rain, indeed, Doc.

I looked toward the glass in the silver tray.

And I was going to bring a tempest down on whomever had killed Noreen Cox.

CHAPTER FOURTEEN

"You have a pronounced what?" Derek pulled at the collar of his shirt like I'd just stripped down to my skivvies right there in front of his desk.

"Thenar eminence," I repeated. I waved my hand in front of me, complete with its neat row of simple, continuous pattern, black stitches.

Addie had been disappointed when she seen them back at the shop. "They didn't have them in pink?" she'd complained.

Now I was back at the police station and in the chief's office. The green glass, crusted with my dried blood, lay in a sealed plastic evidence bag on the desk between us.

"The thenar eminence is the fleshy part of the hand. Right here. Under the thumb. Madame Zorina, excuse me, Noreen Cox, would've called it the Mount of Venus." I gave a fancy little flourish and promptly winced.

I wasn't the only one in pain, though. At the mention of the word "mount," Derek squirmed in his seat. I chuckled inwardly and turned my palm back toward me and examined the now-stitched wound, checking for any impromptu bleeding.

Some blood was, in fact, seeping. Doc had warned me to take it easy, but we all know how very well I take advice. I grabbed a tissue from Derek's desk and gently daubed at the blood. Other than that, the area around the sutures was still a little swollen — a bit black and blue, too — but for my misadventures, I had fared pretty well.

I continued spouting from my burgeoning cornucopia of psychic knowledge. "The Mount of Venus supposedly rules, love, passion, romance… and, um, sensuality."

You know how they say knowledge is power? *Sometimes it's just a pain in the ass.*

My turn to squirm. I drew Derek's attention back to the glass on his desk. "Did you find any evidence of a wine bottle in Noreen's trash?" I asked.

Relief flooded over Derek's features as he eagerly discussed the case. "My people went through the contents of that trashcan with a fine-toothed comb. There was no bottle. Or anything else, for that matter, that offered any insight into her murder."

I slid to the edge of my seat and pointed. "So, that piece of glass right there could be the only link we have to uncovering the identity of at least one of the men that was at Noreen's apartment that night?"

The chief interlaced his fingers behind his head and leaned back in his chair. "Or it could just be a random piece of trash."

"But Iliev insisted that a young man showed up at Noreen's, and he was carrying a bottle of wine."

"And Iliev could be lying. Don't forget, we have his blood at the scene of the crime. And he had access."

"But what about motive? Have you confirmed the motive?"

"Yeah, about that," the chief began. He rummaged through a stack of papers on his desk and pulled out a single page. He handed it to me. I scanned the document as he continued. "You mentioned the guy had a pension for peeking in windows. I ran him through the system. Turns out, the guy has a record. Charge of trespass with intent to peer. Class B misdemeanor. Served six months in Delaware."

"But nothing for violence?" Derek shook his head. "Doesn't mean he didn't do it. Like you said, maybe he decided peeking through windows wasn't enough. He decided to take it one step further, and Noreen wasn't having any of it."

"I don't know. Something tells me Iliev's not our guy."

"Reporter's gut feeling?"

"I suppose you could call it that," I muttered, though it had been a very long time since I had any true confidence in my intuition.

"Tell you what." He picked up the evidence bag. "I'll run this through forensics — see if anything pops. Meanwhile, I have the fellas bringing Iliev in for questioning."

A sharp rap sounded behind us. Kieran Culpepper, one of the chief deputies, leaned in the doorway — clean, cut kid with a dimple in his chin. He hooked a thumb down the hall. "Hey, Chief. We've got him in Interview One."

Derek pushed back his chair and stood. "Great, Culpepper. Thanks. Oh, can you get this to the lab? Have them pull prints. Run them through the system. See if we can get a match." He strode across the room and handed the bag to the deputy, who took it and loped down the hall to complete the task. Derek turned back to me. "You wanna sit in?"

I considered his offer. I looked at my watch. The book club was scheduled to meet this evening at the shop. Shakespeare night. On tap? A Midsummer Night's Beam and Romeo and Juleps. I wasn't at all certain I could trust the dynamic duo to remember to stock up on fresh mint leaves.

But my gut? *It was growling.*

It never even occurred to me it was because I hadn't eaten for 24 hours.

*****

Miroslav Iliev looked like a frightened fish. His eyes darted about the confines of the small interrogation room. I watched him from behind the one-way window — almost like watching hungry piranha at the Mystic Aquarium. I resisted the urge to tap the glass.

"Don't spook the fish, huh?" I jumped at Derek's voice and his uncannily on-point comment. He had strolled up behind me, pen in hand, a legal pad and Iliev's file tucked under his arm. "You ready?"

"As I'll ever be," I replied.

"Okay, but just remember, let me do the talking.

You're a consultant on the case, yes, but I'm still the one with the badge. Keep your theories to yourself in there."

I threw my hands up. "You got it, Chief." He opened the door to the interrogation room.

Every muscle in Miroslav's body tensed as Derek's muscled frame filled the doorway. Derek stepped to the side, holding the door open, revealing my more diminutive form. Miroslav's eyes went from wide and bulbous to narrow and wary.

"You," he hissed and directed a malevolent glare in my direction. He pointed a dirty finger toward me. "She—"

"Is none of your concern, Mr. Iliev." Derek immediately placed himself between me and Addie's smarmy landlord. He placed the pad and file on the table.

Iliev looked nervously at the official folder and adjusted in his seat. "I am under arrest?"

Derek raised an eyebrow. "Should you be?"

Iliev considered for a moment, searching for some subterfuge in Derek's expression. His thin lips sat in a hard line. He crossed his arms and gave a defiant, "No."

It didn't look like Iliev had changed clothes from our meeting the other day. He was still wearing the torn flannel shirt, though I think I spied a fresh tomato sauce stain on his dingy white undershirt. The bruise on his forehead had faded from a dark purple to a sickly yellowish green. His chukkas, the tan nap still the only pristine thing about the man, tapped under the table as his legs bounced in a furious rhythm.

Iliev was nervous—about something.

A harsh squeak pulled my attention as Derek pulled out a chair for me. The unexpected gesture caught me off guard. "Thanks," I murmured as I sat.

"You are *policija*, then?" Iliev asked me. He snorted and that Adam's apple bobbled as he swallowed. It made my gut churn for different reasons altogether.

"No, she is not," Derek interjected before I could reply. "Miss Romano is a consultant on this case."

Iliev slumped in his chair. "Is too bad."

"And why is that, Mr. Iliev?" Derek asked and flipped through his notes without looking up. "I was hoping, maybe, she had... handcuffs?"

"Mr. Iliev, you are already in enough trouble."

Iliev scowled. His black brows twisted into one long slash across his pale, greasy forehead. "So, I guess you no want the room, then."

Derek tossed me a confused look. I shake my head vehemently. Iliev shrugged. "Is okay. How you say — not my type, anyway."

Derek swung his attention back to Iliev immediately. "And what about Noreen Cox, Iliev?" He tossed a sheaf of crime scene photos across the surface of the table. "Was she your type?"

I looked down at the photos. They were all taken from different angles, but they all showed the same thing — Noreen Cox's body, her arms and legs splayed at awkward angles, blood splattered across the rug and scattered tarot cards from the injury to her head. It was everywhere. A pool of it had congealed beneath her fanned hair, matting it to the ground as it had dried.

Something nibbled at the back of my brain, but I

112

couldn't quite put my finger on it. Iliev let out an audible groan. He crushed his eyes closed and pushed the stack of photos back to Derek. I picked up one photo, tilted it this way and that, examining it from every angle.

Owwwooooooooo!

That old hound dog howled.

What are you sniffing at, boy?

"Please," Iliev begged. "I cannot."

"What's the matter, Miroslav? Can't stand to see what you've done?" Derek tapped the official file. "We have your blood, which places you at the scene. We know you've got a record. We know you like peeking into ladies' windows. Maybe, after all this time, it just wasn't cutting it for you anymore. Here's what I think happened. I think you went over to Noreen Cox's apartment and tried to put the moves on her, but when she shut you down, you put her down."

Iliev shook his head vigorously. "No, no, no. I have told you. I only went for to collect the rent monies. When she did not answer the door, I open only to check. And that is when… that is when…"

Iliev's eyes rolled back into his head, exposing the whites.

CHAPTER FIFTEEN

Iliev stiffened, then collapsed to the floor like a downed marionette.

Derek exhaled through his nose and rubbed his temples like he could already feel the migraine forming. "Fantastic." He flicked on the intercom. "Somebody get Bernie in here before I have to file more paperwork."

The door swung open a moment later, and in strutted Bernie Russo. Don't ask me why, but he had a tweed vest over his green scrubs and another bow tie so loud it practically honked. His face brightened the second he saw me.

"Zoe!" He pulled me into an Old Spice bear hug. "How are you?" He stepped back and wiggled his bushy eyebrows. "More importantly, how is the demigoddess that is Dorothy Richards?"

"Dot is fine."

"Wonderful. Wonderful. Oh, how I long to wrap my legs around..."

"Ahem," Derek coughed.

"Oh. Right." Bernie straightened his bow tie. "You know, life was a lot more fun before HR. So, to what do I owe this summons?" he asked.

Derek pointed. "Fainted. Fix him."

Bernie's gray eyebrows arched over thick glasses as he sized up the heap of Iliev on the floor. "Let me guess. Another one taken down by the horror of municipal lighting?" He squatted, poked Iliev's cheek, and muttered, "Yup. Still ugly." He checked Iliev's pulse, lifted an eyelid, then shook his head. "Nope. Not a stroke. No signs of seizure. No aneurysm—unless bad fashion choices count as neurological trauma."

Bernie stood up and nudged Iliev's limp form with his shoe. "Hey, Sleeping Beauty, you dead?" He sighed. "Well, this is boring. And I retired from boring. He's not dying, which is kind of a shame—I was hoping for something interesting." He turned to the officers and jerked his thumb toward the door. "Haul him onto the autopsy table in the next room. If he wakes up dead, at least I won't have to move him."

Derek sighed. "That's not funny."

Bernie shrugged. "You're right. It's hilarious." Two officers hefted Iliev's limp form like an overgrown sack of potatoes and carried him down the hall. I followed, gripping my bandaged hand as they plopped him onto the sterile aluminum slab of the medical examiner's table.

Iliev's arms flopped outward, and his head lolled to the side in a dramatic flourish. If I didn't know any better, I'd say he was auditioning for a crime procedural.

Bernie tugged on a pair of latex gloves with a snap, leaned over Iliev, and just as he was about to prod his forehead—Iliev shot upright with a desperate, rattling gasp.

Bernie stumbled backward so fast he nearly took down an entire tray of scalpels. "Holy hell! Now my patients are rising from the dead!"

Iliev blinked, wild-eyed, then looked down at the gleaming steel beneath him. His skin went an alarming shade of gray. "Is this... is this where you cut the bodies?"

Bernie, never one to miss an opportunity, grinned wickedly. "Oh, yeah. And guess what? The last guy on that slab... never made it out."

Iliev let out a strangled yelp and flailed in an attempt to scramble off, sending a kidney dish clattering to the floor. I bit the inside of my cheek, doing a poor job of hiding my amusement.

Bernie turned to me with a smirk, adjusting his bow tie. "So, tell me, Zoe... Dot's still single, right?"

Bernie's flirtation came to an abrupt halt when a fresh, sharp sting flared in my palm. I hissed through my teeth and glanced down at my bandaged hand. The gauze had turned a deep, alarming shade of red. Iliev followed my gaze. His breath hitched. His eyes went as round as dinner plates. His knees knocked together. And then—like a house of cards in a stiff breeze—he collapsed.

His head smacked against the cold aluminum table with a loud, metallic thunk. The entire room winced in unison.

Bernie groaned. "Again? Really? The guy folds faster than a cheap lawn chair."

I ignored him, my mind churning. Something

116

about this didn't feel staged. I stepped closer, examining Iliev's pale, sweaty face. His body was slack, his breathing shallow but steady. My gut twisted — not with worry, but with realization.

"He's not faking," I murmured.

Derek scoffed, arms crossing. "You're telling me our number-one suspect just happens to have a habit of fainting on command?"

I shook my head. "Not on command. But look at the timing." I lifted my bleeding hand as evidence.

Bernie tilted his head. "You think he's got… vasovagal syncope?"

"Bernie!" Derek hollered. "Cut it out! I will call HR on your ass!"

Bernie blinked. Then realized Derek thought he'd just spit out a twenty-dollar naughty word. "No, no, no." Bernie grinned, rubbing his hands together. "Vasovagal syncope. Basically, our guy here faints like a Bridgerton cast member at the sight of blood."

Bernie, now fully invested in his own personal amusement, rubbed his hands together like a villain in a silent film. "Time for a highly sophisticated medical experiment."

I had a bad feeling about this. With the glee of a man who enjoyed chaos far too much, he plucked a blood specimen jar from the nearest shelf and gave it a vigorous shake — like a macabre maraca.

I grimaced. "Bernie, that's… gross." He grinned, holding the sloshing vial up like he was unveiling a fine bottle of Bordeaux. "Science is often gross, my dear."

Iliev groaned from the table, shifting slightly. His

eyelids fluttered open, unfocused and dazed.

Bernie, fully committed to his bit, leaned in and tilted the jar closer. "And now... for our thrilling conclusion..."

Iliev's gaze landed on the swirling red liquid. His pupils dilated. His face lost all color. His lips parted in silent horror. And then—he was out.

Boom.

Iliev hit the metal table again, his skull connecting with an even louder thunk.

Bernie clapped his hands together. "Ladies and gentlemen, we have a diagnosis!"

I smirked. "The man's not a killer. He'd never survive the sight of his own crime scene."

Derek muttered, "I hate that this actually makes sense."

Bernie leaned in, smirking. "Come on, Chief. Admit it. You love when I'm right."

Derek glared. "You're insufferable."

"That's what the last Mrs. Medical Examiner said." Bernie winked. "But unlike her, you keep calling me back."

I chuckled, but as my gaze fell on Iliev's limp body sprawled across the autopsy table, something nagged at me. If Iliev wasn't the killer... Then who the hell was at Noreen's apartment that night? And whose fingerprint was on that glass?

The case just got a whole lot murkier.

CHAPTER SIXTEEN

We were down a suspect, and Madame Zorina was just getting deader. The case called for a reboot, so I suggested a caffeine run. Chief Cody — Derek — agreed. Personally, I think he was just hoping to avoid another run-in with Arthur about the absentee flamingos.

Derek and I settled into a shaded corner of Sift Bake Shop's patio, the scent of fresh pastries wafting through the air. The Mystic River gleamed under the late morning sun, boats bobbing lazily at the dock. The gentle clinking of cups and cutlery blended with the distant hum of a drawbridge siren. It was almost peaceful.

Almost.

"You know," Derek mused, watching the bridge start its slow ascent, "this bridge has been opening and closing since the 1920s. One of the last remaining bascule bridges of its kind. People come from all over just to see it in action."

Did that include a killer?

I stirred my coffee, watching the swirling ripples of cream dissolve into the dark liquid. "It's like this whole town is a time capsule."

His gaze flicked to me. "That a good thing or a bad thing?"

I hesitated, then shrugged. "Depends on what's trapped inside."

Derek chuckled, but there was an undercurrent of something unspoken. Something neither of us was willing to poke at just yet.

The bridge groaned, its gears churning as it lifted higher, exposing the sailboat passing beneath. The sun caught the water's surface, sending shifting diamonds of light skittering across our table. The moment stretched — quiet, easy, but edged with something else. A lull before the next storm.

I traced the rim of my cup, frowning as I watched a seagull swoop low over the dock, hoping to snatch an abandoned pastry crumb. "So that's it? We're ruling out Iliev?"

Derek exhaled sharply, leaning back in his chair. "We don't have a choice. The guy keels over at the sight of blood. Even if I still think he's a slimy bastard, he's not our killer."

I thought of Iliev's limp form sprawled across the autopsy table, the sickly pallor of his face, the way Bernie had gleefully waved a blood vial like some demented carnival barker. The whole thing had been ridiculous. But it had also been undeniable.

"Then we go back to square one," I said, setting my cup down with a soft clink. "Motive, not means. Who wanted Noreen dead?"

Derek drummed his fingers against the tabletop, his eyes scanning the bustling marina as if the answer might be bobbing out there among the sailboats. "And who wanted her silenced."

That word sat heavy between us. Silenced. It shifted the whole equation. Noreen's murder wasn't just a crime of passion or a robbery gone wrong. Someone had wanted her gone—permanently.

I arched an eyebrow. "You sound like a man who's dealt with plenty of people who needed silencing."

Derek smirked, but his eyes lacked their characteristic twinkle. He turned his cup absently between his hands, his gaze drifting toward the water. "You could say that." His voice was lighter than his expression. "New York had no shortage of them. The kind of cases that crawl under your skin and set up shop. The ones that make you second-guess your own instincts."

I watched him carefully, noting the tension in his jaw, the way his fingers tapped a restless rhythm against his coffee cup. "That why you left?"

He exhaled slowly, as if weighing his words. "That, and I got tired of the noise. The chaos. Thought I'd come to Mystic for some peace and quiet." He let out a short, humorless laugh, shaking his head. "Between flamingos and psychics, though, I've got my hands full."

A smirk tugged at my lips. "You forgot murder."

He huffed. "Oh, yeah. And murder." His gaze flicked to me. Something unreadable passed through it. "Guess I didn't really escape much after all."

I took a sip of my coffee, letting the weight of his words settle. "Guess not."

He gave me a side glance. "You know, I don't get it. You were good. I mean… really good. That series on the psychics? That was some of the best investigative work I've read."

A dull ache bloomed in my chest, slow and heavy. I hadn't thought about that work in a long time—hadn't wanted to. "That was a long time ago."

He studied me, waiting. Patient, steady.

I sighed. "It wasn't just about exposing frauds. One case—one in particular—got to me." I hesitated, the memories stirring like something restless and unwelcome. But there was no point in holding back now. "The sweetheart scam."

Derek leaned in. "Go on."

I wrapped my hands around my cup, letting the warmth ground me. "There are psychics who don't just scam people out of money. They scam them out of themselves. They build trust, forge connections, fake relationships." I swallowed. Hard. "Pretend to be in love with their marks." Derek's brow lifted. "Sometimes they succeed in draining their bank accounts while they're at it. And by the time the victim realizes what's happened, they've lost everything—sometimes more than just money." I only hoped the pain in my heart didn't show on my face.

Understanding dawned in his eyes. "And you think Noreen was running that kind of con?"

I met his gaze, my pulse quickening. "I think it's possible. And if she was… we need to figure out anyone and everyone she was conning."

I drummed my fingers against the table, my mind

spinning through the possibilities. "Noreen had clients. Rich ones. What if she was working an angle with one client in particular? What if she got too deep?"

Derek frowned, his cup pausing halfway to his lips. "Who?"

I met his gaze. "Orson Tobit."

His brows shot up. "You think she was scamming him?"

I nodded. "It fits. He's wealthy. Private. And if she played him right…"

Derek shook his head, setting his coffee down with a dull thud. "No way. That man has too much self-respect."

"Maybe. But what if she convinced him someone was his soulmate?"

"Sera?" Derek exhaled sharply, his skepticism warring with the possibility. "That's a hell of a con. He didn't even meet Sera here."

"I don't know. New York's not that far away." I leaned forward. "Think about it. If she was running a sweetheart scam, Orson would be the perfect target. He's got old money, a reputation to protect. If he thought she was the real deal and then found out she wasn't—"

Derek ran a hand over his jaw. "That's a hell of a motive."

"Exactly." I sat back. "If Orson Tobit realized he was being played, we're not just looking at another suspect."

Derek nodded grimly. "We're looking at our most powerful one yet."

My heart skipped a beat.

Derek leaned forward, voice dropping. "Listen, Zoe. If Tobit's involved, we tread carefully. That man's got influence. Money. Connections. You don't just go accusing him without solid proof."

I nodded. "Agreed."

His eyes narrowed. "That means no snooping."

I sipped my coffee. "Of course."

His sigh told me he wasn't buying it.

A slow smile spread across my lips. "I promise I won't snoop, but I do already have a reason to stop by the ranch."

Derek arched a brow. "Oh?"

I leaned in. "Sera's Dom Perignon order. It's going straight to Tobit."

Derek stared at me. "You're going to deliver champagne and interrogate a potential murderer?"

I grinned. "Let's call it multitasking."

I set my cup down and drummed my fingers against the table, mind working through the tangled mess. "But here's what I don't get—if Tobit found out Noreen and Sera were scamming him, why is he still going through with the wedding?"

Derek exhaled through his nose, rubbing his jaw.

"Maybe he doesn't know the full story."

"You're thinking he may not know about Sera's involvement," I finished.

Derek's silence was enough of an answer.

I sat back, staring out at the sailboats bobbing along the Mystic River, their crisp white sails stark against the blue. If Noreen had set this whole thing in motion, playing matchmaker for a price, then it was highly likely Sera had been in on it from the start.

And if Orson found out?

That changed everything.

The pieces were starting to fit together—just not in a way I liked.

"Hm." A pensive expression came over Derek's face.

"What?" Derek sighed and drained the last of his coffee, setting the cup down with a decisive clink. "Whatever game Noreen was playing it ended with her dead. If Sera was in on it, she might've had a reason to want her out of the picture."

Orson's fiancée. His supposed soulmate. The woman set to marry into one of the wealthiest families in town.

My stomach twisted.

Derek checked his watch. "You should get going. I've got a report to file, and you've got a delivery to make."

I nodded absently.

"Zoe." His tone sharpened. "I meant what I said. If Tobit finds out you're poking around, he won't like it. And if Sera really is part of this scam…"

"…then she won't like it either." I met his gaze. "Yeah, I got that part."

He studied me for a moment before sighing. "Be careful."

I gave him a half-hearted salute and grabbed my bag.

As I returned to my shop, the weight of the coming afternoon settled over me. Ninety-nine bottles of

Dom, a suspicious engagement, and a woman who might not be as lucky in love as she wanted the world to believe.

I needed to finish prepping the order before heading to Tobit Ranch. And if I was lucky, I'd squeeze in a few answers before I left.

I just hoped I wasn't asking the wrong questions.

CHAPTER SEVENTEEN

I paced the length of my office, my fingers drumming against the clipboard in my hand. Ninety-nine bottles of Dom Perignon. A small fortune in bubbles.

My small fortune.

I glanced at my phone, my stomach tightening at the balance in my business account. Mortgage payment looming. Overdraft waiting to happen.

"Deliver the champagne, get paid, keep the shop, and — oh yeah — casually dig into a possible killer's secrets while I'm at it. No big deal."

I set the clipboard down and rubbed my temples. The weight of it all settled on my shoulders like an overstocked shelf ready to collapse.

Ah, well. One good con deserves another. Noreen had worked her angles, but like I suggested to Derek, I had my own.

Sera's engagement party was my way in.

The engagement party was set to be the type of spectacle people whispered about for years. If Orson

Tobit and Sera had something to hide, it would be buried somewhere in that gilded estate, among the imported floral arrangements and champagne towers. All I had to do was play my part—polite, professional, just a wine supplier dropping off a high-ticket order. No ulterior motives.

And while I was there, I'd be looking for anything—anything—that tied Orson or Sera to Noreen's apartment.

A sound plan. Logical. Simple... until I stepped out of my office, clipboard in hand, and my stomach dropped.

I'd forgotten something.

Something worse than my dwindling bank account.

Boisterous voices. Obnoxious laughter.

Oh no.

Book club.

I stepped out of my office and into absolute chaos.

Dot stood behind the counter, looking far too pleased with herself. My gaze dropped to the empty hors d'oeuvres tray in front of her.

Again.

No wonder I was broke. I needed to cut these things back to once a month.

I scowled. "Dot. Tell me you didn't."

She popped the last bruschetta into her mouth. "I regret nothing."

Before I could respond, the door banged open, and Addie barreled in, arms full of bright red bags.

I squinted.

Were those… ketchup chips?

"No worries! I've got it covered!" she announced, nearly upending a wine rack as she skidded to the counter.

I blinked. "What. Is. That?"

Addie dumped the bags down with pride. "Hors d'oeuvres!"

Dot and I exchanged a look.

Addie huffed, like she was put out for having to explain the obvious. "Dot said tonight's wine pairs well with Italian food. Ketchup is made from tomatoes. Spaghetti sauce is made from tomatoes. Same thing."

Her expression said, "Duh."

I dropped my head into my hands.

Addie sighed, clutching a bag to her chest. "Besides, it gave me an excuse to see Tom. God, he's so freaking cute. He keeps these in the butcher shop — imports them from Canada. Apparently, you can't get 'em around here. Says they're his favorite." She sighed dreamily. "Wish I was his favorite."

Dot snorted. "You're a lost cause."

I crossed my arms, still shooting Dot a warning glare, but, speaking of lost causes, I knew one when I saw one. I let it go and turned to Deidre, who was already perched on a barstool, flipping through a fashion magazine like she didn't have a care in the world.

"So," I said, leaning on the counter. "Any updates on the hair dye bandit?"

Deidre exhaled dramatically, tossing the magazine onto the counter. "Chief Cody came by earlier, asked a bunch of questions, took notes, did that whole serious cop thing—"

She smirked, smoothing her already perfect hair bump. "Frankly, I hope the case takes him forever. Serious is a good look on him. That man could put me in cuffs anytime he wants."

I groaned. "Glad to see you're handling the situation with absolute professionalism."

"Oh, please," she scoffed. "I don't even have time to worry about it! Everyone and their grandma are coming in for blowouts and sets this weekend. Phone's been ringing off the hook with appointments."

I arched a brow. "That busy, huh?"

Deidre scoffed, tossing her magazine onto the counter. "What did you expect with the Tobit-Hawking engagement party? It's like the Mystic Met Gala, doll. Custom ice sculptures, designer dresses, champagne fountains—hell, for all I know, there's gonna be a golden carriage rolling up by sundown. I ain't got time to cry over a robbery."

I sighed, rubbing my temples as the weight of the day pressed against me. "Remind me again—what exactly did they take from your shop?"

Deidre threw up her hands like I'd asked her to solve a complex equation. "Just a bunch of dye and developer. But not even the good stuff."

I blinked. "So, what, like pink? Purple?"

Addie scowled at me.

Deidre scoffed. "Nope. Besides, I hardly stock stuff like that since I left Jersey. My customers all wanna be Barbie these days. You know what shades they took?"

I shrugged. "Surprise me."

Deidre held up her manicured fingers, ticking off the list. "Chestnut brown. Perlino cream. Mahogany bay." She let out an exasperated huff. "Borrrrring."

I frowned. That was… *weird*.

Dot smirked from behind the counter, stirring her tea. "Maybe someone out there's going for a very understated ombré."

Deidre shuddered. "Honey, if you're stealing dye, at least steal something with a little pizzazz."

I chuckled, shaking my head, but something about it nagged at me. Those colors—why did they sound familiar? It wasn't just random. It meant something.

I filed it away for later, pushing the thought to the back of my mind. Tomorrow, I had some champagne to deliver.

*****

The late afternoon sun was still warm as I steered my van up the long, winding driveway of Tobit Ranch, an estate that screamed old money and tight security. White-fenced pastures stretched out on either side, perfectly manicured, as if even the horses were held to a higher standard of living.

I eased toward the main gate, rolling down my window. A uniformed guard peered at me over the top of his clipboard.

"Delivery," I said, tapping the clipboard holding the invoice for the ninety-nine bottles of Dom Perignon. "Engagement party order for Sera Hawking."

The guard gave me a once-over before nodding. "They're expecting you. Just pull around to the back entrance near the loading dock."

I feigned casual interest. "Any idea where I can find Miss Hawking? She needs to sign off on the order."

He shifted his weight, glancing down at his clipboard. "She's probably down at the stables. Just got a new stallion in last night. Manny brought it in around midnight, and Miss Hawking likes to check them out first thing."

Midnight?

That *was… interesting.*

I kept my expression neutral. "Manny?"

"The stud manager." The guard scratched the back of his head, already disinterested.

"Right. Thanks."

I almost put the van in drive, but my mind was spinning.

"Excuse me?" I called the guard back over.

"Yeah?"

"Midnight seems kind of late to be receiving horses."

The guard gave an "I-just-work-here" shrug. "Manny says it's better for the horses. Keeps 'em calmer. Not so much traffic and noise."

Made sense.

"Okay. Thanks." I shifted gears and pointed the car toward the loading dock.

I wiped the sweat from my forehead, my arms aching as I stacked the last crate of Dom Perignon onto the loading dock. Ninety-nine bottles of champagne, and not a single one had magically carried itself inside.

Next time, I was hiring a delivery guy.

A shrill whinny shattered the stillness. My head jerked toward the stables.

I'd promised Derek I wouldn't snoop.

Okay, maybe just a little snooping.

I dusted off my hands and wandered toward the sound, keeping my steps light. The barn doors were ajar, the scent of hay, sweat, and oiled leather thick in the air.

The light inside was dim, golden slants of sunlight filtering through high-set, dust-streaked windows, illuminating floating motes. It was expensive in the way that only old money could afford — meticulously kept stalls, polished brass fittings, and the unmistakable tang of wealth that somehow lingered, even in a place full of manure and horse sweat.

Inside, Sera stood in a whispered conversation with a tall, broad-shouldered man whose presence seemed to suck the air from the barn.

Must be Manny.

He was built like a prizefighter, his dark eyes sharp beneath a furrowed brow. His tan skin was roughened by years of sun exposure, his forearms corded with muscle as he leaned against the stall door, arms crossed in a stance that screamed control. There was a dangerous stillness to him, a restrained power that made it clear — if he moved, it would be deliberate, calculated, and final.

I crept closer, the scent of leather and earth filling my lungs, straining to catch snippets of their conversation.

"...time the development perfectly," Sera said, urgency threading her voice.

"I still say it's risky," Manny muttered back, his deep voice carrying an unmistakable edge of doubt.

Development? What development?

I leaned in for a better angle—and my foot clipped a metal feed bucket.

It clattered to the ground, the clang ricocheting through the barn like a gunshot.

Heart pounding, I dove behind a stack of hay bales, barely daring to breathe.

Silence.

Then—a sharp intake of breath.

Manny shifted, the barn's dim light casting shadows across the hard planes of his face. His jaw clenched, his gaze flicking toward my hiding spot.

"We'll finish this later," Sera said, her tone clipped, wary.

Her heels clicked against the barn floor, each step precise and deliberate as she strode out.

Manny didn't move right away. Instead, he stood there, unreadable, the weight of his stare thickening the air.

Then, just as slowly, his fingers uncrossed from his arms, dragging along the stall door in a way that sent an uneasy prickle up my spine.

He turned his head slightly, just enough to scan the barn.

Like he knew someone was there.

I pressed myself against the hay, heart thudding against my ribs. And waited.

Oh, for the love of Christmas, Zoe! Suck it up!

I stepped out cautiously, clearing my throat to announce my presence.

Manny spun, startled, just as the white stallion he was leading inside reared up violently, letting out a piercing whinny. My heart lurched as the massive horse's hooves struck the air, thrashing dangerously close to where I stood.

Manny's grip tightened on the reins, his muscular arms straining as he pulled the horse down. "Whoa. Easy." His voice was low, steady, full of command. The stallion snorted, stomping the dirt in protest before finally settling under Manny's firm hand.

Manny's head snapped back toward me, his dark eyes flashing with irritation. "Are you trying to get yourself killed?" His voice was sharp, edged with something I couldn't quite place. "You never sneak up on a horse, especially one this high-spirited."

I lifted my hands in surrender. "Didn't mean to startle anyone."

Manny huffed, muttering something in Spanish under his breath. His focus shifted to the magnificent animal, his hands running over the opalescent coat in smooth, practiced strokes.

"Beautiful horse," I said, trying to appear casual.

"Perlino," he answered, brushing a speck of dust from the stallion's flank. "Cost us a fortune. I've had him outside all morning, so he didn't kick the walls down."

I tilted my head. "Must take a lot of experience to handle a horse like that."

Manny narrowed his eyes slightly, as if deciding whether to engage. "Been around them my whole life," he finally said. "Worked the rodeo circuit for a while."

I latched onto that. "Whereabouts?"

His hesitation was brief but telling. "Down South. Louisiana mostly." His hands didn't stop moving, brushing along the horse's powerful frame, but his shoulders tensed ever so slightly.

My gaze drifted to his arm, where his sleeve had slipped just enough to reveal a tattoo partially obscured under an elaborate inked Madonna and Child. Beneath it, bold lettering peeked through the faded edges of an older tattoo—R-E-E-N.

My pulse quickened.

I played it cool. "Nice ink."

Manny froze, his fingers pausing mid-brush before he yanked his sleeve down with a little too much force. "It's personal," he said tersely.

I held my ground, pushing just a little. "I'm curious."

Manny's eyes flicked to mine, wary now.

I took a calculated risk. "Did you know Noreen Cox?"

His reaction was immediate. His posture shifted, stiffening ever so slightly. His gaze turned icy.

"Never heard of her," he said, too quickly.

I squared my shoulders, refusing to let Manny's barely veiled threat rattle me. "So, Manny," I said, keeping my tone light, "do you usually get midnight deliveries, or was this horse special?"

His grip on the brush tightened, the bristles dragging roughly over the stallion's flank. His knuckles turned white, his broad shoulders tensing beneath his fitted shirt.

For a long moment, he didn't answer. Just the slow, methodical strokes of the brush against the horse's gleaming coat. When he finally spoke, his voice dropped low, quiet—a gravelly whisper that sent a shiver down my spine.

"Lady, you've got a way of asking questions that don't need answers."

The stallion shifted beneath his touch, muscles twitching, ears flicking back in unease, as if sensing the tension coiling between us.

Manny finally turned his gaze to me—dark, unreadable, edged like a honed blade.

"I'd keep that curiosity of yours in check," he continued, voice even, measured, but carrying the unmistakable weight of warning. "You never know when you'll spook something bigger than you can handle."

I froze. The space between us seemed to shrink, his towering frame casting a long shadow. For a moment, the only sound in the stable was the rhythmic crunch of the stallion's teeth on hay.

Then, just like that, the tension snapped.

Manny resumed his brushing with careless ease, as if nothing had passed between us. But the air still hummed with the ghost of his words.

Before I could respond, a familiar voice echoed from the stable entrance.

"Everything good?"

Manny's stance relaxed instantly, but the warning in his earlier words still hung thick in the air between us.

The rhythmic brushing of the stallion's coat slowed as Manny's body tensed. His grip on the brush went rigid, like he was bracing for something.

Then—like the flick of a switch—his entire stance shifted.

Orson Tobit had entered the barn.

CHAPTER EIGHTEEN

Gone was the simmering hostility, the barely concealed menace in Manny's voice. Now? His shoulders squared, but not with aggression. With obedience.

Manny stood at attention like a soldier answering to his commanding officer.

"Yeah, boss," Manny said quickly, voice smooth but just a little too tight. "Just getting things settled. I'm going to check that the staff is mucking out the stalls." He jabbed a fat thumb behind him before stalking away.

Orson barely acknowledged him before turning that sharp, assessing gaze onto me.

"Miss Romano, isn't it?" His voice was polite, confident, but there was an undertone that hadn't been there at the police station. Something lighter. Almost... amused.

"That's me," I said, keeping my posture easy, casual. "Just delivering the champagne for Sera's party."

Orson grinned as he dusted off the sleeve of his immaculate button-down, looking every bit the carefree billionaire hosting Mystic's most extravagant affair.

"Ah, yes. My fiancée has expensive tastes." He let out a charming, well-rehearsed chuckle, shaking his head like a man who had never once questioned his life choices. "Sometimes I think she spends it faster than I can write the check, but she's worth it... one hundred percent."

It was too smooth.

The last time I'd seen Orson, at the police station, he'd been on edge—controlled but irritated, like he couldn't believe he was wasting his time answering questions about a dead psychic.

Now? He was cool. Relaxed. Like none of it had touched him at all.

Like the murder of Noreen Cox had already been handled.

I smiled politely, playing along, but my mind was spinning. Manny's reaction to my questioning. The tattoo. The connection to Louisiana. And Orson's too-perfect attitude shift.

Either Manny was hiding something about Noreen—or Orson knew exactly what had happened to her.

I wasn't sure which was worse.

I steadied myself, the tension from my exchange with Manny still buzzing beneath my skin. My instincts wouldn't let it go. The way he tensed at Noreen's name, the too-quick denial—it all felt off.

"Everything alright, Miss Romano?" Orson prodded. "You seemed a bit... rattled."

I forced a light laugh. "Fine. Just had a little misunderstanding with your stud manager."

Orson *tsked*, shaking his head like I'd simply complained about the weather. "Manny can be... intense," he admitted, pausing just long enough for me to notice. "But he's a necessary asset."

Necessary asset. Not a great worker. Not a trusted hand.

That hesitation, that carefully chosen phrase — was Orson smoothing over an employee's temper? Or covering for something much worse?

Orson gestured smoothly toward the path leading away from the stables. "Come on, let me show you around. Might help clear your head."

It wasn't really a suggestion.

I hesitated for half a beat before falling into step beside him. Or, rather, a half step behind — because that's how he wanted it.

The estate stretched around us like something out of a high-society magazine spread. The paddocks were pristine, the grass so perfectly manicured it looked airbrushed. Historic stone barns, each with their own copper plaques, gleamed under the midday sun. Even the horses seemed carefully curated — every muscle, every glossy coat a testament to money and breeding.

"This place has been in my family for generations," Orson said, his voice rich with nostalgia. "My grandfather built the original stables after the war." It sounded well-practiced. Polished.

And yet, while his words painted a sentimental picture, his actions told another story.

Orson wasn't just walking with me—he was steering me. A hand barely raised, a shift in his stride—subtle cues, small but intentional.

This wasn't just a casual tour.

This was control. And I had the creeping suspicion he gave this tour to anyone who needed... managing.

Orson gestured toward the galloping horses in the field. "As you can see, what started as a modest homestead is now poised to be one of the most prestigious breeding operations in the country." His voice carried the weight of legacy, each syllable polished like a well-worn coin.

I let my gaze sweep across the estate—an empire built on old money and bloodlines, its history woven into every brick and blade of grass. But something didn't quite fit.

"It must have been wonderful growing up here," I prompted.

Orson gave a small, knowing smile. "Yes. I suppose it would have. I was lucky to spend summers here, at least. The rest of the time, it was boarding school in England, then university at Oxford. My father had a vision—one that didn't involve me mucking stalls." He exhaled, glancing toward the house. "I wasn't meant to come back. Not until he got sick."

There it was. The outsider. The heir who hadn't been groomed for the throne.

Loneliness flickered beneath his carefully composed façade, but was it genuine? Or just another polished detail of his personal mythology?

I studied him, weighing the possibility. If Orson had spent his life on the outside looking in, how easy had it been for someone like Noreen to see the gap—and exploit it?

I tilted my head, keeping my voice light. "And how did Sera come into the picture?"

Orson's expression softened, his lips curving with something close to nostalgia. "Thought everybody knew. Madame Zorina, of course."

"She introduced you?" I prompted.

"No. She saw it," he corrected, as if that made all the difference. "I was in a bad place—tired, restless. Taking care of father, no other family alive... this estate might as well have been a gilded cage. And then, one day, I was visiting Father's grave out at the cemetery and I bumped into this strange, wild-looking woman."

"Zorina."

He nodded. "Zorina. She told me I was stuck. That I was finding it difficult to move forward in my life. I found it odd that such a bizarre woman—a complete stranger at that—could be so perceptive." His gaze drifted into the distance like he was remembering. "But then she said the oddest thing. She said I would find a way." Orson turned to face me. "And somehow, I found that strangely comforting." He resumed walking. "But as quickly as she had appeared, she left. Imagine my surprise when I got to my car and discovered a flat tire! Trouble moving forward indeed! And no jack in the car!"

"Really? That sounds awful."

"Oh, don't worry. She was spot on about 'finding a way'. Manny happened by the cemetery at just the right time. He wasn't working for me then, but I flagged him down and he helped me change the tire. Anyway, we got to talking. I told him about the horse farm, and turns out he had experience and was looking for work. It was truly serendipitous."

More like suspicious.

"Imagine my surprise when I saw Zorina again — this time in town — and discovered she was, in fact, a psychic! She had been so uncannily accurate with her predictions at the cemetery, I wondered what other insights she might have. Before long, I was a regular client." He paused again. "But more than that. She became… my friend."

He fell silent, and I noticed the muscle in his jaw working.

Being suckered by a stranger was painful enough — but betrayal by someone close… that left deep wounds.

"Zorina told me I'd meet my soulmate. An Englishwoman, appearing in the most unexpected place. And from that meeting, I would start to build a family. After so much time alone, that's all I really wanted."

"And you believed her?"

"I had no reason to doubt her. And, of course, she was right."

He chuckled, shaking his head. "Funny thing, though — I lived in the UK for years, but when I met Sera, I couldn't quite pin down where in England she was from. Her accent was a little… muddled." He waved it off with an affectionate smile. "But when you know, you know."

I returned his smile, but my mind was already working.

That was a red flag.

If Orson, a man who had spent years in the UK, had trouble placing Sera's accent, there was a reason. Either she'd traveled enough to pick up an inconsistent mix — or she wasn't English at all.

I tucked the detail away. If Sera's "accent" had been part of the con, then Zorina hadn't just been matchmaking.

She'd been writing the script.

I kept my tone light. "Did Zorina tell you anything else?"

"She warned me there'd be challenges," he admitted, gaze drifting toward the distant paddocks. "Not everyone would support my relationship."

His fingers brushed absently over the iron gate as we passed, his posture still composed, but there was something there — something beneath the surface. A hesitation. A weight.

I tilted my head. "Did that worry you?"

His smile was quick, automatic. "Nothing worth having comes easy." But his fingers tightened on the gate for half a second too long before he let go.

A well-rehearsed response. A line he'd told himself enough times to make it sound true.

I studied him, filing it away. Was this just defensiveness? The natural reaction of a man whose fiancée had been doubted from the start?

Or had those doubts begun creeping in before Noreen was killed?

145

If Orson had questioned Sera, even just a little, then Zorina's warning hadn't been a prediction.

It had been a preemptive excuse. A shield to keep him from looking too closely at the woman she'd placed in his path.

We reached my van, and for the first time, Orson hesitated. It was barely a pause, the kind most people wouldn't catch—but I wasn't most people. The shift was subtle, like the moment a horse flicked an ear back before deciding whether to bolt or bite.

Until now, he'd been smooth, the perfect host, leading me exactly where he wanted. But now, his gaze flicked to the crates of Dom Perignon stacked neatly in the back of my van, and something in his demeanor tightened.

Interesting.

"This must be it," he said, a little too deliberately, as if confirming something to himself.

I leaned against the open door, watching him. "All ninety-nine bottles, just like Sera ordered. You'd think she was stocking a palace."

Orson huffed a laugh, but it was offbeat. "She likes things done right."

Right. Because nothing says elegance like more champagne than the town's entire annual budget.

His fingers skimmed the edge of a crate, thoughtful. What was it about this order that had him uneasy? A simple delivery shouldn't make a man like Orson Tobit pause.

Unless it wasn't simple at all.

146

The sharp click of heels against the stone path cut through the air like a well-timed cue. Right on schedule.

Sera swept into view, all sunshine and champagne wishes, her arm slipping effortlessly through Orson's. "There you are, darling!" she cooed, her voice like honey drizzled over something just a little too polished. Her eyes flicked to the crates stacked neatly beside my van, and for a split second—just a flash—there it was. Calculation.

She recovered quickly, letting out an exaggerated gasp. "Oh! Is that my champagne?"

I crossed my arms, leaning casually against the van. "Ninety-nine bottles of Dom on the wall," I said, deadpan. "A small fortune in bubbles."

Sera clapped her hands together, practically vibrating with glee. "Orson, you really do spoil me," she purred, pressing a quick kiss to his cheek. If I didn't know better, I'd think she was laying it on just a little too thick.

Orson chuckled, though his gaze lingered on the crates a moment longer. "Only the best for my fiancée."

I watched Sera carefully. The way she touched him, the way she performed excitement. This wasn't just about champagne. It was about optics. And I was starting to think she'd been running this script for a long time.

Sera reached for one of the crates with all the enthusiasm of a game show contestant claiming a grand prize. But the moment her fingers curled around the rough wood, she let out a sharp yelp, dropping the crate back onto the stack with a dramatic flourish.

"Ouch!" She cradled her hand, inspecting her palm like she'd been mortally wounded.

Orson's reaction was instant. "Let me see," he said, his voice laced with concern as he reached for her hand.

And that's when it happened.

Subtle — so subtle that most people wouldn't have caught it. But I did.

Sera flinched. Not dramatically. Just the barest, instinctual pullback before she forced herself still, allowing Orson to take her hand in his.

"Darling, you need to be more careful," Orson murmured, brushing his thumb over her skin as he inspected the invisible injury.

Sera laughed, but it was breathy, brittle. "It's just a splinter."

I tilted my head, watching the way her shoulders tensed under his touch. What kind of soulmate recoiled from their "one true love"?

Either Orson had chilly hands, or Sera's devotion wasn't nearly as deep as she wanted him to believe.

I pulled a clean handkerchief from my pocket and handed it over. Sera accepted it with the grace of a tragic heroine, dabbing at the minuscule bead of blood like she'd barely survived a duel.

"Such a nuisance," she sighed. "I swear, I'm always getting hurt."

Orson frowned, still hovering. "Maybe we should have Doc Keating take a look—"

"Oh, don't be silly." Sera waved him off, smiling through her supposed agony. "It's just a little splinter."

A little splinter and a big performance.

Then her eyes flicked to the invoice in Orson's hand. In a move so smooth it could've been choreographed, she plucked it from his fingers before he could so much as blink.

"Oh, honey bunny," she crooned, tucking the paper against her side. "You have so much on your plate already. Shouldn't you be reviewing the bloodstock auction list? Still a few more horses to buy if we want Tobit Breeding to be the name in the industry."

Orson hesitated — just a fraction of a second — but that was all it took.

I watched the shift happen.

Sera wasn't just managing an injury. She was managing him. And the money.

For the briefest moment, Orson didn't move. His fingers flexed at his sides, and something unreadable flickered across his face. Not quite defiance, not quite doubt — but close.

Sera smiled sweetly, still clutching the invoice. "Darling, we can't afford distractions right now. The auction is crucial." Her voice was honeyed reassurance, but there was steel beneath the sugar.

I waited. Watched.

Orson could take the paper back. Demand to see the final total, insist on handling his own finances.

He didn't.

Instead, his shoulders loosened, his gaze softened, and just like that, the resistance was gone. He nodded, exhaling through his nose. "You're right," he murmured. "There's a lot to finalize."

Sera beamed, pressing a kiss to his cheek — an effortless display of affection that felt anything but.

I shifted my weight, hiding my smirk behind a sip of coffee.

That hesitation? That fleeting moment of pushback? It was small, but it was real.

And it told me something important.

For all the perfect, polished appearances, Orson Tobit wasn't fully under Sera's spell.

Not yet.

Which meant there was still room for doubt.

And doubt had a nasty habit of unraveling even the most well-crafted lies.

Sera turned to me, her smile as bright and empty as a showroom chandelier. "And you simply must come to the party," she purred, her fingers smoothing over the invoice like she hadn't just hijacked the conversation — and Orson's wallet.

I returned her gaze, my smile just as polished. "Wouldn't miss it."

It wasn't a lie, exactly. I had every intention of being at that party. Just not for the hors d'oeuvres.

Sera's expression didn't falter, but I caught the flicker of something behind her eyes. Not excitement. Not generosity. Calculation.

She wanted me there.

Which begged the question: Why?

If she'd sensed I was poking around, this could be her way of keeping me close. A controlled environment. A chance to watch me just as much as I was watching her.

Or maybe—just maybe—there was something at that party she needed me to see.

I adjusted my grip on my clipboard, feigning casual indifference. "Should be quite the event."

Sera's smile sharpened. "Oh, it will be."

For once, we agreed.

I just wasn't sure if I'd be the guest of honor... or the next one on someone's hit list.

As Sera turned, she tossed the handkerchief back to me. "Thanks, darling." Dismissive. Done.

I caught it, eyes snagging on the tiny smear of red. Barely there, but impossible to ignore.

Sera thought this was over.

I watched her go, heels clicking, posture perfect, slipping her arm through Orson's like nothing had happened.

But something had happened.

The flinch. The control. The careful script.

She thought the bleeding had stopped.

I looked at the stain, dark against the fabric.

She was wrong.

It was just beginning.

CHAPTER NINETEEN

I sat at the counter at Read Between the Vines, the scent of coffee and old books mingling as my latté cooled, and I scrawled notes across my legal pad. My pen tapped against the wood in a steady rhythm, my mind a storm of names, places, and half-formed connections.

Dot, perched on her usual stool, was absorbed in a champion-horse-themed crossword, her pencil poised like a weapon. Addie lounged nearby, twirling a pen between her fingers, watching us with the disinterest of someone debating whether to cause trouble or take a nap.

"Zoe!" Dot piped, her eyes bright. "Seven letters. Winner of the 1973 Triple Crown."

"Secretariat," I answered absently, flipping my pad and scribbling: *Sera, Manny, tattoo, timing, robbery, chestnut, mahogany, cream.*

"That's it!" Dot crowed, scribbling the answer down with a triumphant grin. "Next one—nine letters. 'A flashy equine feature.'"

"Coat color," I muttered, my focus locked on the

tangled mess in front of me.

Dot beamed. "You're on fire, kid! Okay, how about this: Eight letters, 'a sport that combines precision and elegance'?"

"Dressage," I replied, my pen never stopping.

Addie raised an eyebrow, smirking. "Wait, are *we* solving the puzzle, or is *Zoe*? What exactly are you doing, Dot?"

"I'm providing moral support," Dot declared, unbothered. She filled in the answer and tapped her pencil on the last clue. "Here we go—ten letters. Starts with an 'R'. Horse that likes to run by the inside rail."

"Rail runner," I said automatically, still flipping through my notes.

Dot leaned back, setting down her pencil with the satisfaction of a woman who had conquered worlds. "Done! You know, they can't make a one of these I can't beat!"

Addie snorted. "Yeah, because you didn't just outsource the whole thing."

Dot waved a hand dismissively. "Jealousy is a terrible thing, Addie. I'll still let you bask in my crossword glory."

I paused, glancing up from my notes. "What color was Secretariat?"

"Chestnut," Dot answered promptly.

I frowned, staring at my scribbles again. *Chestnut, mahogany, cream.* The same shades that had been stolen from Deidre's salon. The same shades as—what? A horse? A person? The pieces refused to click, swirling just outside my grasp.

Dot stretched, pleased with herself. "This was a good one. Keeps my brain sharp for bingo night."

Addie muttered, "Pretty sure Zoe's the sharp one around here."

"Speak for yourself!" Dot shot back, then patted the counter. "I think I deserve a celebratory cup of tea from Alice's."

Alice in the Village wasn't just a tea shop. It was a Wonderland-themed, sensory overload of a café tucked into Olde Mistick Village. The place was all whimsy and delicate teapots, walls stacked with tins of exotic blends that smelled like mystery and temptation. Dot treated it like a second home.

She turned to Addie. "I take mine with honey."

Addie huffed but stood anyway, rolling her eyes. "I swear, one of these days, I'm gonna make you *earn* these little errands."

Dot ignored her and turned to me. "What do you take in yours?"

"Cream," I murmured, the word lingering on my tongue. My mind was still stuck on the colors. *Chestnut. Mahogany. Cream.*

Before I could dig deeper, the shop door swung open.

Tom walked in. Addie walked out.
More like tripped out... right over her tongue.

"Hey," Tom greeted, placing a small bag on the counter. "Thought you might like these. Truffles from the chocolatier downtown."

I blinked at the unexpected gesture. "Tom, you didn't have to."

He shrugged, casual as ever. "Figured you deserved something sweet."

His grin was easy, but his eyes weren't idle. They scanned the counter, drifting over my notes.

"You're still on this?" he asked, nodding at my scribbles.

"Yeah, but it's not quite making sense," I admitted. "I'm pretty sure Orson's stud manager, Manny Denis, has something to do with it, but I can't quite put my finger on it. One thing I *do* know? The guy's 265 pounds of bad attitude in boots."

Tom tilted his head, considering. "Hmm. Manny sure sounds like a scary guy, but maybe you're looking too far afield. Sometimes the answers are closer than you think."

I narrowed my eyes. "Closer how?"

He shrugged again, too nonchalant. "I don't know. Just… sometimes people hide in plain sight. Especially the ones who seem to have everything all tied up neatly. They might be more… complicated."

His eyes drifted down toward the counter. My gaze flicked to my legal pad and to what lay next to it.

Plain sight, huh?

Dot's newspaper lay folded on the counter, and my eyes landed on a front-page article below the fold. A staged, glossy photo of Orson Tobit and Sera Hawking, locked in what was meant to be an effortless, romantic embrace. But Orson looked stiff — awkward. Out of place. And Sera? All smiles, her charm so polished it practically gleamed.

"Doesn't get much more plain than the front

page," I muttered.

The bell above the door jingled again. Chief Cody strode in, a manila folder in hand. It was like Grand Freakin' Central Station in here today.

Almost like I never left New York.

Derek nodded at me and gave a curt head bob to Tom. "Sawyer."

"Chief." Tom pulled himself to his full six-foot-two height.

Derek paused a moment, then rolled his shoulders back and placed the file on the counter in front of me — right on top of Orson and Sera's photo. "Got something for you."

I opened it, scanning the contents. The words confirmed what I already suspected. Iliev was officially cleared as a suspect.

"I knew it," I said, exhaling.

Tom raised an eyebrow. "So, where does that leave you now? Any new leads?"

Derek shot him a sidelong glance. He answered warily. "Still looking. Just takes time to unravel."

The two men eyed each other silently for a few moments before Tom pushed the bag of truffles across the counter toward me. "Well, I should get back to work. Hope the chocolate inspires something good." He levered himself over the counter and planted a kiss on my cheek. "Not that you need any more sugar, because you are already unbelievably sweet."

I nodded absently as he walked out — my brain melted.

Derek watched him go, arms crossed, his scowl

carrying more weight than usual.

"He seems…"

…*gorgeous, yummy, a moment on the lips, forever on my hips…*.

"…helpful," he muttered flatly.

"He's harmless. Just likes to chat," I mumbled.

Derek didn't look convinced. "Maybe. Promise me you'll stay sharp, Zoe. Not everyone's as harmless as they seem."

"Why, Chief Cody… do I detect a little jealousy?" Dot needled.

"Who? Me?" Derek cleared his throat. Loudly. He tugged at his collar. "I don't know what you're talking about, Mrs. Richards."

I snickered. Personally, I was enjoying watching somebody squirm in Dot's hot seat for a change. I stole a quick glance at the reddening police officer.

Was he jealous, though?

Believe me. Enquiring minds wanted to know.

Ah, well. Time to save the poor guy from himself.

I drummed my fingers against the counter, thoughts swirling. "I was thinking. We don't know for certain yet that Sera was in cahoots with Noreen. But let's assume, for a minute, she was. Orson made a comment about Sera spending his money like it's water. And considering how much he shelled out for Noreen's — Madame Zorina's — uh, 'advice,' I wonder if that didn't sit too well with Sera."

Dot perked up. "You think Little Miss Soon-to-be-Tobit got sick of playing second fiddle to a psychic?"

I shrugged, glancing at my legal pad. Sera's name

157

was now circled twice.

"Tom said something about Sera being… complicated. And honestly, the way she and Manny were whispering at the stables, it felt like there was more going on. What if—"

The bell jingled wildly. I looked up, half-expecting, half-hoping it was Tom again.

Nope. Just Addie, balancing cups of tea.

Darn.

"Wait a second," Derek cut in. "Are you really saying Sera might've had something to do with Zorina's death? That's a pretty big leap. First, you think Orson might be involved, and now you're pointing fingers at his fiancée? With what proof?" His arms crossed, a skeptical shake of the head. "You're playing with fire, Zoe."

"I know," I conceded. "But when I'm onto a story, I'm like a hound dog with fleas. I just have to keep scratching until I get at it."

Derek sighed, his expression softening slightly. "Just remember what happens when you scratch too hard."

I arched a brow. "What's that?"

"You bleed," Derek stated pointedly, his gaze flicking down.

I followed his stare, my stomach tightening.

A faint pink stain was seeping through my bandage.

CHAPTER TWENTY

Morning arrived reluctantly, dragging its feet through the dusty blinds of my bedroom and slapping me awake with a soft beam of golden light — the kind that should have been peaceful, but mostly just annoyed me.

I groaned, rolling onto my stomach, only to meet resistance.

A foot.

A foot that did not belong to me.

"Addie," I muttered, my voice thick with sleep.

A snore answered. Deep. Unapologetic. And entirely in my personal space.

I squinted at the ceiling, debating whether I had the energy to shove her off my bed or if it would be easier to set the house on fire and start over.

Instead, I sighed and kicked at the mass of blankets sprawled next to me. "Get out."

Another snore. More of a growl, really.

This was my life now.

My charming little bungalow — the one I'd picked for its quiet street, weathered Cape Cod shingles,

exposed brick, and perfectly imperfect bookshelves —
had officially become a crash pad for wayward strays.
And at the moment, the resident stray was Addie, who
had commandeered my bed like a human-shaped
barnacle after insisting that her temporary stay would be
"just a couple of nights."

I could only hope.

I sat up — rubbing the fog from my brain — last
night's thoughts still tangled between sleep and
wakefulness. Horses. Manny. Colors. Sera. Orson... it all
looped in my head, refusing to settle.

I needed coffee. And space.

A loud rattling snore rumbled from beneath the
covers.

Lots of space.

I swung my legs over the edge of the bed, only to
hear a soft thud as Addie's foot — still half-tucked in my
blanket — hit the floor.

She groaned, shifting but not quite waking. "Is it
morning?"

"No, it's the apocalypse." I shoved her shoulder.
"Get out of my bed."

"Rude," she mumbled, barely peeling one eye
open. "Is there coffee?"

"There will be if I survive the next five minutes."

A knock at the door cut off whatever comeback
she was brewing.

I frowned and squinted at the clock. Too early for
the mail.

Too late for a serial killer.

Addie lifted her head, hair a tragic mess.

160

"Expecting someone?"

"No."

But as I made my way to the door, rubbing the exhaustion from my face, I had a sinking feeling I knew exactly who it was.

And sure enough — when I swung it open, there he stood.

Tom.

Grinning like a man with a plan.

And holding an obnoxiously oversized picnic basket.

I crossed my arms, eyeing the basket like it had personally offended me. "What's all this?"

Tom set it down with an unnecessary amount of flair, flipping the lid open just enough for me to catch the scent of fresh bread and something distinctly buttery. He held up a blanket, vibrant and patterned — the kind you'd see draped over a perfectly curated Instagram picnic.

"Thought you could use a break," he said, that infuriating grin firmly in place. "Fresh air, good food, and," he shook out the blanket, letting it billow between us before cocking an eyebrow, "a little sunshine therapy."

I smirked, shaking my head. "I don't have time for sunshine therapy, Tom. I'm — "

"Obsessing?" he cut in smoothly, the glint in his eye warm but knowing.

I opened my mouth to argue. Closed it again.

Because he wasn't wrong.

Last night had been a carousel of half-formed theories, of rearing horses, and crystal balls, of puzzle pieces that refused to fit. And maybe, just maybe, I was wearing myself down to the bone over something that still refused to make sense.

Tom just stood there, watching me watch myself come to that realization.

And the worst part?

I hated that he knew me that well. And yet, I knew next to nothing about him.

"Come on," he coaxed, lifting the basket onto the counter. "I've got all the local favorites."

He opened the lid wider, revealing an array of local delicacies. A loaf of crusty sourdough from Nana's Bakery, its golden surface dotted with sesame seeds. A wedge of creamy cheese from Mystic Cheese Company, the aroma rich and inviting. A jar of wildflower honey from the hives at Stonewall Apiary, glistening amber in the morning light. And nestled beside them, a bottle of crisp apple cider from B.F. Clyde's Cider Mill, condensation already forming on the glass.

"You really went all out," I said, unable to keep the surprise from my voice.

He shrugged, a casual lift of one shoulder. "Figured you could use a little spoiling."

I glanced at the spread, then back at him. The tension in my chest loosened just a fraction.

"Fine," I relented, trying to sound exasperated. "But just for a little while."

Tom's grin widened, victory gleaming in his eyes. "Deal."

As he turned to set up the picnic, I couldn't help but feel a flicker of gratitude. Maybe a break wouldn't be the worst thing in the world.

Tom, undeterred, nudged the basket closer. "Come on, just an hour. I promise it won't kill you."

I narrowed my eyes. "You sure? Sunshine exposure can turn the fair-skinned into Red Hots."

"I happen to like Red Hots. But I brought SPF 50, just in case. And snacks. Good ones."

I sighed, relenting. "Fine."

Before he could answer, a door creaked behind me.

Addie, wrapped in a blanket, hair a tangled mess, shuffled in like she'd been personally wronged. "Wait. You're *leaving*?"

Tom grinned. "Just borrowing her for a little while."

Her eyes flicked to the basket, then to me. "A surprise picnic? Seriously? *I* have been hinting for *days* for a scenic date, and she just—" She flailed a hand at me. "—*exists* and gets gourmet snacks and fresh air?"

I blinked. "I get fresh air all the time."

Addie scoffed. "The walk between here and Read Between the Vines does *not* count."

Tom was smirking now.

She squinted at him. "Wait a second. Where are you taking her?"

I turned to him. "Yeah. Where *are* we going?"

Tom just smiled. "You'll see."

*****

The marina shimmered under the afternoon sun,

the salty breeze tangling in my hair as I stepped onto the dock. I stopped short when I saw *it* — Tom's boat, freshly polished and tied off like it had belonged to him forever.

A *boat*.

I shot him a look. "*This* is the picnic spot?"

Tom just grinned, setting the basket down before stepping aboard with an ease that suggested he'd been born at sea. "You're the one who keeps saying I need a hobby." He held out a hand. "Come on, city girl. It won't bite."

I hesitated, eyeing the deck like it might betray me. I could handle high-speed chases in a New York cab, but trusting Tom *not* to capsize this thing? Questionable.

Still, I took his hand and stepped on.

Minutes later, we were drifting, the hum of the marina fading behind us. Tom stretched out, arms behind his head, while I picked through the picnic spread. I popped a strawberry into my mouth, savoring the burst of sweetness, the gentle rock of the boat lulling me into something dangerously close to relaxation.

Tom watched me, smirking. "You look like you're actually enjoying this."

I arched a brow. "Don't spread rumors. I have a reputation to uphold."

His grin deepened, but I barely noticed. Because despite the sunshine, despite the wine, my mind wouldn't let go.

Tom dipped another plump red strawberry in fresh whipped cream and held it up for me to take a bite.

I licked my lips… and froze.

Cream.

Tom noticed the shift in my expression, his easy smirk fading just a fraction. "You've gone quiet. What's on your mind?"

"Horses."

Tom huffed a laugh. "Horses? That's a turn."

I grabbed my phone, scrolling through an article I'd bookmarked earlier. "Did you know some bloodstock horses are worth millions?"

Tom nearly choked on his wine, coughing as he set the glass down. "*Millions*? Like, plural?"

I nodded. "Champion lineage, stud fees — it's a huge business. Breeders invest up front, but they make it back over time. Hundreds of thousands per session, sometimes more."

Tom let out a low whistle. "Hell of a business."

I tilted my head, chewing my lip. "And some horses? They're bred for a *look*. Perlinos, for example — their creamy coats are stunning but high-maintenance. They're sensitive to the sun, need special care. Most owners keep them covered or limit their exposure."

His gaze sharpened. "Where are you going with this?"

"I saw one at Tobit Ranch. The day I delivered the champagne. Manny had just brought him in." I leaned back, staring at the sky, shielding my eyes from the bright yellow sun. "No blanket. No sunscreen. Outside all morning. But not a single sign of sunburn."

Tom frowned. "That's odd."

I nodded. "Yeah. And odd means *something*."

Tom's grip tightened around an apple, his knuckles whitening just a fraction. "Maybe Manny's

165

just… good at his job."

I studied him, the way his fingers flexed, the measured way he kept his voice even. "Or maybe something's off."

He took a slow, deliberate bite, chewing longer than necessary. "That's a lot of what-ifs, Zoe."

I didn't respond right away. Just watched as his fingers tensed before he finally set the apple down with too much care—like he had to *think* about it.

"Reporter's habit," I murmured.

Tom exhaled through his nose, forcing a laugh that didn't quite reach his eyes. "But you're not a reporter. You own a bookstore and a wine bar." His jaw tightened ever so slightly before he caught himself, schooling his features back into easy amusement.

The air between us shifted, subtle but noticeable. The teasing lilt in his voice didn't match the tension creeping into his shoulders.

"You know what? You're right. And that's not what today's about." I picked up my wine, swirling it lazily.

Tom's gaze lingered on mine, something unreadable flickering beneath the surface. The teasing was gone now, replaced with a quiet intensity that sent a slow, deliberate shiver down my spine.

He reached for his glass, but instead of taking a sip, he traced the rim with his thumb, his focus still locked on me. "I've noticed you do that," he murmured.

I arched a brow. "Do what?"

"That thing." He gestured vaguely. "When you're close to figuring something out—when the pieces are clicking together. Your voice drops, your eyes sharpen... it's like watching a storm gather."

I swallowed, suddenly too aware of the space—or lack of it—between us. The gentle rock of the boat had shifted us closer, his knee brushing mine, his arm stretched along the bench seat behind me.

"Is that a compliment?" I asked, keeping my voice steady despite the warmth curling in my stomach.

Tom smirked, tilting his head. "Maybe." He reached out, tucking a stray piece of hair behind my ear, his fingers lingering just a second too long. "Or maybe it's just an observation."

The air between us thickened, charged with something electric.

My breath hitched as his fingers traced the side of my jaw, slow and deliberate, his touch feather-light. "Zoe..." His voice was lower now, rougher.

I didn't pull away. Didn't break the moment.

Because maybe, just maybe, I didn't *want* to.

Tom leaned in.

A sharp, wet splat shattered the moment.

Tom jerked back, brow furrowing. I blinked, trying to process what had just happened. Then— realization dawned.

"Oh my God," I whispered, horror dawning as my gaze traveled past Tom's shoulder. A thick, unholy smear of white and gray dripped down his sleeve.

Tom froze. "Tell me that's not—"

"It absolutely is."

His jaw tightened, his body rigid as he turned his head, glaring up at the sky like he could summon vengeance upon the airborne menace that had so rudely intruded.

A seagull, utterly unrepentant, circled overhead before flapping lazily away, leaving nothing but chaos in its wake.

I bit my lip, failing spectacularly at holding in my laugh.

"Oh, you think this is funny?" Tom arched a brow, his expression equal parts unimpressed and amused.

I nodded, covering my mouth. "I mean... considering the timing?" I gestured vaguely between us. "Yeah. A little."

Tom exhaled, shaking his head as he reached for a napkin, dabbing at the mess with the resigned acceptance of a man who had lost a battle he never signed up for. "Well, that's one way to ruin the mood."

"The seagulls of Mystic have impeccable comedic timing."

Tom shot me a look, then flicked a glance at the horizon. "Alright, sunshine therapy's over. Let's head in before I get targeted again."

Still laughing, I helped him gather up the picnic supplies, the moment between us shifting back into something easy, something familiar. Whatever had sparked before?

Gone.

At least, for now.

The boat glided smoothly into the marina, the gentle hum of the motor blending with the sounds of lapping water and the occasional cry of a gull—one I was sure was still laughing at Tom's misfortune.

Tom cut the engine, moving with practiced ease as he tied off the lines. I busied myself gathering what was left of our picnic, brushing away stray crumbs and folding the blanket. The earlier tension between us had evaporated, replaced by something lighter, easier.

Tom turned, rubbing at his shoulder with a grimace. "Gonna take a full shower and a moral cleanse after that."

I smirked. "Try holy water."

He let out a low chuckle, reaching for the basket. "Thanks for indulging me today."

I hesitated, then smiled. "Yeah. It was… nice."

His eyes lingered on mine, unreadable for half a beat, but he didn't push. He just nodded before stepping onto the dock. "See you later, Romano."

I watched him go, feeling something strangely unresolved. Then my stomach grumbled.

Strawberries. I should've packed more strawberries. Or at least stolen the rest before he left.

I sighed, dropping onto the now-empty seat. My fingers drummed against my thigh, restless. My mind circled back—*cream.*

Not just in the strawberries. In the Perlino stallion.

I was onto something. I knew I was. The horse had been standing in full sunlight when I arrived at Tobit Ranch. No protection. No shade. No sign of sunburn, despite everything I'd read about the breed.

That horse hadn't been outside all morning. *No way in hell.*

I scrambled for my phone, fingers flying as I searched. I needed more information on that horse.

169

Because if it wasn't where Manny said it was...

Then where the hell had it been?

The pieces were coming together—too slowly for my liking, but they were coming.

I reached for my phone, swiping it open to make a call, and—I froze.

One new text. No name. No number. Just a single line of warning, glaring up at me in stark letters.

Walk away, Romano. Before you get trampled.

The words sent a flicker of something cold through my chest. Not a suggestion. Not even a warning.

A threat.

I swallowed down the instinctive rush of adrenaline and forced my mind to steady. Someone was watching me. Tracking my movements. Maybe they'd seen me at Tobit Ranch. Maybe they knew I'd been asking too many questions.

A quick glance around didn't reveal any curious eyes. But that didn't mean I wasn't being watched.

I inhaled slowly, my grip tightening around the phone. Someone wanted me scared.

Bad luck for them.

I wasn't scared.

I was curious.

And now?

Now I knew I was closer than ever.

CHAPTER TWENTY-ONE

I never meant to get tangled up with another case, let alone another man.

Now, sitting in my car outside the police station, my hands tucked deep into my coat pockets — takeout cooling in the bag on the seat beside me — I felt the pull of two people in opposite directions. Tom, all effortless charm and magnetic energy, and Derek, quiet steadiness, a man who didn't try to pull me anywhere at all.

One made my pulse quicken; the other made me feel like I could finally exhale.

And yet, hesitation clung to me like the bitter chill in the air.

Because I'd been here before — chasing a story, caught between instinct and emotion, and blinded by both. And I'd paid for it.

Back in New York, I thought I knew the game. I thought I knew *him*. A source I shouldn't have trusted, a man who spun me a story just believable enough to make me fall. By the time I learned the truth, it was too late.

I pushed the thought away.

This wasn't New York. And I wasn't that same

woman.

I opened the car door, grabbed the bag of food, and walked toward the station, where Derek waited, and with him, the case that refused to let me go.

Maybe I hadn't learned a damn thing.

The evening breeze nipped at my fingers as I locked the car. My mind was still tangled in the silent tug-of-war between Tom and Derek, but it wasn't why I was here.

I pulled my phone from my pocket, scrolling back to the anonymous text that had slithered onto my screen earlier that day:

You never know when you'll spook something bigger than you can handle.

A chill that had nothing to do with the night air prickled down my spine.

Manny Denis had said almost the exact same thing to me at the stables. A casual warning... or a veiled threat?

I couldn't shake the memory of the way he'd looked at me — part wary, part knowing. The tattoo on his arm, half-hidden beneath the worn cuff of his sleeve, nagged at me like an unsolved riddle.

I'd done a deep dive into prison tattoos for an article once — spent weeks interviewing former inmates, decoding ink that spoke of loyalty, debts, faith, and fear. Tattoos often told stories. You just had to know how to read between the lines.

My eyes narrowed. What story was Manny's tat telling?

And then there were the letters.

R-E-E-N.

That flash of faded ink I'd glimpsed near his wrist. Not the Madonna and Child. Something else. Something unfinished.

REEN... was it part of a name? A word? A warning?

I stepped inside the police station, the low hum of late-night duty filling the quiet space. A few officers were scattered across desks, drinking stale coffee and pushing through reports. The overhead fluorescents cast everything in a washed-out glow.

Derek's office door was open.

He was hunched over his desk, sleeves rolled up, stubble darkening his jaw. The usually composed chief looked... almost approachable like this, like he belonged more in a worn-out leather jacket than a uniform.

I lingered for a moment, taking him in before I cleared my throat.

He glanced up, brow furrowing before his expression softened slightly. "You bring peace offerings?"

I lifted the takeout bag. "Truce via noodles. Thought you could use a break."

His mouth quirked, but his eyes stayed sharp. "I could. But something tells me this isn't just a social call."

I sank into the chair across from him, placing the bag between us. "You'd be right. I've been thinking about Manny Denis."

Derek leaned back, watching me. "Tobit's stable hand?"

"Yeah. He's got this Madonna and Child tattoo on

his arm. It's often a nod to faith, redemption… or even family. Sometimes, it marks someone who feels abandoned but still clings to hope. But mostly I've been thinking about it because it's a common prison tat." I hesitated. "I think Manny did time. Maybe in Louisiana."

Derek exhaled, rubbing a hand along his jaw. "If he did, there's one place that would make sense."

I raised a brow.

"Angola Prison." He reached for his laptop, typing quickly. "It's got a reputation. They even hold a rodeo there—prisoners ride bulls like they got nothing to lose."

I leaned forward. "And you think Manny was there?"

Derek's eyes met mine, something unreadable in them. "It's possible."

The Angola Prison Rodeo.

Vivid images formed in my mind—rough men gripping ropes, dirt swirling in the air, the thunder of hooves, the desperate need to prove something, to feel something, even from inside a cage. I glanced at Manny's file, my fingers tapping absently on the table. If he had been there, if Angola had shaped him, what did that mean for the case?

Derek exhaled, rubbing a hand along his jaw. "How about we eat first—before your 'truce via noodles' turns into a war crime?"

A welcome shift. I pulled the takeout containers from the bag, handing him his. As I popped mine open, Derek's voice cut through the quiet.

"Dim light suits you, you know."

I paused, chopsticks hovering mid-air. He wasn't

looking at me, not directly, but there was something in the way his fingers lingered on the edge of his container.

I smirked, recovering. "Careful, Chief. You're dangerously close to flattering me."

His lips twitched—like a man debating whether to let himself smile. Instead, he just shook his head.

"Just an observation."

We sat in comfortable silence for a while, wrangling our *udon* with chopsticks, stealing glances across the desk.

Derek reached for the *wasabi* at the same time I did, our hands brushing over the small plastic cup. I froze for a second, my fingers still resting against his. His skin was warm, rougher than I expected—like a man who knew how to fix things with his hands, not just file reports.

He didn't pull away immediately, either.

A beat passed. Then another.

I cleared my throat, curling my fingers back. "Go ahead, Chief. I would never want to stand in the way of a man's effort to spice things up."

Derek huffed a quiet laugh, popping the lid off. "Generous of you."

The moment broke, but something about it lingered as he wiped his hands on a napkin and turned back to his laptop.

"So, you think Manny was at Angola?" he said, voice shifting back into business mode. "Let's find out."

He typed a few quick commands, pulling up the Louisiana Department of Corrections database. I leaned in slightly, watching as he searched for former inmates,

Angola records, anything that might link Manny Denis to the notorious prison.

A few hits came up.

"Here we go. Emanuel Denis." Derek's mouth puckered. "Hm. Well-rounded convict. Fraud. Assault with a deadly weapon. Counterfeiting."

Then Derek's fingers stilled on the trackpad.

"Look at this."

I followed his gaze to a grainy, years-old photo of Angola's infamous prison rodeo. Rows of men in worn denim, hands gripping bull ropes, their faces set with something between defiance and desperation.

Derek tapped the screen. "There was a scandal— illegal horse sales. Some rodeo officials were smuggling stolen horses under the radar."

I leaned in closer, my breath hitching. "And you think Manny knew about it?"

"With his rap sheet," Derek's jaw tightened, "I think he might've been part of it."

Derek scrolled through the old rodeo article, his expression tightening. "Illegal horse sales... stolen animals funneled through the rodeo circuit, sold with forged papers. The operation ran for years before anyone caught on."

I leaned in, my pulse kicking up a notch. "So, what if Manny learned from it?"

Derek glanced at me. "Learned what?"

I gestured toward the screen. "The bait-and-switch scam. Only instead of moving stolen horses, what if he was counterfeiting them?"

Derek arched a brow. "Like a Louis Vuitton

knock-off, only horses?"

I exhaled sharply. "Think about it—papers can be forged. But what if he took the scheme a step further? What if they weren't just lying about the bloodlines? What if they were physically altering the horses to look like champions?"

Derek muttered a curse under his breath. "Jesus."

But I barely heard him—I was already pushing forward, piecing together fragments of memory.

Then it hit me.

Zorina's prediction.

"You feel stuck. Trapped. Like nothing you do can move you forward."

At the time, Orson had thought she meant his life. His financial struggles. The weight of failure pressing in from all sides. Ambiguous like any run-of-the-mill horoscope.

But what if Noreen had planned every step of this? What if she orchestrated her prediction into reality?

The flat tire. Orson's frustration, the helplessness of being stranded.

And then—Manny Denis, stepping in like fate itself. The guy with just enough horse experience, conveniently looking for work.

I went still.

Orson hadn't just been conned. He'd been set up from the start.

Sera's voice came back to me, low and matter-of-fact.

Shouldn't you be reviewing the bloodstock auction list? Still a few more horses to buy if we want Tobit Breeding to be the name in the industry.

My breath slipped out in a whisper. "Oh, my God."

Derek's eyes snapped to mine. "What?"

I opened my mouth, then shut it.

The Perlino.

The high-dollar auction horse. The one that should have been sunburned in a matter of hours.

But it hadn't been.

Because its pale coat wasn't natural.

I met Derek's gaze, the final piece clicking into place. "Orson wasn't buying top-tier bloodstock. He was buying junk horses dressed up to look like champions. And he didn't even know it."

Derek leaned back in his chair, exhaling. "And Manny, Zorina, and Noreen Cox were pocketing the difference."

I swallowed hard, my pulse hammering. "Noreen wasn't just running a sweetheart scam. She was playing chess. And Orson was her king."

Derek watched me, his expression unreadable. "You're relentless, you know that?"

I barely heard him.

Because that only left one question.

If the king was in checkmate...

Who killed the queen?

CHAPTER TWENTY-TWO

I still felt wired, flushed — more alive than I had in a long time.

Whether it was the rush of the case or the man sitting too close, I wasn't sure.

I curled my fingers into a fist, grounding myself as Derek leaned back, arms crossed. "It's brilliant, Zoe. But right now? It's still just a theory."

I exhaled sharply, my momentary high fading. "You don't believe me?"

He shrugged. "I think it's a damn convincing story. But stories don't hold up in court. We need proof. Something tangible linking Noreen, Manny, and — if you're right — Sera."

The words stung more than they should have. Because I knew he was right.

I shifted my focus to the screen as Derek scrolled through old Angola records, scanning photos from the rodeo archives. Rows of spectators in faded images, some leaning forward, some half in shadow.

And then...

I leaned in. "Wait."

Derek stopped scrolling.

There.

The grainy photo captured a section of the bleachers. Among the crowd, a familiar face sat near the front.

Noreen Cox.

I swallowed. "That's her."

Derek's voice lowered. "Well, there's your connection."

She was no psychic. She'd been part of this.

From the very beginning.

A rush of thoughts tangled in my mind, disjointed but urgent. And then it clicked.

The library.

Noreen's first stop in Mystic.

I sucked in a breath. She hadn't "valued the written word" like Mrs. Potter surmised — she was researching her mark.

Looking through obituaries.

Making sure Orson Tobit was exactly who she needed him to be.

My throat tightened. A man like him — abandoned, lonely, and sitting on a fortune.

She hadn't found him.

She had chosen him.

Talk about a gift horse.

Then — another echo.

Iliev's words filtering back through my memory.

A big man. Visiting Zorina the night she died.

I stilled.

Iliev hadn't known her by the name Noreen. He'd

only ever called her Zorina. But they were the same woman. A woman Manny Denis knew.

And had known for a long time.

My heart pounded.

Zorina — Noreen — was tied to Manny through Angola. And Manny fit the description Iliev had given me.

I sat back, pulse hammering in my throat. "Derek." My voice came out quieter than I expected. "What if Manny killed her?"

Derek was already watching me. His expression unreadable.

"If she was the chess master," he said, tapping the screen, "and she ended up dead… someone didn't like how she was playing the game. Or was tired of being a pawn."

His words sat heavy between us.

I bit the inside of my cheek.

If Manny had killed Noreen, why let me snoop around? Why warn me instead of silencing me?

Unless…

Maybe the con wasn't played out.

I clenched my jaw. "So much for true love, huh?"

Derek huffed a quiet breath, but it was humorless.

Neither of us spoke.

Suddenly, the stakes felt even higher.

And I had the sinking feeling we were only scratching the surface.

The photo nagged at me, like a half-formed thought just out of reach. I narrowed my eyes, studying the figures on the screen.

Noreen sat in the stands, her gaze fixed on the action below. But it wasn't just her presence that pulled at me. It was the girl beside her.

Lanky frame. Long, dark hair.

A shadow of familiarity stirred in my gut.

"Does it look like… Sera?" My voice was quiet, almost uncertain. "But as a brunette?"

Derek frowned. "Nah. No way."

But I wasn't so sure.

The girl was younger, maybe mid-teens, but there was something about her jawline. The way she tilted her head, the sharp edge of her profile. The same subtle arch in her brows, the same high cheekbones.

I chewed my lip, tilting my head. "It's there, Derek. Look at the shape of her face. The way she holds herself."

Derek leaned in, scrutinizing the image. His hesitation was small, but I caught it.

I wasn't imagining this. I kept staring at the screen.

Derek let out a slow breath, rubbing his jaw, still scrutinizing the image like he could will a different answer into existence.

I swallowed. My fingers absently brushed my coat pocket, and that's when I felt it—the soft, crumpled cloth.

My breath caught.

Without a word, I pulled it out and handed it to Derek.

He took it automatically, then froze, quickly rubbing his mouth. "What? I have wasabi on my face?"

I chuckled, shaking my head. "No. You said a

good story's not worth its salt without evidence. Well," I gestured. "It's evidence."

His expression sobered as he unfolded the handkerchief. The once-white fabric was marred with a dark, rust-colored stain.

I met his gaze. "Bernie needs to run that against Zorina's blood."

Derek's brows pulled together. "You think it's a familial match?"

I exhaled. "If Sera's Zorina's daughter, the sweetheart scam makes way more sense."

Derek ran a thumb over the fabric, his jaw tightening. "Damn."

I crossed my arms, watching his expression shift — calculation, doubt, and something like reluctant acceptance.

"If I'm right," I murmured, "this wasn't just about money. It was personal."

Derek let out a slow exhale, folding the handkerchief with surprising care. "I'll get it to Bernie first thing in the morning."

I nodded, but my pulse was already thrumming. *It was looking like a new queen was on the board.*

Derek placed a hand on my shoulder. It was brief — just the weight of his palm, steady and grounding. But it was enough.

I looked up.

His eyes met mine, warm and steady, searching for something. Or maybe just making sure I wasn't about to spiral down another rabbit hole.

I wasn't sure I could move if I tried.

A breath of silence stretched between us, thick with something I didn't want to name.

I swallowed, forcing a nervous laugh. "Don't worry, Chief. I'll leave the badge-wielding to you."

"Derek." His lips twitched, but he didn't step back right away. His hand lingered for a fraction of a second longer, like he wasn't entirely convinced. "Please."

Finally, he exhaled, dropping his arm as he leaned against the desk. "See that you do."

I cleared my throat, looking anywhere but at him, but the warmth of his touch still buzzed under my skin.

I should have felt relieved when the moment passed.

Instead, I felt like I'd just walked away from something I wasn't ready to admit I wanted.

What had started as a sweetheart scam had spiraled into something far more dangerous, tangled in old cons, stolen bloodlines, and a murder that didn't feel like the last move in the game.

I dragged a hand through my hair, exhaling slowly. "Yeah." It was all I could manage.

Derek studied me for a beat, his expression unreadable. Then his voice dropped. "Just don't go chasing this alone."

I glanced at him, my first instinct to brush it off with something light, a teasing remark to break the tension.

What, you worried about me, Chief?

But the words caught in my throat.

Because he *was* worried. And that mattered more than I wanted to admit.

I nodded instead. "I won't."

A lie.

We both knew it.

But Derek just exhaled, jaw ticking slightly, before pushing away from the desk and escorting me to the front door.

We stood there in silence for seconds that seemed like hours. Then he did something I didn't expect. He leaned in and kissed me on the cheek. "Goodnight, Zoe.

I struggled to find my voice. When I did, it came out like a squawking chicken. "Goodnight, Chief Cody."

He frowned. I swallowed. "I mean... Derek."

He smiled and opened the door, and I stepped out into the night.

I heard the door close behind me. The night air was cool, but the quiet felt too thick, pressing in like a held breath.

I walked toward my car, my keys clutched tight. The lot was nearly empty, just a few scattered vehicles under the humming glow of the streetlights. My boots scuffed against the asphalt, the sound louder than it should have been.

A breeze swept through the lot, rattling a stray paper cup along the pavement.

I glanced behind me.

Nothing.

Still, the feeling clung to me — an itch at the back of my neck, a whisper of movement just outside my line of sight.

I reached for my door handle...

A sudden rustling near the curb snapped through

185

the silence.

I tensed, heart pounding, then…

"Three now. Gone clean in the night."

I spun, my pulse hammering, only to find Arthur O'Leary standing beneath a flickering streetlamp, hands on his hips, scowling at the sky.

My breath rushed out. "Arthur. Jesus."

He barely looked at me, shaking his head. "They got more of my flamingoes."

I let my head fall back against my car with a shaky laugh. "Arthur, I—"

But he was already muttering about organized crime and shuffling toward the sidewalk, his flashlight bouncing in the dark.

I exhaled, sliding into the driver's seat and locking the doors.

Maybe I *was* getting paranoid.

I pulled out of the lot, winding through Mystic's quiet streets. The town looked different at night, the usual charm of its historic buildings and mom-and-pop storefronts dulled by the eerie stillness.

The glow of the Mystic Drawbridge reflected off the dark river below, its towering iron frame casting long shadows against the water. Even at this late hour, the soft hum of the current was constant. Mystic Pizza, usually packed with tourists grabbing a slice of its movie-famous pie, sat dark and shuttered, its neon sign flickering faintly in the window.

I passed Bank Square Books, its warm, inviting display of new releases now just a quiet front of glass and dark wood. The usually bustling sidewalks of Main

Street were empty, the cobblestone paths slick from an earlier rain. The scent of salt lingered in the air, mingling with the faint trace of fried seafood from the Sea View Snack Bar down by the water.

Even Olde Mistick Village, which during the day was all colonial charm and cheerful boutiques, felt eerie now — shadows pooling beneath the eaves, the carved wooden sign creaking in the breeze.

The roads were nearly deserted, only the occasional porch light flickering on as I passed, casting strange shadows across the sidewalk.

By the time I turned onto my street, the feeling had almost faded.

Then I pulled into the driveway.

The second I cut the engine, bass rattled through my windshield, muffled but unmistakable.

Addie.

I shook my head, letting out a half-smile as her off-key wailing filtered through the house windows, colliding with whatever pop anthem she had on full blast.

"My neighbors are gonna love me," I laughed, stepping out of the car.

For a moment, it felt normal again. Safe.

And then I saw it.

A thick, heavy envelope leaned against my front door.

YOUR LUCK'S RUN OUT.

The words were bold, blocky... angry.

A lump formed in my throat as I ripped it open.

A heavy iron horseshoe tumbled out, hitting the

porch heels down.

The unluckiest position of all.

I wasn't laughing anymore.

CHAPTER TWENTY-THREE

The scent of espresso, old paper, and a trace of red wine curled in the surrounding air, familiar and warm, but the iron horseshoe sitting between our coffee cups felt anything but. It lay there cold and heavy, the envelope beside it like a loaded threat.

YOUR LUCK'S RUN OUT.

Addie eyed the horseshoe like it might grow fangs. "Could be a prank?"

Dot, unimpressed as ever, stirred honey into her tea with a slow, deliberate motion. "Not with a message like that. And not with you stirring up the town's dirt like a stick in a hornet's nest."

I exhaled, tapping my nails against my cup. "Which is why tomorrow night is important."

Manny was still the strongest suspect—his aggression, his history, his connection to Zorina. But Orson? He had motive. Money. The size to match the killer.

Dot gave me a knowing look. "So, what's the plan?"

I leaned forward. "Sera's party. Both men will be

there. It's the best chance to press them both."

Addie frowned. "Cody won't like that."

I shrugged. "Which is why he doesn't get an invite."

Dot smirked. "And who does?"

I hesitated. "Tom."

Dot's face lit up like she was sending me off to prom. "Oh, that's lovely. I knew that boy had potential."

Addie let out a dramatic snort. "You're picking the guy who owns a beat-up truck and probably a drawer full of expired Taco Bell sauce packets?"

"Careful," Dot warned playfully. "Your bitter is showing."

I grinned. "What? He's charming. Even if he likes weird snack food."

Dot clasped her hands. "Oh, this is so exciting!"

All I had to do now was ask a question. How hard could it be? I used to ask questions for a living.

So, what had my knees knocking now?

You're afraid of the answer.

Shut it, mom.

*****

When he wasn't at the butcher shop, I found Tom exactly where I expected — half-buried in his boat's engine, forearms slick with grease, tanned skin glistening in the late afternoon heat. His shirt had been discarded over the railing, forgotten, leaving broad shoulders and a lean torso that looked like they belonged in some vintage, sepia-toned postcard — *Mystic's Finest Catch.*

Not that I noticed.

Much.

He glanced up as I stepped onto the dock, wiping sweat from his brow with the back of his hand, the movement making the muscles in his arm flex just enough to be distracting. The late sun caught on something around his neck — a glint of gold resting against his collarbone.

His gaze flicked over me, slow and amused. "Romano," he greeted, voice all lazy warmth. "You here to admire the view, or did I forget to pay a tab somewhere?"

I crossed my arms, shoving aside the flicker of heat low in my stomach. This was work. Just work. "Got plans tomorrow night?"

Tom arched a brow. "You askin' me on a date?"

I scoffed. "It's not a date."

"Right."

"It's a business arrangement."

"Uh-huh."

I exhaled. "I'm sure you've heard — Sera's throwing some big champagne-fueled party for her engagement." A frown puckered his full lips, so fleeting I almost dismissed it as a smirk quickly took its place. "Rich people. Fancy clothes. An opportunity to ask the right questions."

Tom leaned against the side of the boat, his arms crossed — his smile edging just enough into dangerous territory to make my pulse quicken. "And you need a date for this… interrogation?"

"More like cover." I cleared my throat. "If I show

191

up alone, Sera will hover. If I show up with Derek, I might as well bring a flashing 'I'm Investigating You' sign."

His smirk deepened. Then, before I could process the movement, he was suddenly closer.

Too close.

A single step, and the already narrow dock felt impossibly smaller.

His voice dropped, quiet but teasing. "And what about me? You trust me not to blow your cover?"

I swallowed. He smelled like sun-warmed wood, engine grease, and something else—something clean and distinctly male that sent heat curling up my spine.

"You were the only pick."

His grin widened, but instead of stepping back, he reached past me, gripping the dock railing just behind my hip. Not touching me, exactly, but suddenly bracketing me in place.

The scent of saltwater clung to the air, mingling with the distant briny bite of the tide.

"Guess that means I gotta say yes," he murmured.

I blinked up at him, suddenly very aware of the hard press of his forearms, the way his sun-browned throat moved as he swallowed.

A challenge flickered in his gaze. He knew what he was doing.

I refused to be the first to back down. "Guess it does."

For a second, the only sound was the distant call of seagulls, the gentle lap of water against the hull.

Then, just as easily, he leaned back, breaking the

moment.

"Better go shine my boots," he said with a wink.

I exhaled — only just then realizing I'd been holding my breath.

"Just wear something that doesn't look like it was used to wipe engine grease," I muttered, stepping past him.

"Can't make any promises."

I rolled my eyes, but before I could leave, the light caught the chain at his throat again — just for a second, just enough to make something in my gut twist.

A gold medallion.

Old, worn with time. The figure etched into the metal was just barely visible, a woman's face solemn and saintlike.

Something about it snagged at me, but before I could place why, he stretched, rolling his shoulders — and the medallion disappeared beneath his collar.

I shook off the thought.

Bigger things to worry about.

Like the fact that I still felt warm from where he'd been standing.

*****

I stared into my closet like it was some kind of mystical abyss.

I was going to Sera's party to investigate. To get paid. Not to make a statement.

And yet, here I was, holding up a strapless dress in one hand and a push-up bra in the other, as if either was crucial to solving a murder.

I huffed and shoved them back into the closet. *Not a date, Zoe.*

I reached for my go-to sleek black number — professional but understated — only for the hanger to catch, dragging half my wardrobe out with it. A cascade of rejected fashion choices puddled onto the floor.

Perfect. Just what this night needed. A sign from the universe that I should stay home in pajamas and eat peanut butter straight from the jar.

I scrolled through my messages while kicking a rogue sequin-covered top out of the way.

Dot: *A little effort never hurt anyone.*

Me: *It's not that kind of party.*

Dot: *Neither was my cousin's retirement party, but now she's engaged to her financial planner.*

I groaned, tossing my phone onto the bed.

I wasn't dressing for Tom. Or Derek. Or anyone but myself.

But when I pulled on a deep green dress that was cinched just right at the waist, my traitorous brain whispered.

Wouldn't hurt if Tom noticed.

I ignored it.

Buttoned my coat.

Time to get to work.

*****

Tom showed up cleaned up and dangerous.

No butcher's apron, no grease-streaked boat work

194

clothes. A real suit. Not stiff or corporate but tailored just enough to make a girl forget how to breathe.

The charcoal jacket fit those broad shoulders like it had been made for him. The deep blue dress shirt — no tie — was open just enough at the collar to show a teasing hint of skin. Polished dress shoes, no scuffs. A belt that actually matched.

And — God help me — he'd shaved.

The golden medallion — Saint Sarah I could now see — still glinted at his throat, a quiet, personal detail in all that well-dressed charm.

He stepped inside and stopped cold.

His breath hitched. Just a fraction. Like he forgot how to use his lungs.

His gaze dragged over me, slow and deliberate.

The deep green dress. The way it hugged my waist. The soft curl in my hair.

Heat flared behind his eyes, something unreadable but unmistakable.

Then — barely a whisper.

"Beautiful."

Oh, no. No, no, no.

It was hot. Oh, Lord, was it hot.

Why was it suddenly so hot?

I resisted the urge to fan myself with Dot's napkin. Or strip naked. Not that. Definitely not that.

Well, okay… maybe later…

Zoe Marie!

Dot, entirely unbothered by the sheer hurricane of tension in the room, clapped her hands together. "Stand up straight. Let me see you."

"I *am* standing up straight."

"You're slouching."

Before I could react, she reached out, smoothing my collar with meticulous, mom-like care. Then — horror of horrors — she licked her thumb and rubbed my cheek.

"Dot!" I jerked back, mortified.

"You had too much blush," she tsked, entirely oblivious to the fact that I was currently on fire.

Tom finally snapped out of it, his lips twitching at the corners. "Guess I gotta agree with Dot on this one. You're so beautiful, you don't need anything on."

One… two… three shocked faces.

Tom's eyes flew wide. "Oh, no! That's not what I meant. Damn! I just meant you're so pretty, you don't need makeup." He jammed his fist downward. "Me and my big mouth!"

I shot him a look. "You sure you wanna be seen with me?"

His voice dipped low and dangerously smooth.

"Oh, trust me, Romano. That ain't the issue."

Oh, for the love of God.

Dot clutched her heart, looking between us like she was watching the last scene of a rom-com. "I'm going to take pictures."

"Nope." I grabbed Tom's arm, shoving him toward the door before she started picking out wedding invitations.

Dot's voice followed us, sing-songy and delighted. "Smile for the camera!"

Tom slid into the driver's seat, grinning like he had all the time in the world.

"You *sure* this isn't a date?"

I groaned, breathing in the scent of his cologne—crisp notes of sea salt and bergamot, softened by driftwood and white musk—and yanked my seatbelt across my chest. "Just drive."

"We'll see you there!" Addie called out.

Tom's laughter rumbled low in his throat as the engine purred to life.

Trust me… that wasn't the only thing purring.

CHAPTER TWENTY-FOUR

Tobit Ranch looked like it had been ripped straight from a *Town & Country* spread. Except tonight, it wasn't just for show. Twinkling string lights draped from the beams of the wraparound porch, casting a soft golden glow over a graveled drive that made no damn sense. Sleek, black Bentleys and Teslas sat bumper to bumper with rust-speckled minivans and at least one old Ford truck missing a side mirror. Near the barn, I was pretty sure I spotted a beat-up station wagon with a 'I'm a Connecticutie' bumper sticker.

Inside, the mansion-turned-ballroom was a strange, hilarious collision of wealth and small-town charm. Crystal chandeliers sparkled above the polished hardwood floors, casting reflections on the crowd that absolutely should not have been in the same room together.

Sera and Orson reigned over the party like Mystic's most unlikely royal couple — she, a vision in ice-blue silk, her blonde hair swept into a flawless chignon, the diamond at her throat winking with every graceful tilt of her head; he, a good two decades older, thick around the middle, his tux straining just slightly at the buttons, the sheen of sweat on his brow suggesting he'd rather be anywhere but stuffed into formalwear and making nice with people who whispered behind his back.

There were the Whitmores, the Bensonhursts, the old-money elites — dripping in diamonds, sipping Dom Pérignon like it was hydration therapy — kept their distance from the townies. And the townies? They didn't care.

I passed by Bernie, Mystic's medical examiner, at the buffet table, holding a paper plate stacked three inches high with bacon-wrapped shrimp. I raised a curious eyebrow.

"So, my rabbi's gonna kill me," he mused, mid-chew. "But these things are amazing!"

Further down the room, the Mystic Book Club ladies had taken over the bar.

Mrs. Potter, the librarian, sniffed at the cocktail menu. "This is ridiculous. If I wanted a drink that tastes like a flower, I'd go outside and lick the azaleas."

"Speak for yourself," Addie snorted, stirring her gin and tonic. "I'm three sips away from making some really bad life choices."

And then there was Deidre.

Dear, chaotic, Deidre.

I spotted her before I even heard her, because how could I not? A walking disco ball of Jersey Shore ambition. The gold-sequined gown clung to every curve like a second skin, the slit creeping dangerously high. Her platinum hair was teased to somewhere between "glamorous" and "in need of tower clearance." And the heels?

Six inches. Too tall. A disaster waiting to happen.

"I swear to God," Deidre huffed. "You'd think these people never saw a beautiful woman before."

Tom let out a low whistle. "Oh, she's gonna wipe out."

I shot him a look. "Don't be mean."

"I'm not being mean. I'm being observant."

We stepped deeper into the party. I glided into the atmosphere effortlessly. Tom?

Tom was a different story.

Sure, he'd cleaned up well — his dark suit tailored just enough to hint at the strength beneath, the deep blue of his shirt complementing the sharp lines of his jaw. But there was no disguising the slight furrow of his brow as he eyed the hors d'oeuvres like they might attack.

A passing server offered him a tray. "Sea urchin mousse with beluga caviar?"

Tom barely resisted a full-body shudder. "Yeah, no."

I smirked, lifting my champagne. "Aren't you hungry?"

Tom shrugged, stuffing his hands into his pockets. "If my stomach gets louder than Deidre's outfit, I'll slip out to my truck for some real food."

I sighed, taking a sip of my drink. "You're impossible."

He grinned, but before he could respond — Deidre let out a dramatic shriek.

I turned just in time to see it.

Deidre's heel slipped. A precarious wobble. A flailing arm. A server ducking for cover. And then— Deidre went down like a chandelier in a windstorm.

Her arms pinwheeled, and in a glorious, slow-motion spectacle, she crashed into the nearest catering station.

Hard.

Glasses toppled. Shrimp cocktails went flying.

A single shrimp skittered across the floor and came to rest at the toe of Sera's Manolo Blahniks. Her lips tightened into a hard, thin line.

Meanwhile, a collective gasp rippled through the crowd. Some guests winced. Others sipped their drinks, watching like it was free entertainment.

"Oh, my God!" Mrs. Potter cried. "Should we call a doctor?"

"Only if he's single," Deidre mumbled from the tile.

Before I could react, Tom was already moving.

"Stay put," he murmured as he brushed past me. I watched, against my better judgment, as he moved through the crowd like he belonged everywhere and nowhere at once.

He knelt beside Deidre, all calm efficiency. He checked her ankle and looked carefully at her pupils. She'd conked her head pretty hard, though I was fairly certain the hairspray had provided a solid helmet of protection. His strong hands stayed steady as he helped her to her feet—the same hands that had helped me after I'd been injured.

A reminder.

Tom knew how to handle things.

And while he was busy patching up the sequined hurricane, I turned my attention to something much more important.

At the bar, gripping a half-empty glass of scotch, looking tenser than anyone had a right to at a party.

Manny.

I squared my shoulders. Time to get some answers.

Manny looked like a man with too much weight on his shoulders and too little patience to carry it. He stood at the far end of the bar, swirling the whiskey in his glass like it held the answer to all his problems. His eyes flicked toward the exits between slow, calculated sips. He was waiting. For what—or *who*—I wasn't sure.

I slid into the space next to him, setting my champagne flute down with an easy clink. "Didn't peg you for the Dom Pérignon type."

Manny let out a dry chuckle, but there was no mirth in his eyes. "Didn't peg you for someone who gets invited to parties like this."

I smirked. "Mystic's full of surprises."

He shot me a sidelong look, slow and assessing. "Yeah. Some less welcome than others."

I ignored the bait. "Speaking of surprises, you left in a hell of a hurry the other night."

Manny's grip on his glass didn't tighten, but the pause before his next sip told me I'd hit a nerve. "What can I say? You and I run in different circles."

I tilted my head. "Do we? Because lately, it seems like we keep bumping into each other. Me, you...

Zorina." I let the name hang between us, waiting for the reaction.

Manny exhaled through his nose, swirling the whiskey again. "You're digging in places you don't belong, sweetheart."

Sweetheart. Cute.

I kept my expression even. "Funny. I thought the same thing when I found a horseshoe on my table with a less-than-friendly note." I sipped my champagne. "Tell me, Manny. That your brand of intimidation?"

His smirk didn't falter, but something flickered behind his eyes — something quick and unreadable. "You think I've got time to send love letters?"

"Maybe not. But I think you've got a vested interest in me backing off."

Manny's smirk faltered for a fraction of a second — barely long enough to register — before snapping back into place. "You don't know what you're talking about."

"Horses."

Manny finally turned to face me, his voice dropping just low enough that I had to lean in. "Listen close, Romano. Zorina played a dangerous game with the wrong people. You think you know what happened, but you don't. And if you keep poking around, you might end up on the losing side, same as her."

That pulse of warning thrummed through my veins, but I kept my expression neutral. "That sounds like a threat."

Manny smirked again, but this time, it was sharper. "Nah. That's just friendly advice."

I watched him for a long moment, waiting for him

to crack. But he was good — used to being questioned, used to talking around things without ever really saying anything.

Still, he was running out of patience. I could see it in the set of his jaw, the way his knee bounced once under the bar.

I leaned against the counter, keeping my tone conversational. "Just one more question before you disappear on me — where were you the night Zorina died?"

Manny's entire body tensed. Not much, but enough.

He let out a slow breath, setting his glass down with an audible *clink*. "Not my problem what happens to a woman who plays games she can't win."

That wasn't a denial.

I opened my mouth to press further, but he was already on the move, turning sharply and striding toward the patio doors leading to the stables.

I hesitated, watching him go. Follow him or press Sera?

Manny was running... metaphorically, anyway.

Sera was still standing right there.

Decision made, I straightened my dress and turned toward Mystic's reigning queen.

Sera stood near the French doors leading to the patio, her ice-blue gown catching the light like she'd been dipped in moonlight and diamonds. She looked untouchable, elegant — the perfect society princess in the perfect setting. But when I sidled up beside her, the tension in her shoulders told me she wasn't as composed as she wanted to appear.

I swirled my champagne, keeping my tone light. "Gorgeous party. Must've cost a fortune."

Sera didn't look at me. "Orson wanted me to have it." Her voice was crisp, measured. "Big, lavish. Something Mystic wouldn't forget."

"Well," I mused, scanning the room, "between the Dom Pérignon and Deidre taking out a catering station, I'd say, mission accomplished."

Sera let out a breath, something too sharp to be amusement. "That woman is a menace."

I smirked. "She's consistent, at least." I let the moment settle before shifting gears. "Speaking of consistency, I ran into Manny earlier. Just as tall, dark, and broody as the last time I talked to him. Although tonight... tonight, he seemed a little... on edge."

That got her attention. She turned, but only slightly. "Manny's always on edge."

"Mm." I took a sip, watching her over the rim of my glass. "It's funny, though. I'm a little on edge myself. The other night, someone left me a little gift on my doorstep—a horseshoe. With a message." I tilted my head. "YOUR LUCK'S RUN OUT."

Sera finally looked at me fully, her gaze sharp but unreadable. "And you think Manny had something to do with it?"

I shrugged, letting the silence do the work.

Her eyes flicked away, out toward the stables, just for a second. Just long enough to mean something.

I didn't press. Not yet. "See, I have a hard time believing Manny acts alone. He's more of a... team player." I let the words sink in before adding, "Not a quarterback. More of a defensive lineman. Not the one making the plays, but the one protecting the real shot caller."

Sera's expression didn't change, but the subtle way her jaw shifted told me she didn't like where this was going.

"You see, I'm pretty sure Manny and Zorina had known each other for quite some time." I noticed her eye twitch. I continued. "How about you?" I let the pause stretch, my voice dipping just enough to keep her on edge. "How long did you know Madame Zorina… or should I say, Noreen Cox?"

Sera's lips parted, but no sound came out.

That was it. The moment.

Not shock—*recognition.*

She covered quickly, reaching for the nearest champagne flute and taking a deliberate sip. When she finally spoke, her voice was smooth, almost bored. "I don't know what you're fishing for, but you certainly won't find it here."

And then she was gone, slipping through the doors in a flurry of silk and tension, striding across the patio toward the stables.

I watched her go, that brief pulse of triumph mixing with something darker. I didn't have proof—yet—but she knew more than she was letting on.

And as I turned back to the room, my eyes landed on Orson.

He was standing across the ballroom, watching me.

Not drinking. Not talking.

Just watching.

A cold weight settled in my stomach. I lifted my champagne glass to my lips, pretending I wasn't rattled, but the bubbles tasted suddenly sharp against my tongue.

Something was shifting. The pieces were moving.

And I wasn't sure if I was the one playing the game — or the one about to be played.

Time to find out.

CHAPTER TWENTY-FIVE

I didn't have to go to Orson.

He was coming to me.

Fast.

For his bulk, the man cut through the crowd like a blade, each step measured, deliberate. His face was flushed — not with liquor, but with the type of heat that came from barely restrained fury. A bead of sweat clung to his temple, catching in the chandelier light as he approached. The whiskey glass in his hand barely wobbled, though his grip on the crystal looked tighter than it needed to be.

The party hummed around us, oblivious to the shift. Addie was at the bar, halfway through a martini and laughing too loudly at one of Arthur's long-winded stories. Dot had finally arrived, her cocktail dress clashing spectacularly with the practicality of her orthopedic Cobbie Cuddlers. The sight should've been amusing. But the moment Orson locked eyes on me, the atmosphere changed.

"Miss Romano." His voice was pleasant, controlled — but the steel beneath it was unmistakable.

"You always make it a habit of harassing the host's fiancée at his own party?"

I let my champagne flute dangle between two fingers, considering. "Harassing? That's a strong word."

His smirk—if you could call it that—was sharp and humorless. "Not as strong as the one I'd prefer to use."

I didn't blink. "I ask questions. That's what I do."

Orson let out a chuckle—low, mirthless, the kind that belonged in a poker game where the stakes had just been raised. "That's one way to put it."

I tilted my head, keeping my voice light. "And you? You ever ask yourself any?"

His whiskey swirled in the glass, slow and controlled, like he was considering whether this conversation was worth his time. "Such as?"

I leaned in slightly, just enough to look like I belonged in this glittering world of chandeliers and Dom Pérignon, but not so much that he'd mistake me for someone who played by its rules. "Like why a woman like Zorina would come sniffing around a man like you?"

The muscles in his jaw tensed, just for a second. Not much, but enough.

Behind him, Dot copped a squat on a barstool while reaching for a canapé from a passing tray. Arthur, still mid-monologue, barely noticed. Addie, however, had turned just slightly, her martini hovering near her lips, eyes flicking between us like she was watching a slow-moving car crash.

"I know exactly what you're implying," Orson said, his voice even, but his grip tightening around the glass.

I held his gaze, letting the silence stretch. "Do you?"

That's when I saw it — something else hiding behind the swirling rage in his eyes.

Pain.

I reached out and gently took his hand. He didn't pull away. "Do you, Orson? Because the way I see it, you were probably getting played. Have you ever wondered, even once, how much of what she told you was true?"

Orson's smile faltered — just a fraction, just enough. He yanked his hand away.

A hush had settled in our corner of the party, a quiet pull of curiosity from the surrounding guests who had learned that, when I started asking questions, things tended to unravel. Mrs. Potter, who had edged her way closer under the guise of inspecting the drink menu, gave an impatient little huff.

"First place she went was the library," I continued. "Spent a good long time poring over those old records — obituaries, wedding announcements, birth certificates."

"She's right, you know," Mrs. Potter piped up, her eyes flicking to Orson with barely veiled judgment.

Orson turned his gaze toward me, his grip on his glass tightening. "That so?"

I tilted my head. "It is. You see, that day at the cemetery? That wasn't chance. It wasn't divine providence. It was planned."

Something dark danced behind his gaze.

"Just like her prediction that Manny would show up," I continued. "That wasn't luck, either. Manny and

210

Madame Zorina — Noreen Cox — already knew each other."

Orson took a slow sip of his whiskey, processing. "You're suggesting Zorina... targeted me?"

"I'm not suggesting anything," I said, setting my champagne flute down with deliberate ease. "I'm saying it outright."

He exhaled through his nose, a sharp breath that barely masked the simmering tension beneath the surface. "Careful, Romano. You're on thin ice."

I leaned in just enough to make sure he saw the glint in my eyes. "Thin ice cracks, Mr. Tobit. But so do a lot of cons."

I could feel the old familiar rush of pursuing a story, when you reached that pivotal moment that sent you rushing headlong toward a riveting conclusion.

But then I also heard a voice inside my head, husky, warning me not to overstep — especially with a man as powerful as Orson Tobit.

Derek's voice.

But the siren call of my reporter instincts outweighed any inkling of self-preservation I may have had.

"I don't know about you, Orson, but that would make me furious," I said, tilting my head. "If I found out I'd been played like that? Strung along, used? I'd want to do something about it."

His jaw flexed, a slow grind of molars.

I stepped in just a fraction, voice dipping lower. "How about you, Orson? Did you want to do something about it?" I let the silence stretch. Then — *the* question.

"Where were you the night Noreen Cox was killed?"

The muscle in his cheek jumped as he seethed.

"I wasn't even in Mystic that night." His voice was clipped, measured. "I was on my damn boat."

I raised an eyebrow. "Convenient."

"Check the dock records," he growled. "I left before sunset and didn't come back until well after midnight."

I held his gaze, watching for cracks. His hands were loose at his sides, but his posture was rigid.

For a moment, I thought I had him. That flicker of doubt, the crack in the armor—I saw it. But just as quickly, Orson Tobit sealed himself off. He exhaled slowly, shaking his head like a man who had already decided I wasn't worth listening to.

"You reporters," he murmured, taking a measured sip of whiskey. "Always so sure of yourselves. Always willing to wreck lives for a good headline."

The words slithered through the space between us, deceptively soft, razor-sharp beneath the surface.

My breath caught. It was barely a hitch, a fraction of a second, but he saw it. His gaze sharpened like a predator scenting blood. He didn't know everything about me, but he knew enough.

Enough to go for the throat.

I could feel the quiet shift around us, the way the room tilted ever so slightly in Orson's favor. Some guests were watching outright now, their interest sharpened, eyes darting between us like spectators at a prizefight.

I smoothed my expression, reached for my champagne flute like the hit hadn't landed. "I care about the truth. Don't you?"

Orson's smirk didn't waver, but I caught the way his fingers curled tighter around his glass. A tell. A man clinging to the version of events that suited him best.

Or that he desperately needed to believe.

"I care about what's mine," he seethed.

Orson exhaled slowly, shaking his head like he'd finally had enough. He straightened his jacket, smoothed down his tie, then leveled me with a look as sharp as a well-honed knife.

"You've overstayed your welcome, Romano. Time for you to leave."

It wasn't a suggestion. *It was a verdict.*

The words settled between us, heavy with finality. Around us, the party continued — laughter, clinking glasses, the gentle hum of an expensive string quartet — but it all felt distant, hollow.

I didn't move. Didn't flinch.

Orson lifted his glass, took a slow sip, then set it down with a quiet, deliberate *clink* — a sound that landed like a gavel, final and absolute.

"By the way..." His voice was smooth, almost lazy, but the glint in his eyes was sharp as a blade. "Consider your invoice ripped up."

There it was. The kill shot.

Why, oh why, hadn't I listened to Derek?

All the time, the effort, the logistics — gone. The profit margin I'd carefully calculated? *Nonexistent.* A full shipment of Dom Pérignon that I had personally facilitated, signed off on, and now had no hope of seeing a cent for.

And Orson? He knew exactly what he'd done.

I forced my expression to remain neutral, but my grip tightened around the stem of my champagne flute. I wouldn't give him the satisfaction of a visible reaction.

Across the room, I caught the subtle shift of movement — some guests still mingling, oblivious — others well-tuned into the unfolding drama. Mrs. Potter frowning in disapproval, Addie whispering something to Arthur. Dot, observing, eating anything and everything that didn't eat her first. Even Diedre, who had hobbled back in, watching us like the last episode of a reality show.

But before I could fully absorb the blow — a scream tore through the night.

I suddenly wondered...*where was Tom?*

CHAPTER TWENTY-SIX

Sera burst into the ballroom like a shot fired from a gun.

The glacial composure, the practiced poise — gone.

Her ice-blue gown was askew, the delicate silk bunched where she had gripped it in her fists. Her golden hair, once an intricate masterpiece, had come loose in places, stray tendrils sticking to her damp forehead. But it was her eyes that turned the air brittle.

Wide. Wild. Utterly wrecked.

The party didn't stop immediately. The orchestra still played, laughter still hummed — but the shift was undeniable. A ripple of silence moved outward as people sensed it. The disruption. The fracture in the night's carefully curated perfection.

Sera's chest rose and fell like she'd run a mile in heels. Her gaze swept frantically over the sea of guests, desperate, searching — until she found him.

Orson.

He had just straightened from his final, cutting words to me, the last of his whiskey swirling untouched in his glass. But at the sight of Sera, his entire body tensed, his grip tightening like he was bracing for impact.

Sera staggered forward, nearly collapsing into his arms. Her breath hitched, her fingers clutching desperately at the front of his tuxedo.

"He's—he's—"

Her voice cracked on the last word. Terror. True, unfiltered terror.

A single glass slipped from someone's hand, shattering against the polished floor. A small, startled sound—but in the stunned silence that followed, it might as well have been a gunshot.

And then, in a voice so small it barely belonged to her…

"He's dead."

The room leaned in, collective breaths suspended in midair. The weight of the moment crushed against my chest.

My knees nearly buckled. I caught the back of a chair, fingers digging in hard. My heart pounded against my ribs, a frantic, pulsing drumbeat of panic.

No. No, no, no.

Where was Tom?

The world tilted. The walls of the grand ballroom—glittering with chandeliers, alive with murmuring guests—began to close in. My breath caught in my throat.

This wasn't happening.

Then…

"MANNY'S DEAD."

Sera's words slammed through the room like a bullet-shattering glass.

A collective gasp. A ripple of stunned horror. Someone's champagne flute slipped from their hand, crashing to the floor.

Beside me, Bernie muttered a sharp Yiddish curse.

Dot shot him a look, pressing her lips together. "Bernard. Not the time."

But Bernie only shook his head, reaching for his whiskey. "You're right. But it is definitely the time for another 50-year-old Macallan."

Across the room, Orson didn't move.

His grip on Sera tightened, his jaw rigid, but his face — a man built on control — had gone ashen.

And then, finally, as if the weight of Sera's words had just hit — the ballroom exploded into chaos.

"Where?" Orson growled.

Sera pointed, limp-wristed. "The stables."

Orson was already moving.

His grip was white-knuckled on Sera's wrist as he yanked her forward, shoving through the frozen crowd. His expression was unreadable, but the force in his step — the sheer determination in his movements — was like a wrecking ball clearing a path.

My instincts screamed.

I shook off my shock just in time to see the tide shift — guests moving, murmuring, stepping toward the patio doors. The pull of morbid curiosity was impossible to fight. This wasn't just a scandal anymore. It was blood on the floor.

Bernie groaned. "I should've eaten dessert first."

Dot whacked him on the arm. "Move, Bernard. You're not dying in a tux."

I wasn't waiting for them. I was already pushing forward, dodging between clusters of partygoers clutching their pearls and their drinks. My mind raced ahead of my body, already trying to piece together the scene I hadn't yet seen.

Manny was dead.

But where? How? And, more importantly… who was next?

I stepped outside, the warm glow of the ballroom cutting off behind me. The air outside was thick, humid — too still for what I knew was waiting.

The stable doors loomed ahead. Dark. Open. Waiting.

And somewhere inside, beneath that black, yawning entrance — a body was cooling.

I wasn't sure what was going to happen once we got closer to the stables but, lucky for me, I didn't have to.

Bernie might've been semi-retired, but the second we reached the entrance, he snapped back to the job like he'd never left it. He strode ahead of the crowd, his voice sharp and commanding, cutting through the rising tide of chaos like a scalpel.

"Everyone stay back!" He lifted a hand, his usual dry humor gone, replaced with the steel of an old pro who'd seen too many bodies in his time. "We don't need a herd of footprints messing up the scene."

"Scene?" Addie echoed, clutching Arthur's arm. "Bernie, what do you — ?"

"I mean what I said." His eyes, sharp despite his years, flicked to the stable doors. The air inside felt thick.

Heavy. Charged. "We go in slow. We don't touch a damn thing."

Sera quivered like a live wire. "Orson—"

"I've got you." Orson's hand tightened around her arm, his face a mask of barely contained fury and something dangerously close to fear.

Bernie's attention swung to me. His gaze scanned my face, my stance—like he was assessing whether I could handle what we were about to see. Whatever he found there must've satisfied him, because he gave a single, clipped nod.

"You, Tobit, and Sera. No one else." He turned back to the growing cluster of guests, his voice dropping into an authority that brooked no argument. "The rest of you? Stay put. Last thing I need is a bunch of rubberneckers contaminating the scene."

I heard the murmurs, the shifting feet, the quiet but urgent whispers flying between the guests, and the high-pitched whinnies and snorts of nervous horses from within.

Dot crossed her arms, huffing. "No one wants to get trampled by a spooked stallion, anyway. I might be old, but I'm not stupid."

Bernie shot her a look. "Dot, not but thirty minutes ago, you were two glasses deep and betting on who would fall down first on the dance floor."

She sniffed and looked at Deidre. "And I was right."

Bernie sighed. "Stay. Put."

And then, with a last glance at the three of us, he stepped inside the stables.

Orson followed, his grip on Sera never loosening.

I braced myself.

Then I stepped over the threshold — into the thick, stifling air of the stables.

The moment I stepped inside, the world tilted.

The horses were frantic. The air vibrated with their fear. A chestnut mare pawed at the ground, nostrils flaring, white-ringed eyes wide with distress. A gray gelding threw his head, slamming against his stall door hard enough to rattle the hinges. Somewhere deeper in the stable, a horse screamed — a high, keening sound that sent my nerves into overdrive.

The scent hit me next. Blood. Thick. Metallic. Soaking into the hay, clinging to the humid night air.

Bernie muttered another curse, but I barely heard him over the chaos. Orson stormed behind him, dragging Sera in his wake. Her heels skidded against the dirt floor, but she didn't resist. She just kept staring — wide-eyed, hollow — at the thing no one should've had to see.

Manny lay sprawled in the middle of the aisle.

His body twisted, his limbs at unnatural angles. His chest, unmoving. His eyes wide and glassy, reflecting the dim stable light. A dark, ragged smear of crimson cut across his torso, soaked deep into the trampled straw.

The Perlino, Seriatim, reared back in his stall, striking the wooden divider with his hooves. His coat was slick with sweat, his ears pinned flat, his sides heaving.

I swallowed hard, forcing my brain to work past the visceral jolt of horror. Something about the scene felt... wrong.

Orson's breath came harsh and unsteady. "Good God."

Sera let out a broken, choking sound and staggered back, gripping the stable door like it was the only thing holding her up.

So much for not touching anything.

Her breath hitched. She gagged once, hand flying to her mouth, then turned her face away.

And me?

I took a step closer.

Because whatever had just happened in this stable, I was almost certain it hadn't been an accident.

It was murder.

*****

We stepped out into the night air again. The sharp sound of sirens wailed. Someone had called the cops.

A sudden commotion sounded through the crowd.

Footsteps, fast and uneven, crunching through the gravel drive.

"Zoe!"

I spun, just in time to see Tom barreling toward me, eyes wide, breath coming a little too fast, like he'd been running. He gripped my arm, firm but not rough, his fingers pressing into my skin just enough to ground me.

"What the hell happened?" His voice was low, urgent. "I was coming back and—" His gaze flicked to the cluster of guests standing stiff on the patio, then to the stables, where light now spilled from the open doorway. "What's going on?"

I exhaled sharply, my heart still hammering from the night's relentless turns.

"Manny's dead."

Tom's face dropped.

Dead air stretched between us, just a fraction too long before he found his voice. "What? Dead?" His throat worked through a swallow, his grip on my arm loosening. "How—?"

I shook my head. "We don't know yet, but it looks like he got trampled by one of the horses."

Tom let out a breath, dragging a hand through his hair. "Jesus." His gaze flicked to Orson and Sera, just outside the stable, their silhouettes framed against the harsh light. "I thought this was supposed to be a party."

I turned my attention back to him, my reporter instincts finally catching up.

"Where were you?"

His expression froze, just for a beat. Then he rubbed the back of his neck, shifting his weight.

"I, uh—" A humorless chuckle. "I got hungry."

I frowned.

Tom sighed, shaking his head. "I couldn't stomach the idea of all that fancy food, so I slipped out to my truck." His lips tugged into a sheepish smirk. "Figured if I was gonna suffer through all this, I deserved at least a bag of comfort junk food."

My stomach twisted.

"All the comfort food in the world's not gonna help Manny," I said, wry but sharp.

Tom's smirk faltered.

Before he could answer...

"Zoe."

Chief Cody.

Derek.

I barely had time to register his approach before he was in front of me, his eyes raking me over, head to toe, like he was checking for injuries.

"Are you hurt?" His voice was firm but laced with concern. "Did you see anything? What happened?"

I barely shook my head before he fired off another.

"Who was with you?"

I opened my mouth, but Tom stepped forward.

"Don't worry, Chief." His voice was easy, casual — too casual. "She's been right by my side all night."

A cold flicker of doubt whispered through me.

But you weren't, were you?

Derek cut his eyes to Tom, scanning him like he was just now registering his presence.

"I'll be sure to see that Zoe gets home safely," Tom offered.

Before anyone could say another word, "Everyone that lives at Zoe's, right? Because that would be AWESOME!"

Oh, Addie. My "temporary" roomie.

She barreled in from the sidelines, hands gesturing wildly, eyes as wide and manic as a kid on a sugar high.

"What an insane night, am I right?" She let out a shaky laugh, her jewelry jingling.

Tension shattered.

And just like that, the night lurched forward

223

again.

But I was afraid it was about to run me over flat.

CHAPTER TWENTY-SEVEN

Sleep was a lost cause.

Every time I closed my eyes, I saw Manny — his body twisted in the straw, his lifeless eyes reflecting the dim light of the stable. The scent of blood clung to my skin long after I'd left the scene, burrowing into my brain, refusing to let go.

I had stayed at the stables as long as Chief Cody allowed, watching the officers comb the area, taking statements, measuring hoofprints in the churned-up dirt. Then, like everyone else, I'd been dismissed — sent home with no answers, no closure, just the echo of Sera's scream and the growing suspicion that none of this was over.

Morning came too soon. I barely touched my coffee, the bitterness doing little to shake off the exhaustion gripping my bones. But curiosity had always been stronger than self-preservation, and there was only one place to get the answers I needed.

The Groton Police Department.

Derek.

I parked out front, stepping onto the sidewalk just as a gust of wind rolled in from the coast. The sky was heavy with storm clouds, thick and brooding, as if Mystic itself was holding its breath. The calm before the inevitable downpour.

Inside, the station was awake with movement — officers on calls, phones ringing, papers shuffling. But above it all, one voice cut through the air like a blade.

Orson Tobit.

I slowed my steps as I approached Derek's office. The door was cracked open just enough for me to catch the scene inside.

Orson stood near Derek's desk, his face red, his posture tight with fury. He jabbed a finger toward Derek, his voice laced with something sharp and desperate.

"You've let this amateur sleuth make a mockery of me and my family!"

My brows lifted. I wasn't expecting fan mail, but this was something else.

Orson's hands clenched at his sides, veins popping at his temples. His anger didn't just stem from irritation. This was panic.

And then — he dropped a bombshell.

"Sera's beside herself. Talking about going back to England."

I stilled.

That was new. And judging by the way Derek's posture stiffened behind his desk, it was news to him, too.

Back to England?

That didn't sound like a grieving woman trying to

226

escape painful memories. That sounded like a guilty woman running.

A woman getting out before the walls caved in.

I edged closer, just out of sight, heart hammering in my chest as Orson's voice rose again, vibrating with fury.

"You need to sideline her, Cody. Now. She's a liability to this investigation, and I won't stand for it."

Sidelined? Oh, I'd like to see him try.

I inched forward, my pulse pounding in my ears, waiting — watching.

Derek had yet to say a word. From my vantage point, I could only see the stiff set of his shoulders, the way his fingers drummed once — just once — on the desk. Not a man caught off guard. A man thinking.

And thinking hard.

Finally, he exhaled, slow and measured. "If you're so worried about your fiancée's reputation, Orson, maybe you should be asking yourself why she wants to run."

The words landed like a slap.

Orson's back straightened, his breath a sharp inhale. "What are you implying?"

Derek didn't blink. "I'm not implying anything." A pause. "Yet."

I took another step forward.

Let's see what else Derek had to say.

He didn't answer right away.

Instead, he exhaled sharply and rubbed a hand over his face. The movement wasn't just frustration — it was exhaustion, a man who had spent too many hours chasing answers that refused to come clean.

For a split second, I saw it. The doubt.

Maybe he wasn't completely sold on Orson's demand. Maybe he was wrestling with how much truth had tangled itself in my theories.

But Orson wasn't finished.

He leaned in, voice dropping to a dangerous register. "You have no control over her, Cody. That's a problem."

Silence.

The kind that stretched thick and suffocating.

Then, without waiting for a response, Orson spun on his heel, his footsteps sharp against the tile.

I barely stepped aside in time.

He didn't just pass—he loomed, stopping just long enough to look at me, his dark gaze simmering with something just short of fury.

"Enjoy your little investigation, Ms. Romano," he murmured. "While it lasts."

A chill ghosted over my skin.

Then he was gone.

The heavy glass door swung shut behind me, muffling the chatter from the front desk. Myrna's voice still carried, crisp as ever, no doubt giving someone an earful while picking through her box of donuts.

Derek let out a sharp sigh, pinching the bridge of his nose like he was holding his skull together. His desk was its usual disaster—case files in disarray, half-drained coffee, a notepad scribbled on so furiously the pen had torn through the paper.

I folded my arms. "What the hell was that about?"

"Exactly what it sounded like."

"So, what—Orson throws a tantrum, and now I'm cut out?"

Derek's expression darkened. "Zoe, you've been poking around in sensitive matters, making accusations without solid proof."

I scoffed, stepping closer. "Orson was getting taken for a ride! The rodeo connection, that conversation I overheard about 'development'? They had to be talking about altering the horses' appearances! Forget 'sensitive matters'—that's motive."

Derek's jaw flexed. He wasn't looking at me anymore—his gaze had drifted to the desk, fingers tapping once, twice. He knew it too.

His hands pressed against his desk like he needed to physically ground himself. "We don't even know for sure Sera is Zorina's daughter," he said, his voice taut. "I haven't gotten the DNA results back from Bernie yet. And nothing's popped on the fingerprint from the glass either. Without something to compare it to, it's worthless."

I scoffed, throwing my hands up. "Okay… so we don't have definitive proof, but we sure as hell have enough to be asking the right questions."

His exhale was sharp, measured. A breath you take when you're trying to keep a lid on something that's about to boil over. "Manny's death was an accident," he said, slower this time, like maybe if he said it with enough conviction, I'd believe it. "Trampled by a spirited horse."

My patience snapped. "Was it? Or is that just what

you're telling yourself?"

His mouth flattened into a hard, unyielding line. The muscles in his forearms tensed, his hands curling into fists at his sides. A charged silence stretched between us, thick enough to cut.

Derek wasn't just frustrated—he was angry. Not at me. Not entirely.

At the situation. At himself.

At the fact that deep down, he knew I was right.

I gripped the edge of Derek's desk, leaning in just enough to force his attention. My voice dropped low, steady. "You want to know how I know I'm on the right track?" I met his gaze, unwavering. "Someone threatened me."

Derek stilled.

"Twice, now," I continued. "Someone told me to back off. Basically said this won't end well for me."

The air in the office shifted. The tension that had been simmering between us hardened into something sharper, more dangerous. Derek's fists unclenched, but his posture changed—no longer stiff with frustration, but wired, bracing.

Then, before I could take another breath, he moved.

He stepped around the desk, close enough that I had to tilt my chin to hold his gaze. His nearness was a challenge, a warning. "You didn't tell me this?" His voice was lower now, controlled—but beneath the control, something darker lurked.

I exhaled sharply. "I was going to." I shook my head, biting back the urge to step away. "But I figured you'd react exactly like this."

"Damn right, I am."

Derek's face was unreadable, but his body told another story. His breathing was steady — but the corded muscles in his forearms popped and flexed.

"What did they say, exactly?" His voice was low, clipped, but there was something dangerous curling beneath it.

"Walk away, Romano. Before you get… trampled."

The air between us turned razor sharp.

Derek went completely still. The unnerving stillness that came before a storm.

I didn't stop. "And then I got a note. A note with a horseshoe." My voice was steady, but my pulse wasn't. *"Your luck's run out."*

I heard his teeth grind.

And then he moved.

He turned abruptly, pacing away from me, his movements tight and agitated. His back was to me, but I could see the tension radiating from his frame, the barely leashed fury threatening to snap.

I swallowed. "This isn't just about me investigating, is it?"

No answer.

Derek exhaled sharply through his nose, pressing his hands flat against his desk, his head dropping between his shoulders.

The silence between us was thick. Heavy.

Then, finally, "I pulled you into this."

His voice was low, raw. Like he hated the words. Like saying them out loud made them real.

231

Something twisted inside me.

Because I realized—Derek wasn't just angry. He wasn't just frustrated.

He was blaming himself.

And worse... he was frightened.

I blinked, thrown off.

Derek's voice was raw. "You wouldn't be in danger if I'd just—damn it, Zoe." He shoved a hand through his hair, his breath coming sharp. "If I had just kept you out of this, you wouldn't have a target on your back."

I stared at him. I'd expected anger. Frustration. Maybe even an order to stand down.

But not this.

Not the guilt.

Not the way his voice sounded stretched—like the last bit of jam scraped over too much bread.

I swallowed, suddenly unsure of what to say. His words hit hard, heavy, and unrelenting.

"Derek..." I started, softer than I meant to.

He let out a breath, shaking his head. "No. You don't get it. I should have known. Should have seen it coming. And now Manny going down like that—hell, the second you started digging—I should have realized they'd come for you."

I hesitated, something twisting inside me. Was that why he was trying to push me away? Not because of Orson's tantrum. Not because I was stirring up trouble.

Because he was scared. Scared of what might happen to me.

And maybe, just maybe... scared of how much that

mattered to him.

Derek pushed off the desk, dragging a rough hand through his hair. His expression was set, his stance braced—like he'd already made peace with the fallout.

"You're done, Zoe. This isn't a request. Stay out of it."

The words hit harder than I expected. My mouth opened, but nothing came out at first. Then...

"Derek, you can't—"

"I can. And I am." His voice was final. Cold. A door slamming shut.

A prickle of heat climbed my spine, my pulse kicking up a notch. "So that's it? You're just cutting me out?"

He exhaled sharply, looking away. "I'm protecting you."

I scoffed, the sound harsher than I intended. "That's a neat excuse."

His eyes snapped back to mine. "You don't get it, do you? This isn't a game, Zoe." His voice dropped, rough with something unreadable. "This is real. You've got a target on your back, and if anything happens to you because of this—" He broke off, shaking his head like he couldn't even say it.

Something in his expression twisted, raw, and unguarded for just a second.

I swallowed hard. "I can take care of myself."

But even I wasn't sure I believed it.

I let out a slow breath, leveling my gaze at him. "You're wrong, Derek. You know there's more to this."

For a second, something shifted in his expression.

A flicker of hesitation. Of knowing.

Then, just as quickly, he shut it down. "Not anymore. Not for you."

A slow, incredulous laugh escaped me. "You're serious?"

"As a damn heart attack."

I studied him, searching for some sign that this was just another argument we'd circle back to later. But there was something different this time. A finality in his stance, a weight in his voice that I wasn't sure I'd ever heard before.

He wasn't just pushing me away. He was shutting me out.

"So, that's it?" I asked. "You're really cutting me off?"

Derek exhaled sharply. "Zoe, I don't want—" He stopped himself, pressing a hand to his forehead before letting it drop. "I can't do this with you."

I squared my shoulders. "Well, lucky for you, I don't need your permission to keep going."

His gaze snapped to mine.

I held it. And then, with deliberate precision...

"Chief Cody."

For a beat, Derek didn't move.

Didn't breathe.

The switch to his official title had landed harder than I expected. A line drawn in the sand. His mouth parted slightly, like he was going to say something— maybe take it back, maybe double down—but in the end, he said nothing at all.

So, I turned and walked out.

The station doors swung shut behind me, the cool morning air doing nothing to temper the heat simmering beneath my skin. I pressed a hand to my chest, trying to will my heartbeat back to something resembling normal.

It didn't work.

Derek had shut me out. Completely.

I paced a few steps, dragging in a sharp breath, but it didn't help. If anything, the weight of it all sank deeper. Not just the case. Not just the danger.

He thought he was protecting me.

That was the worst part.

I pulled out my phone, my thumb hovering over the screen.

I stared at my phone, debating my next move.

He wanted to shut me out? Fine.

That just meant it was time to call in a second opinion. Someone with a little less patience for protocol — and who didn't balk just when things were getting… interesting.

I tapped the screen, lifting the phone to my ear.

The line rang once. Twice.

Then, with a sigh that sounded both exasperated and oddly delighted, the voice on the other end answered.

"Well, this oughta be good."

CHAPTER TWENTY-EIGHT

The air outside the medical examiner's office carried a crisp bite, the scent of asphalt and fading sunlight settling over the quiet street. I shifted on my feet as Bernie locked up, his keys jingling softly in the stillness.

He turned, leveling me with a look. "Now, tell me again — does this involve me getting fired, arrested, or both?"

I mustered up my best innocent expression. "Possibly all of the above."

Bernie sighed, already exasperated. "Figures."

"But," I continued, "it could also involve dinner with Dot."

His brows lifted. "Dot? My blue-haired angel?"

"Dinner," I drawled, "maybe dessert. Just imagine the charm offensive you could unleash."

Bernie scratched his chin, pretending to mull it over, but I saw the gleam of interest in his eyes. "Tempting," he admitted. "But what exactly are we doing?"

I hesitated, then exhaled. "I need to get onto the

Tobit Ranch. Derek would kill me if he knew, and Orson would rather set the dogs on me."

Bernie studied me for a beat, weighing his options.

Then he nodded. "Beats fly-fishing." he hesitated, rubbing the back of his neck before heading toward his van. "I actually just left a message for Chief Cody. I've got the results of that bloodwork."

Something in his tone made my stomach twist. "And?"

"Your guess was spot on." He let out a breath. "Sera Hawking is, indeed, the daughter of Madame Zorina."

Sonofabiscuiteater.

I had suspected, but hearing it confirmed sent a shock through me. If Sera was Zorina's daughter, that meant she wasn't just some innocent bystander caught in the crossfire—she was part of the legacy. The scam. The lies. And if she had as much to lose as I now suspected... she had a damn good motive to keep the grift running—or silence anyone who threatened it.

Bernie must've seen the wheels turning in my head, because he gave the side of the van a sharp slap, snapping me back to the present. "We'll tell the Chief together later," he said, with the casualness that told me he knew exactly how much trouble I was about to drag him into.

Then, with a sigh, he yanked open the van's back doors.

"But first," he said, motioning inside, "you get to play 'dead body'."

He held up an empty body bag. I smiled wanly

and groaned.

*****

I tried not to think about the fact that I was zipped inside a body bag.

The vinyl pressed against my arms, sealing in the warmth of my breath, making the space feel tighter by the second. My heartbeat was embarrassingly loud in my own ears, thudding against the stillness like a telltale drumbeat. The air inside the bag was stale, heavy with the faint scent of disinfectant and something vaguely plastic, and no matter how carefully I breathed, I couldn't shake the nagging sensation of being suffocated.

Bernie's voice rumbled from the driver's seat. "I can't believe I let you talk me into this."

"Just stay calm," I whispered, the sound muffled in the tight space.

"Easy for you to say," he muttered. "You're not the one who's gonna get fired from semi-retirement. I'll be forced to take up something awful… like golf."

I felt the van slow. The engine's hum deepened, vibrating against the metal floor beneath me. Then— light. A bright flash slicing through the darkness as the guard stepped forward, sweeping a flashlight beam over the windshield.

Bernie rolled down the window. "Evening."

The van barely rocked, but I felt every shift. My pulse climbed as the guard's footsteps scraped closer.

"What brings you back?" the guard asked.

"Think I left my medical bag in the stable when I picked up Manny's body," Bernie said, casual as ever.

The pause stretched. Then the beam of the

flashlight swept lower. Over the cargo hold.

Right over me.

I held perfectly still, lungs burning with the effort of not making a sound.

The guard grunted. "Busy night?"

Bernie shrugged. "Yup. Dropping this one off on my way home. What's a guy gonna do? People are just dying to spend time with me."

A beat of silence. Then — mercifully — the guard stepped back. "Okay. Head on in."

The van lurched forward. I let out a slow, measured exhale.

Bernie muttered under his breath, "Nobody gets me."

Bernie eased the van to a stop near the stable's side entrance, cutting the engine. The stillness pressed in immediately. Out here, away from the house, the only sound was the restless shifting of horses in their stalls, the occasional snort or stamp of a hoof echoing from inside.

Inside the van, I squirmed against the bag, then kicked lightly against the zipper. "Bernie."

With a sigh, he climbed into the back and yanked the zipper open. Cool night air rushed in, and I sat up fast, taking in a deep breath.

Bernie arched a brow. "You good?"

"Let's see… been playing dead for twenty minutes, breathing in the recycled scent of my own panic? Yeah. Peachy."

I swung my legs over the edge of the van and hopped down, giving myself a full-body shake, as if I could physically rid myself of the heebie-jeebies. "Never doing that again."

Bernie snorted. "Yeah, well, maybe don't make a habit of sneaking into crime scenes."

I ignored him, turning toward the stable. It loomed in front of us, its wide double doors yawning open like a waiting mouth. The night swallowed the far end of the space, deep shadows stretching between the stalls, the usual golden glow of the overhead lamps dimmed to a skeletal flicker.

I took a step inside. The familiar scent of hay, leather, and manure greeted me. But underneath it, something else.

Something sharper that I hadn't paid attention to before.

The smell was chemical.

Like ammonia.

I frowned, sweeping my flashlight over the stalls.

Something was different tonight. And I intended to find out why.

The smell vanished under the earthy musk of horses filling my nostrils. I stepped lightly, my footsteps muffled by the well-worn planks beneath me. The stalls stretched out in orderly rows, their occupants shifting restlessly in the dim light, watching me with silent, liquid eyes.

A mahogany bay lifted its head as I passed, its dark coat gleaming under my flashlight beam. Its nostrils flared, ears flicking in my direction before it let out a quiet snort, as if sensing something was off. Further down, the Perlino stallion stood motionless, his pale cream coat almost ghostly in the low light, his blue eyes eerie and unreadable.

Hard to believe he'd killed a man less than twenty-four hours ago.

I swallowed, gripping my flashlight tighter.

I think I'll stick to riding the horses at the Watch Hill Carousel.

Forcing myself to move on, I swept my light along the walls of the stalls. The beam skated over wooden planks, pausing when something glinted back at me.

I narrowed my eyes. A screw stood out in the light — shiny, new, untouched by time or dust. I waved the beam over the remaining three screws in the plank. All unmarred silver.

Bernie leaned in, his breath warm against my shoulder. "That's... weird."

My pulse ticked faster. I let my eyes rove over the hardware on the nearby planks.

Weathered nails — red with oxidation. I swung the flashlight beam back to the shiny screws. "Why replace the hardware in one plank?"

The wood was the same, aged like the rest of the stable. But someone had removed and reinstalled this plank recently — and with easily removed hardware.

Someone had been hiding something.

I slipped my pocket knife from my jeans and flicked it open.

Bernie hitched an eyebrow. "You carry a pocketknife?"

I shrugged. "I was a Girl Scout. Be prepared."

Bernie snorted. "Yeah, I think that's the Boy Scout

motto."

"Yeah? Well, dated a few of those, too." The blade caught the faintest glint of moonlight as I knelt.

Bernie let out a strangled whisper. "You're not—"

I ignored him, already setting the tip against the first screw. It gave easily, barely more than finger-tight. I worked quickly, my pulse drumming louder with each turn. The last screw dropped into my palm, and I wedged my fingers beneath the plank, prying it free.

The wood groaned softly, the sound lost beneath the shifting stir of the horses. My flashlight beam sliced into the hollow space behind the plank.

Rows of plastic bottles.

My breath hitched.

Bernie crouched beside me as I pulled a handkerchief from my pocket, wrapping it around my fingers before carefully lifting one of the bottles.

The label read: Perlino Cream.

I reached for another. Mahogany Bay.

And the last: Chestnut Brown.

Bernie let out a slow exhale. "That's the dye."

I nodded, my stomach tightening. "The dye stolen from Myrna's."

I carefully opened one of the half-used bottles, wincing at the sharp ammonia odor inside.

He frowned. "If the cops searched this place, how'd they miss this?"

"They weren't looking for it," I murmured.

And someone had made sure it was just hidden enough.

I resealed the bottle and carefully slid them all

back into the hollow space, making sure they were positioned exactly as I'd found them. My handkerchief remained wrapped around my fingers as I worked — I wasn't about to add my prints to the evidence.

Bernie shifted beside me, his weight making the old floor creak. "Okay. We found what we came for. Can we go now?"

Ignoring him, I lifted the wooden plank and lined it up against the opening. The screws were small, their threads still sharp from being recently removed. I pressed them back into place and twisted each one in, careful not to over-tighten. If I stripped them, it'd be obvious someone had tampered with the panel.

Bernie let out a quiet groan. "Tell me again why I let you rope me into this."

"You were promised dinner with Dot," I reminded him, tightening the last screw.

He muttered something under his breath about questionable life choices. I stepped back, studying my work. The wood looked untouched, the screws no shinier than before.

Perfect.

Bernie exhaled. "Alright. We're done."

I shook my head. "Not yet."

He groaned. "Of course not."

The sharp crack of a kick against a stall wall made me flinch. Bernie yelped. I held a cautionary finger to my lips.

The atmosphere felt suddenly charged with electricity. A gelding near the entrance let out a rough, irritated snort, ears pinned back. Another horse stomped, its tail swishing hard enough to stir up bits of loose straw.

Something had them riled up.

Bernie shifted his weight, glancing from stall to stall. "They're not usually like this, right?"

"No." I stepped closer to the mahogany bay, his muscles twitching as I neared. He wasn't just jittery — he was on edge. His ears flicked back and forth, listening, anticipating.

A stallion at the far end let out a sharp, high-pitched whinny, pawing at the ground, nostrils flared. Another snorted hard, jerking its head as if trying to shake off a bad feeling.

"They're agitated," I murmured.

Bernie edged closer to me. "Yeah, and I don't think it's us making them that way."

A shiver worked its way down my spine. If it wasn't us...

Then what were they reacting to?

"They're definitely spooked," I admitted.

"So am I," Bernie mumbled.

"We should get out of here," I whispered, my nerves stretched too thin. The horses' unease was contagious, pressing against my own instincts to flee.

Bernie didn't argue. He turned toward the exit, but as I moved to follow, my flashlight beam skimmed across the floor — then stopped.

A flash of red, half-buried in straw.

I crouched, brushing the straw aside, fingers closing around the crinkled object. A chip bag.

Not just any chip bag.

Ketchup-flavored.

Bernie peered over my shoulder. "That's…
random."

I turned it over. Both ends were blown open, not
just torn, but split wide. Like someone had forced them
apart in one quick motion.

A prickle crawled up my spine.

This wasn't just litter.

Ketchup chips. Impossible to find around here
unless you went out of your way to get them.

I swallowed, my grip tightening on the bag.

Bernie stepped back—and cursed under his
breath.

"Damn it." He scraped his boot against the floor,
grimacing. "Freaking used chewing tobacco."

I wrinkled my nose. A dark wad sat mashed into
the floorboards, the pungent scent sharp in the air.

"Disgusting," I muttered, stepping around it.

Bernie shook his head, still scraping at his boot.
"Some people."

I huffed a laugh, distracted. "Yeah, like Addie—
always chewing gum. I swear, her gum pops scare me
half to death."

The words barely left my mouth before something
clicked.

A sound. A feeling. A memory snapping into
place.

I looked down at the chip bag in my hand. Both
ends ripped wide open.

A pop.

A sharp, unexpected noise.

245

Horses were skittish creatures. The security guard at the gate had said it himself—loud sounds could spook them, send them into a frenzy.

My stomach dropped.

I turned the bag over again, my fingers smoothing over the crinkled surface, my pulse hammering in my ears.

Manny's death. The sudden, violent trampling.

What if it hadn't been an accident?

What if someone had made sure that horse lost its mind?

What if someone had *popped* the bag—on purpose?

A chill crawled up my spine, slow and insidious.

The chip bag crinkled in my grip, both ends blown open. The horses, restless and on edge. The dyes hidden away like a dirty little secret.

And Tom.

Tom, who loved ketchup-flavored chips. Tom, who had come in the shop and bought a bottle of chardonnay from Dot the day before Noreen Cox died. Who hadn't been around at all when Manny died.

My breath caught in my throat, my pulse an unsteady staccato. I didn't want to believe it.

Not him.

I forced myself to breathe, to think. There had to be another explanation. Coincidence. A mix-up. Someone else who liked ketchup chips.

But the suspicion had rooted itself in my brain, and no matter how I tried to shake it, it wouldn't let go.

I looked at the chip bag again, at the torn ends, at the way the straw had half-buried it. A pop—loud

246

enough to spook a horse. A horse powerful enough to kill a man.

My stomach lurched.

Was it possible? Had Tom been here that night?

Had he done something unforgivable?

A fresh wave of unease swept over me.

Because if he had—*what did that mean for me?*

I clutched my phone so tightly my fingers ached. I should call Derek.

But I hesitated.

This wasn't proof. Not really. Right now, this was just a story in my head. A chip bag, some hair dye, and a gut feeling.

And if I was wrong about Tom—if I accused him of something this awful and had to look him in the eye after—could I live with that?

My pulse thudded, hard and insistent, as I forced a deep breath. "Let's go."

Bernie didn't move. "Zoe, maybe we should—"

A sound cut him off.

Voices.

Close.

Every muscle in my body locked up.

Footsteps crunched over the gravel drive outside, slow and deliberate. Someone was coming. I shoved the chip bag into my pocket without thinking.

Rookie move, Romano.

But I had more important things to worry about right now.

Bernie shot me a look, panic flickering behind his thick glasses. "Please tell me you have a plan."

I did.

It was called running.

I sucked in a sharp breath and grabbed Bernie's sleeve, yanking him toward the nearest empty stall.

"Hide," I whispered.

And then the voices grew louder.

The flashlight beam skimmed past our hiding spot, pausing for a fraction of a second. My breath lodged in my throat.

A voice. Gruff. Male. "Hey, you hear something?"

My pulse pounded against my ribs.

Another voice answered, bored. "Probably just the horses. They haven't been right since it all went down."

Silence stretched.

I clenched my jaw, praying they'd just keep moving.

Then—after an agonizing pause—the beam lifted, sweeping lazily across the stalls before moving on.

"Ah, there ain't nothing here. Let's check the west gate."

The footsteps followed, crunching against the wooden floor, growing fainter.

I didn't breathe. Not until the last scrape of boots faded into the distance.

Beside me, Bernie let out a slow, shaky exhale. His glasses had slipped down his nose, and his fingers were gripping the front of his shirt like he was keeping his heart from jumping out of his chest. "We need to get the hell out of here."

I nodded, forcing my legs to work even as the tension in my muscles screamed. "I agree."

We crept toward the exit, every step measured, every sound magnified in the silence.

We made it to the van, where Bernie promptly handed me the keys.

"What's this?" I asked.

"This time," he panted heavily, "*I* get to play the part of the dead body."

And with that, he collapsed in a heap next to the van.

CHAPTER TWENTY-NINE

I sat slumped in the overstuffed armchair at Read Between the Vines, letting the familiar scent of old books, rich coffee, and aged wood settle around me. Normally, this place was my refuge. A sanctuary.

Today, it felt like a trap.

The air was too still. The low murmur of the ceiling fan barely stirred it. I curled my hands around my mug, seeking warmth, but the contents had long since cooled, leaving nothing but the feel of the cold ceramic against my palms.

Across the counter, Dot sat with her crossword puzzle, glasses perched low on her nose. Everything looked the same. The well-worn counter. The lazy curl of steam rising from her coffee.

But something was wrong.

She wasn't writing. Wasn't tapping her pen or muttering about "Twelve across."

She was watching me.

I blinked. "What?"

Dot didn't answer right away. She just kept looking at me, her gaze steady, unreadable.

Finally, she set her pen down. "I was about to ask you the same thing."

Her voice was gentle. Too gentle.

Something inside me twisted.

Because I didn't have an answer.

Not one I wanted to say out loud.

I hesitated.

The words sat heavy on my tongue, waiting, wanting to be spoken. But saying them aloud would make them real. And I wasn't sure I was ready for that.

Dot didn't push. She just reached for the coffeepot, filled a second cup, and nudged it toward me. The scent of hazelnut curled into the air, warm and steady—like her.

"You look like there's something you want to get off your chest," she said, voice light but laced with understanding. Then, with a wry smile, she added, "And I don't mean your sports bra."

A startled laugh escaped before I could stop it.

Dot just sipped her coffee, waiting.

I curled my fingers around the warm mug, staring into the dark swirling liquid like it held answers. I stared at the chip bag—the evidence I'd stupidly removed from the scene—sitting innocuously on the table in front of me.

"I found something out at the Tobit Ranch."

Dot gave a small nod, not surprised.

I licked my lips, trying to choose my words carefully. "Something that doesn't make sense. Or maybe it does, and I just really don't want it to."

Dot set her cup down with a quiet clink. "I see."

And somehow, I think she really did.

I didn't say Tom's name.

Not yet.

Instead, I laid out the pieces. The stolen dye, the horses so spooked they'd nearly taken down their stalls, the chip bag buried under straw — blown open like it had been meant to startle something big. Something dangerous.

Dot listened. Really listened.

She didn't touch her crossword. Didn't glance at the clock. That alone sent an uneasy ripple through me.

My fingers tightened around my mug, the warmth doing nothing to chase the cold settling in my stomach.

"If this all means what I think it means…" My voice wavered.

Dot leaned forward, her expression unreadable. "Then what?"

I stared at my hands, at the half-moons my nails pressed into my palms.

"Then someone I trust — someone I care about — isn't who I thought they were."

Dot exhaled, slow and deliberate. Her lips pressed into a thin line, her fingers steepling under her chin.

Finally, she said, "That's a hard thing to reckon with."

It wasn't comfort. It wasn't reassurance.

But it was the truth.

Dot exhaled through her nose, slow and steady. When she spoke, her voice was softer than usual, but it carried the weight of something solid.

"People aren't stories, Zoe. We tell ourselves what

we want to believe about them and, most of the time, that story holds up." She pulled off her glasses, folding them neatly, her eyes never leaving mine. "But then, every so often, the truth muscles in."

A pit formed in my stomach. Heavy. Unshakable.

I wanted to argue. To say that I knew Tom. That the person I'd laughed with, confided in, let close — he wasn't capable of something like this.

But the chip bag.

The horses.

The timing.

Dot's fingers tapped gently against the counter, pulling me back. "And you gotta decide," she said, "if you're brave enough to look it in the eye."

Brave enough.

Like it was a choice.

Like ignoring it wouldn't make it disappear.

I swallowed hard. "And what if I don't like what I see?"

Dot sighed. "Then, honey, you're just like the rest of us."

Dot sighed and stood, rubbing her arms as if she were warding off a chill that had nothing to do with the air. "I'm gonna light a candle for you."

I blinked. "For me?"

She nodded, already moving toward the cabinet where she kept her small collection of religious candles — mixed in with frosting-covered cupcake ones, of course. "And I'm gonna say a prayer to St. Jude while I'm at it."

Something in her tone made my skin prickle. "St. Jude?"

Dot struck a match, the sulfur scent curling through the air. "Patron saint of lost causes."

My pulse kicked.

Lost causes.

A name echoed in the back of my mind, distant but urgent.

Saint Sarah.

Tom had mentioned her once, so casually I hadn't given it a second thought. Saint Sarah the Black. A Romani patron saint.

My stomach twisted.

Zorina — Noreen Cox — had been Romani. Had Tom learned about Saint Sarah from her? Was that connection deeper than I ever realized?

I gripped the counter, my fingers pressing into the worn wood.

Dot's candle flickered. My thoughts roared.

And suddenly, I knew.

I wasn't just looking at a lost cause.

I was looking at a lost son.

I pressed a hand to my mouth, as if I could physically hold in the thoughts unraveling too fast, too loud.

No.

No, no, no.

This couldn't be right. Couldn't be real.

Because if it was...

Dot was watching me, her brow furrowed, concern written deep in the lines of her face. "Zoe?"

I shook my head sharply. Swallowed hard, forcing down the name that wanted to escape.

Tom.

Saying it would make it real.

I wasn't ready for that.

My fingers curled against my lips, as if they could keep the truth at bay for just a little longer.

This was too much. I needed time. I needed definitive, unassailable proof.

Because if I was wrong — if I let myself believe this and was wrong — I didn't think I'd forgive myself.

Dot reached out, resting a hand lightly on my arm. "You don't have to tell me." Her voice was quiet but firm. "Not until you're ready."

I exhaled shakily, nodding.

But in my gut, I knew.

I would never be ready.

Not for this. Not for him.

The bell over the shop door jangled violently, snapping me back into my body.

Addie burst in, breathing hard like she'd sprinted from the mailbox. Her hair was windblown, her cheeks flushed, and she clutched a white envelope like it was a live wire.

"Zoe," she gasped. "Hey, one of Tom's chip bags. What's that doing here?"

"Zoe found it at the stable," Dot stated.

Addie's mouth puckered in a soundless, "Oh."

She stood in silence for a few seconds, then shook herself alert and slammed the envelope she carried onto the table. "The postal worker just handed this to me. It's from the bank."

My hands were already unsteady, but now they

shook outright as I reached for the envelope.

I ripped it open. My eyes skimmed the words, but my brain refused to process them.

FINAL NOTICE.

The bottom dropped out of my stomach.

Foreclosure.

My breath hitched as the reality slammed into me. I'd been so caught up in the case, the investigation, Tom, that I'd forgotten—I'd let this slip through the cracks.

Orson.

He'd refused to pay for the champagne order. Without that payment, we wouldn't be able to make this payment.

This wasn't a warning.

It was a death sentence.

Dot's voice was quiet, but firm. "How long do we have?"

I swallowed past the burn in my throat.

"Tomorrow."

The doorbell jingled again, too soon, too loud.

I looked up—and froze.

Tom stood in the doorway, hands tucked into his pockets, his stance relaxed, easy—like he belonged here. Like nothing had changed.

Like I hadn't just spent the last twelve hours trying to convince myself he wasn't a killer.

His smile was the same as always—warm, familiar, effortless. A smile that used to make my chest feel light. A smile that had me replaying our conversations in my head long after he'd walked away.

But now, it felt dangerous.

I didn't trust it.

Didn't trust him.

The chip bag burned in my memory. The restless horses. The possibility that Manny's death wasn't an accident.

Churning acid threatened to burn a hole in my belly. I couldn't look at him the same way anymore, not with that seed of doubt burrowing deeper and deeper.

He tilted his head, his smile softening. "Hey, Zoe. You okay?"

The words hit me like a sucker punch.

No. I wasn't okay.

But I had no idea what would happen if I let him see that.

Tom stepped closer, his easy smile never faltering. "Hey."

My throat went dry.

"I was gonna grab some tea," he said, casual, effortless, like this was any other day. Like nothing had changed. "Figured I'd see if you wanted to join."

The normalcy of it was staggering.

My pulse pounded in my ears. Tea. With Tom.

After everything I'd just pieced together.

Dot didn't move. She just watched, her expression unreadable.

Addie, not nearly as subtle, slipped into the back room, throwing me an exaggerated over-the-shoulder stare that practically screamed, What the hell are you doing?

I couldn't breathe. Couldn't think.

I should say no.

I should tell him I was busy. That I had too much on my plate, that I had no time to sit across from him at a café, pretending I wasn't wondering if he'd killed a man.

But the words wouldn't come.

Tom's smile didn't waver. He tilted his head slightly, waiting.

Waiting for me to choose.

For a long beat, I didn't move.

The weight of Dot's stare pressed against me, heavy and knowing.

She cleared her throat. "Well," she said evenly, like she wasn't holding her breath, like she wasn't screaming at me with her eyes. "Seems like you got a decision to make."

Tom tilted his head, waiting. Still smiling. Still him.

"What do you say?"

My hands trembled against the counter.

My mind screamed no.

My heart wasn't sure.

I forced a breath.

And then I heard it — my own voice.

"Sure."

Tom's smile widened. "Great. My truck's outside."

I shouldn't go.

Every instinct told me to stay put, to ask more questions, to not let his easy charm distract me from the truth I was only just beginning to understand.

But I did.

I grabbed my coat, stepped around the counter,

and followed him toward the door.

The bell jingled overhead. The brisk morning air hit my face like a warning.

And as I crossed the threshold, I felt it.

Dot's eyes on my back.

Watching.

Waiting.

Praying.

For a lost cause.

CHAPTER THIRTY

I followed Tom into Alice's in the Village, the whimsical tearoom wrapping around me like a storybook setting I no longer belonged in. The air was perfumed with the sweet, citrusy scent of bergamot—freshly brewed Earl Grey. It mingled with buttery scones and spiced chai. The delicate clink of teacups against porcelain punctuated the low murmur of conversation.

It should have been comforting. Instead, it felt surreal.

The walls were lined with Alice in Wonderland illustrations, the whimsical strokes suddenly too dreamlike, too detached from reality. A teapot chandelier hung above us, casting a warm, golden glow over the pastel hues and mismatched vintage furniture. Tiny bottles labeled "Drink Me" lined the shelves, their curling script a quiet invitation to escape into something easier.

I wish.

Sliding into the velvet-lined booth, I wrapped my hands around the coffee mug the second it hit the table, holding onto its warmth like an anchor.

Tom stretched his arms over the back of his seat, looking as relaxed as ever, like we were just two friends catching up over caffeine. Like nothing had changed.

But something had.

His gaze roved over me, sharp despite the easy smile. "You seem off this morning."

I forced a laugh, hoping it didn't sound as hollow as I felt. "Just tired."

Tom leaned back, one arm draped casually over the back of the booth. His fingers tapped idly against the velvet lining. His expression was casual, but his eyes — those sharp, perceptive eyes — watched me too closely.

"You're a terrible liar," he said, his voice as smooth as the rich espresso between us.

My heart slammed against my ribs.

I forced a breath, curling my fingers tighter around my mug to keep from fidgeting. "I don't know what you're talking about."

Tom smirked, tipping his head slightly. "That's one of the things I like about you."

I swallowed hard, past the lump of unease forming in my throat. This was Tom.

Tom.

The same man who had charmed half the town, who had always been kind, who had — until last night — been someone I thought I could trust.

But trust wasn't a feeling. It was a choice. And right now, I wasn't sure I could make it.

I forced a chuckle, light and normal. "Guess that's why my mom always knew I was the one who ate all the

Oreos."

Tom lifted his coffee to his lips, watching me over the rim as he took a slow sip.

"Probably. Well, that and the black teeth."

I giggled. I couldn't help it.

It's how he made me feel.

A beat of silence stretched between us before Tom exhaled, absently swirling his coffee.

"I'm leaving Mystic."

The words hit harder than I expected. My fingers tightened around my mug, the warmth doing nothing to chase the sudden chill creeping up my spine. "Oh?"

He nodded, gaze flicking toward the window. "I've been thinking about it for a while. Time for a change. Time to start fresh somewhere else."

Fresh. The word sat wrong.

Fresh from what?

But I was almost certain I already knew that answer. I forced a swallow. "Where would you go?"

Tom shrugged. "Haven't decided. Maybe sail south, see where the wind takes me."

South. Not England. Not where Sera had said she was going. So, maybe, at least, they weren't in cahoots.

But still…

I shifted in my seat, my heartbeat knocking against my ribs. "So, just… drift?"

Tom smiled. "That's the beauty of it, isn't it? No ties, no obligations. Just open water and freedom."

Freedom.

I wasn't sure why, but the word sent a ripple of unease through me.

I pressed my mug tighter between my hands, nodding like this was just another conversation. Like I wasn't fighting the urge to run.

The words were out before I could stop them. "You too?"

Tom's eyes flicked up, sharp and assessing.

A slow smile — too slow, too measured — tugged at the corner of his lips. "Too?"

My pulse kicked like a startled horse.

I forced a swallow, but my throat had gone dry.

Tom set his cup down with a soft clink. Casual. Controlled. But I wasn't fooled.

He was waiting.

Watching.

Hunting.

My stomach knotted. I'd played right into his hands.

I scrambled for something, anything, to cover. "I just meant…" I let out a weak laugh. "Seems like everyone's leaving Mystic these days."

Tom tilted his head, considering me. "Everyone?"

I nodded too quickly. "You. People move on, right?"

Tom said nothing. Just studied me, his fingers drumming that maddening rhythm again.

My skin prickled.

Then, after an agonizing pause, he leaned back. Smiled. "Yeah," he said easily. "Guess so."

But something in his eyes told me he didn't believe me.

Not for a second.

263

Tom let the silence stretch. Let it settle. Let me squirm.

Then, softly — too softly — he said, "You were talking about Sera, weren't you?"

My throat closed.

I willed my face to stay blank, but I wasn't sure I pulled it off.

Tom leaned in, his voice a whisper, barely carrying over the hum of the café. "She's leaving, isn't she?"

I forced myself to breathe. To think.

If I denied it outright, he'd know I was lying. If I confirmed it, I might as well hand him a damn map to her front door.

I needed to thread the needle. Carefully.

I shrugged, aiming for casual, but my fingers were still clenched tight around my coffee mug. "I don't know her plans. I'm not exactly a welcome guest on Tobit Ranch right now."

Tom hummed like he was mulling that over.

I willed myself not to react. Not to flinch. Not to let the panic clawing at my insides reach my face.

Tom studied me for a long beat, unreadable. Then — suddenly — he smiled.

"You ever think about leaving, Zoe?"

The shift in conversation hit like whiplash.

I blinked. "What?"

Tom shrugged, like he hadn't just been picking apart my every reaction, like he hadn't been hunting for something in my words. "You ever think about just… getting out of here?"

I forced my fingers to unclench from around my coffee mug. "Mystic?"

"Yeah." He leaned back, stretching one arm across the back of the booth like we were just two friends shooting the breeze. "I mean, you've never really seemed like the small-town type."

I swallowed. "You don't think?"

Tom's lips curved. "I think you're restless." His gaze flicked over me, warm, assessing. "And I think you're too damn smart to stay in one place forever."

I felt like I was standing on a ledge, the ground crumbling under me.

This wasn't casual.

This was a test.

And I had no idea what answer he was looking for.

Tom swirled his tea absently, the ceramic cup making a soft, rhythmic scrape against the saucer. Then he looked up, eyes warm. Inviting.

"Come with me."

My stomach plummeted.

He said it so easily, like he was asking me to go for a drive, not to leave behind everything that had just started to feel like home.

"I mean it." His voice was smooth. Steady. "You're always working your fanny off. You hardly ever do anything for yourself." He leaned in, his gaze locking onto mine. "Come with me, Zoe. Leave Mystic behind. Just us, the boat, open water."

The café walls suddenly felt too close, the air too thick. My fingers clenched around my cup to keep them from trembling.

I should say no. Laugh it off. Tell him he was insane.

But the way he was looking at me—like he could already see me saying yes—had my throat locking up.

"I—" The word barely made it out.

Tom's smile deepened. "No pressure," he said, voice as smooth as a tide rolling in. He reached for his coffee, took a slow sip. "Just think about it."

Like it was that simple.

Like he hadn't just flipped my entire world upside down.

He reached for his cup, taking a leisurely sip, as if we weren't sitting in the middle of a minefield, as if nothing in my world had just cracked wide open.

I nodded, careful, controlled. Then I glanced at the clock on the wall, like I suddenly remembered somewhere I had to be.

Casual. Unrushed.

Tom followed my gaze, then tilted his head. "Gotta get back?"

"Yeah," I said, pushing my chair back. "Early delivery coming in."

Not a lie. Just not the truth that mattered.

I needed to move. Needed to get away from his knowing smile, his careful, watching eyes.

Tom tossed a few bills onto the table, slipping his wallet back into his pocket with the same effortless grace he did everything. Like this wasn't a pivotal moment. Like he hadn't just thrown a grenade into my already crumbling world.

"I'll be around a little longer," he said, casual as ever. "I have, uh, something I need to take care of, but then I'll be shoving off for the next adventure. Let me know if you decide to take me up on my offer."

I nodded, but it felt like someone else moving my head. My heart was hammering so hard I swore he could hear it.

I wouldn't.

I couldn't.

But I couldn't say that. Not yet. Not here.

So, I smiled instead — light and airy — like my stomach wasn't twisted into a thousand knots. "I'll let you know."

Tom's eyes stayed on mine for a second too long, searching, assessing. Then, finally, he nodded. "Hope I see you around, Zoe."

And with that, he turned, stepping out of the café, the bell jingling behind him.

I stood there for a second, watching the door swing shut, my pulse roaring in my ears.

If I was right about Tom, I had even less time than I thought.

The second Tom disappeared out the door, I scrambled from the booth, barely registering the crackle of static electricity as I zipped across the velvet. The café felt too tight, too suffocating, and I needed air. Needed space.

Needed Derek.

I bolted onto the sidewalk, my phone already in hand. My fingers fumbled against the screen as I pulled up his number, but I didn't stop. My pulse was a hammer in my ears, drowning out the hum of morning traffic, the chatter of passing tourists.

It rang. Once. Twice.

Come on. Pick up.

Another ring.

I didn't care if he was buried under reports, knee-deep in another case, or halfway across town—he needed to hear this.

Now.

Voicemail.

A curse slipped from my lips as I stabbed the call button again, pacing hard toward the corner. I needed to keep moving, keep thinking. My gut screamed that I was running out of time.

This wasn't just suspicion anymore.

Tom was planning something.

And if I didn't get ahead of it, I had a sinking feeling someone else was going to end up dead.

I looked down at the bakery case as I headed out the door. A brightly frosted cookie leered at me with bold, red lettering.

EAT ME.

Yeah. That about summed up how I felt.

CHAPTER THIRTY-ONE

I paced outside Alice's in the Village, my phone gripped so tight my fingers ached.

Still no answer from Derek.

Perfect. Just perfect.

The wind had picked up, rolling storm clouds across the sky, swallowing what was left of the daylight. The red, white, and blue bunting the historic committee had started mounting on the lampposts for the upcoming Independence Day festivities snapped in the wind. An ominous sound. The looming black clouds made it feel more like midnight than early evening. Fitting.

A raindrop hit my cheek.

I sighed.

Of course.

A set of headlights swung around the curve. My rideshare.

I climbed in, barely registering the driver's mumbled greeting as I racked my brain for a way to talk my way past Tobit Ranch's gate guard.

Delivery?

No.

Lost dog?

Worse.

Interview?

Please.

By the time the car pulled up to the sprawling estate, I still didn't have a plan.

Didn't matter.

The guard was missing.

I swallowed hard, stepping out of the car. The second my feet hit the ground, the driver was gone, tires spitting gravel behind me.

Don't expect five stars, buddy.

A sharp gust of wind bit through my sweater.

This is such a bad idea.

Which, as my mother will happily inform you, was my specialty.

I eyed the tall iron gate, then the very locked keypad beside it.

Great. No way in.

Except...

My gaze flicked to the left, to a paperbark maple growing just outside the fence line, its peeling cinnamon-colored bark curling like old parchment.

I chewed my lip.

Technically, I could climb it.

Technically.

It wasn't the tallest tree, but it had a thick trunk and a good amount of branches — enough to get me over the fence if I didn't die first.

I glanced down at my Converse. Not ideal.

I placed a careful foot on the lowest branch,

testing my weight. It held.

So far, so good. Although maybe I should have passed on the chocolate croissant at Alice's.

I grabbed hold of the next branch, hoisting myself up.

The bark flaked under my fingers, showering my sleeves with papery curls. I ignored it, climbing higher, my pulse quickening.

Just a little more.

The wind howled, shaking the tree, shaking me.

Don't look down.

I swung my leg over the fence, gripping a sturdy branch for balance.

Then, in true Zoe fashion...

I slipped.

With a yelp, I toppled forward, landing hard in the mud.

Flat on my back.

Staring up at the storm-churned sky.

"Well," I muttered. "That went well."

I wiped a smear of mud off my cheek, shaking my hands out with a grimace.

So much for sneaking in with dignity.

Forcing my breathing to steady, I turned toward the house.

Dark.

Not dim. Not low-lit.

Dark.

The Tobit Ranch house was never dark.

Even at night, porch lights glowed, windows spilled warm yellow onto the front drive, and the kitchen usually stayed lit well past midnight. Someone was always awake.

But now?

Nothing.

A low rumble of thunder crawled across the sky. The wind picked up, kicking dry leaves into little spirals along the dirt road.

I swallowed, my nerves twisting into a tight coil.

Something wasn't right.

A sudden, sharp whinny split the silence — loud, panicked.

My pulse kicked and, from the sound of it, that might not be the only thing.

I turned toward the sound, my stomach dropping.

The stables.

"Great," I muttered, dragging a hand down my face. "Here we go again."

I hesitated for only a second before moving.

Lightning flared behind the thick clouds, throwing long, eerie shadows across the ranch. The wind howled through the trees, rattling the stable doors.

The horses weren't just restless.

They were scared.

#samehere

I picked my way across the graveled drive. The stones shifted beneath my hurried steps. The storm overhead deepened, thick clouds swallowing the last sliver of daylight.

A fat raindrop splattered against my cheek. Another followed, cool and sharp against my bare skin. The scent of wet earth and ozone thickened in the air, a prelude to the coming downpour.

The stable doors loomed ahead—slightly ajar, swaying with each gust of wind. The metal hinges groaned.

I hesitated.

Common sense said turn around. Leave. Get help.

But then common sense never had a firm grip on me.

I swallowed hard and stepped inside—then stopped cold.

The air was thick with the scent of damp hay and sweat. The horses were frantic. Eyes rolling white, nostrils flaring, hooves scuffing against the packed dirt floor. A palomino near the far stall stomped hard, snorting out an anxious breath.

No one else was here.

Was I too late?

Then—a voice.

"Zoe."

My blood ran cold.

I whipped around.

Tom stood in the entrance. His face was shadowed in the dim light. A mask of regret. Of resolve.

And in his hand...

A gun.

CHAPTER THIRTY=TWO

The wind howled through the stable, rattling the walls and kicking up the scent of damp hay and sweat. The horses shifted uneasily, their hooves scuffing against the packed dirt.

But all I could see was the gun in Tom's hands.

"You shouldn't be here," he hissed.

"Funny. I was about to say the same thing to you."

Tom sighed, head tilting slightly, like I was a puzzle piece that almost — but not quite — fit.

"You just couldn't leave it alone, could you?"

I swallowed hard. "You were at Noreen's the night she died." My voice was steadier than I felt. "The glass I found — it was from the bottle of chardonnay you bought from Dot earlier that day. I'm betting it's your fingerprint on it."

A pause. Then Tom gave a small, almost amused shake of his head. "You really are something, Zoe."

My heart hammered, but I pressed on. "You killed her."

Tom exhaled, swirling the gun loosely in his grip.

"I didn't go there planning to." His voice was quieter now, almost wistful. "I wanted answers. I wanted something to make up for the years she left me alone."

"You're Noreen's son."

The sadness that filled his eyes confirmed it.

"She *owed* me." He slapped his broad chest with his free hand. "An explanation, at the very least."

"But she didn't give you one," I whispered.

He let out a hollow laugh. "Oh, she gave me one." His jaw tightened. "She laughed in my face. Called me a mistake. A liability."

The words hit like a gut punch.

"She was good at the con," he continued, voice turning sharp. "But back then, she was still figuring it out. She scammed some retiree in California, drained his savings, then found out she was pregnant. And I was the mistake she never wanted."

I swallowed hard.

"She wound up in Phoenix, latched onto Manny Denis. They stayed long enough for her to have me... then they were gone." His fingers twitched. "Just like that. Left me in the system."

My throat was dry. "And Sera?"

His whole body tensed.

"She was the one she kept."

The bitterness in his voice was razor-sharp.

"How did you find them?" I asked, my voice barely above a whisper.

Tom exhaled slowly. "Three mistakes."

I waited.

"The first?" He reached into his pocket, pulling

275

out a worn, faded photograph. A younger Noreen, smirking, cradling a newborn. "Some nurse at the hospital kept a scrapbook of all the new moms. I tracked the old lady down. She still had the book."

He let the photo linger in his hands before slipping it back into his pocket.

"The second mistake," he continued, voice hollow, "was listing Manny's address on my birth certificate. It took some digging, but I found them." His grip tightened. "And she was still with him. Like nothing had changed."

A lump formed in my throat.

"And the third?" I asked.

His face went stony.

"She opened the door to me."

The gun lifted slightly.

I forced myself to stay still. "You snapped," I whispered.

Tom's expression flickered. "Do you know what it's like to be told you were a mistake?"

The air between us felt suffocating.

"She turned away," he murmured. "I grabbed her arm. She tried to pull back, and I pushed. She fell down the stairs." His voice cracked. "She hit her head on the accent table. Hard. She hit the ground, and the picture frame tumbled and splintered into a billion pieces."

Lightning flashed behind the thick storm clouds, illuminating the shadows on his face. And for the first time, I saw the weight of it all.

The regret. The grief.

But something nagged at me.

276

"Wait." I don't know who the simple word surprised more—me or him. He gave me a funny look.

Okay, Romano. Better explain yourself.

I sucked in a deep breath. "When Addie told me what happened," I began slowly, "she said the police found broken glass under Noreen." My heart pounded. "But you just said the picture frame fell after she did."

Tom's breath caught.

A realization slammed into me.

"You tried to help her, didn't you?"

His fingers twitched on the gun. His whole body seemed to waver for a moment.

"I ran down the stairs," he admitted, voice hoarse. "She wasn't moving. I checked for a pulse. She wasn't breathing, so I tried giving her CPR." He let out a breath that sounded closer to a sob. "I did everything I could. But she was gone."

I swallowed against the lump in my throat. "Your medical training. For the captain's license."

Tom let out a bitter chuckle. "Yeah. Useless in the end, wasn't it?"

The tension in the stable changed, shifting, softening.

For a moment, I saw not a killer, but a son who had been discarded. Again and again. But still, he tried to save her. His mother.

And I almost let my guard down.

Then his jaw tightened. The mask slid back into place.

"She tried to buy me off," he said, quieter now. "Signed over a TBR check. Told me to take the money and go." His lips curled. "At first, I didn't want it. Money wasn't what I wanted." His voice grew distant. "But after she fell… I hesitated. And then I took it."

I felt my stomach tighten. "That's how you bought Captain Talley's boat. That was your *financing*."

Tom nodded.

"But the Ten of Swords…" I whispered.

"I left it in her mouth," he admitted. "I wanted Orson to know he was being scammed… without getting involved."

The last piece clicked into place.

This wasn't about fake psychics or sweetheart scams or horse counterfeiting swindles.

It was about erasing everyone who had taken what should have been his.

I licked my lips, pulse thundering in my ears.

"Tom," I whispered. "You don't have to do this."

Something flickered in his eyes.

Regret. Pain.

Then, resolve.

His finger flexed on the trigger.

"Oh, Zoe… why couldn't you just get on the boat?"

And he lunged.

CHAPTER THIRTY-THREE

Tom's finger tightened on the trigger. My breath caught. Then…

Tires on gravel.

The sound ripped through the tension like a gunshot.

Okay. Maybe poor choice of words.

Tom flinched. His grip faltered, just as red and blue lights slashed through the stable doors, casting jagged streaks of color across the rain-slicked ground.

"POLICE! DROP THE GUN!"

Chief Cody's voice boomed through the storm, rattling the walls of the stable. The doors slammed open, rain gusting in behind him, his gun locked on Tom.

The next few seconds stretched painfully long, the air thick with storm-churned dust and tension.

Tom's entire body tensed.

His breath came hard and fast, his wild gaze

darting between me and Derek. Trapped. Cornered.

The gun twitched in his grasp—just a second. Just enough to make my heart stop.

I sucked in a sharp breath, every muscle locking. *Would he shoot? Would Derek?*

The rain hammered the roof. The horses snorted and stomped, restless and afraid.

Then…

Tom's shoulders sagged.

His grip slackened.

His eyes met mine for the briefest moment. Something shattered behind them.

And then—he let the gun slip from his fingers.

The dull thud of it hitting the dirt rang louder than the storm outside.

Derek moved fast, lunging forward and knocking Tom to the ground, knee digging into his back. The sharp, metallic click of handcuffs snapped through the stable.

"Thomas Sawyer," Derek said, his voice as unyielding as steel, "you are under arrest for the murder of Noreen Cox and Manny Denis."

Tom didn't fight.

Didn't say a word.

Didn't even look at me.

I exhaled sharply, but my breath barely made it out. It was over.

Or at least, it should have been.

"WHAT IN GOD'S NAME IS GOING ON HERE?!"

The bellow shattered the moment like a brick

through a window.

I turned just as Orson barreled into the stable, his expensive loafers kicking up damp hay, his face a storm of disbelief and rage.

His eyes landed on Tom, then the cuffs, then the gun lying abandoned in the dirt.

His face went pale.

"What…" His voice faltered. "What the hell is this?"

I took a shaky breath, still feeling like I might crumple to the ground. "Tom killed Noreen. And Manny. And I suspect Sera was next on the list."

Orson's stunned silence didn't last long. His shock turned to fury.

"My Sera?" He took a step forward, all fire and anger, pointing a shaking finger at Tom. "Is this true?"

Tom finally looked up.

His expression didn't shift. No remorse. No apology. Just the same hard, unreadable mask.

He didn't answer.

Didn't need to.

Orson inhaled sharply, raking a shaky hand through his hair. "Jesus Christ."

The storm growled overhead, wind howling through the open doors.

A sharp, high-pitched buzz cut through the moment.

Orson's phone.

His hand shook as he pulled it from his pocket. He glanced at the screen — then froze.

His jaw locked.

Something was wrong.

"Sera's gone," he bit out.

My stomach dropped. "What?"

Orson's grip tightened around the phone, his knuckles bone white. "Took the jet an hour ago. She's already in the air. On her way back to England, she says."

I wouldn't bet the ranch on that, Orson.

"She knew," I whispered, my voice barely audible over the rain. "She knew this was all going to come crashing down. Orson," I began. "There are a few things we need to talk about."

Derek exhaled sharply, his hand still near his holster. "We'll issue an international alert," he said, voice grim. "But right now, our focus is on the man we've got. Get him out of here."

My gaze flickered back to Tom as the deputies escorted him out.

The man who had unraveled everything.

The man who had almost...

I swallowed hard. My hands wouldn't stop shaking.

"Zoe."

I turned.

Derek stood, soaked from the storm, his dark hair plastered to his forehead.

His jacket dripped rainwater, his badge gleamed under the dim light.

But his eyes?

His eyes were on me.

Something cracked in my chest.

I saw it all over his face.

The way his gaze swept over me, checking for injuries, checking if I was breathing, if I was standing.

His throat worked, his jaw tightening. "Are you hurt?"

I opened my mouth.

Nothing came out.

My hands were still trembling.

I didn't even know if I was okay.

But I nodded anyway. "I'm fine."

Liar.

"How—how did you know where I was, or that Tom..."

"You have Addie to thank for that. Thank God that pink hair dye hasn't seeped all the way to brain just yet. She noticed you left that ketchup chip bag at the shop and figured it was something I needed to see ASAP."

Addie. Of course, it was Addie. Leave it to the human firecracker to pick up a thread I'd completely forgotten about. Maybe I'd start calling her The Pink Sherlock.

But maybe not to her face.

Derek continued explaining. "Yeah, she found me in Arthur O'Leary's garage, where he had hidden his *own* flamingos! Turns out he was having a property line dispute with his neighbor and was trying to pin the whole thing on him."

I shook my head. "Mystic."

"Yeah. Mystic." Derek exhaled sharply, stepping closer. For a second—just a second—I thought he was going to pull me into him. Hold me.

Instead, he clenched his fists, like he was physically stopping himself.

"You shouldn't have come here alone," he said, his voice raw.

Something twisted inside me.

"I didn't exactly have time to consult you," I shot back, my voice shakier than I wanted it to be.

Derek's lips pressed together. His shoulders tensed.

Then — something softened.

He let out a breath, shaking his head. "You're impossible, Romano."

A shaky smile tugged at my lips. "Yeah. I know."

"You did good. Even if you scared me half to death pulling a stunt like this."

I smiled faintly. "Just a hound dog with a couple of fleas."

We stood there, the weight of everything settling between us.

I knew what he wanted to say.

That I'd scared the hell out of him.

That he wasn't sure if he'd find me alive when he got here.

That this could've gone another way.

I knew — because I wanted to say the same things.

But I couldn't.

Not yet.

Not after everything.

So, instead, I let out a breath, looking past him, toward the flashing red and blue lights outside.

"I think I'm ready to go home now."

Derek hesitated. His fingers twitched — like he was debating saying something else. Then he just nodded.

His voice was quiet.

"Yeah. Let's get you home."

Problem was, home was where the heart was…and I wasn't sure where my heart belonged.

EPILOGUE

The inside of the shop was quiet.

Too quiet.

A quiet that let the weight of reality settle in, thick and unrelenting.

A quiet suddenly interrupted by the abrupt pipe and beat of the 5th Connecticut Regiment Drum Corps. The Fourth of July events were warming up all over town, distracting Mystic residents from the scandal and disaster of recent happenings.

I wish they could distract me.

I tapped my pen against the FINAL NOTICE bill spread out on the counter, staring at the total like I could will the numbers to change. They didn't. They just sat there, smug and unwavering, a stark reminder that my little dream of keeping Read Between the Vines afloat was still a very real struggle.

I scribbled some numbers into my notebook. Crossed them out. Tried again. Still didn't add up.

Time to start Googling "How to Live Comfortably in a Cardboard Box."

The bell above the door jingled, and I hastily flipped the bill over as Orson Tobit strode in, the scent of leather and wealth trailing after him. His broad shoulders were slightly slouched, and in one hand, he clutched a checkbook.

That… was unexpected.

"Orson," I greeted warily, straightening. "What brings you here?"

Without preamble, he pulled a pen from his pocket and scribbled something on the check before tearing it out and setting it on the counter.

"For the champagne," he said simply. "It's the least I can do."

I blinked.

How many zeroes was that?

"Thank you?"

Orson let out a slow breath, his gaze flickering to the shelves. "And maybe a little extra for what you did. Exposing the truth."

I tilted my head. "You're surprisingly gracious for someone whose life I just turned upside down."

A dry chuckle. "You made me face some hard truths. Like how much I let myself be blinded by… hope, I guess. I was so wound up in the idea of wanting a family, of leaving a legacy, I let myself be blind to what was right in front of me." He cleared his throat. "I, um, went to see Tom."

I stilled. "Tom?"

"At the jail." He nodded. "Figured someone ought to talk to him. He's got a lot of demons, but he's not beyond redemption. I told him when he gets out, I'll help him find work. Maybe at the ranch."

I studied him, my skepticism softening. "You're a

better man than most, Orson."

He shrugged. "Maybe. Or maybe I just know what it's like to lose everything and still need a second chance."

For once, I didn't have a snarky reply.

Just like that, Orson Tobit—high-society horse mogul, champagne enthusiast, and former fiancé of a scam artist—walked out of my store, leaving me to wonder if I'd just witnessed actual character growth.

Maybe there is hope for my love life after all.

Stranger things had happened.

"Say, Zoe," Dot began. "I'm thinking I like the cheddar better." At least, I *think* that's what she said through the mouthful of Manchego that was supposed to be for tomorrow's book club.

"Dot!" I groaned as she downed the glass of Riesling she'd helped herself to as well.

The bell jingled again, and before I could so much as breathe, Bernie strode in with a bouquet of daisies in one hand and a Dot-approved box of chocolates in the other.

Addie snickered. "Don't look now, Dot, but your boyfriend's here."

Dot barely looked up from her crossword, but I caught the faintest tinge of pink dusting her cheeks.

"Boyfriend?" she huffed. "What in heaven's name are you talking about?"

Bernie grinned. "I'm here to seal the deal."

Oh. Right.

My arrangement with Bernie.

Oops.

Dot finally looked up, eyes narrowing behind her spectacles. "Bernie, what on earth do you think you're doing?"

Bernie's grin faltered. "Didn't Zoe tell you?"

I slunk toward the shelves like I could somehow disappear.

Dot zeroed in on me like a hawk spotting a very guilty, very doomed field mouse.

The daughter you never had — remember, Dot?

Not to be dissuaded, Bernie pressed on, thrusting the bouquet forward. "Let me take you out. Dinner, starlight, the works."

Dot crossed her arms. "Hmm. You'll have to earn it."

She adjusted her glasses and squinted at one of the crossword clues as her personal fan ruffled her curls. "Five letters. A soothsayer or fortune-teller. Starts with 'A.'"

Bernie scratched his chin. "Augur."

Dot raised an eyebrow. "How'd you know that?"

Bernie shrugged. "A man's gotta know things to impress a lady like you."

Dot sniffed, tucking her crossword under her arm. "Fine. One dinner. But don't think this means you've won."

Bernie grinned, offering her his arm. "Oh, I never think I've won, Dot. I just know how to play the long game."

As they strolled toward the door, Addie popped a bubble with a smirk. "Poor guy," she murmured. "He doesn't know what's about to hit him."

Dot paused in the doorway, then glanced back at me. "Thanks for nothing, Zoe."

The door swung shut behind them.

I grinned.

"Beeteedubs... I think I have a line on a new apartment," Addie announced, slinging her bag over her shoulder. "Gonna go check it out. It's a yurt!"

I nearly spewed my coffee across the shop. "Good luck."

And then she was gone, leaving the shop quiet again.

I leaned against the counter, taking in the familiar scent of old books, ink, and just a hint of vanilla from the candle still burning near the register.

Orson's unexpected compassion.

Bernie's charming persistence.

Tom's final, shattered look before they took him away.

It all settled over me in a way that felt both heavy and strangely light.

I thought about Derek.

The way his eyes searched me in the stable. The way his voice shook when he asked if I was hurt.

He had held back, but I had felt it.

I sighed.

Maybe not all mysteries were meant to be solved at once.

Maybe some things—like old wounds, unanswered questions, and the confusing mess of feelings I wasn't ready to unpack—needed time.

A small smile tugged at my lips.

The shop door creaked slightly as the wind rattled against it.

I glanced toward it absently — just as my phone buzzed.

I picked up my phone.

One new text.

DEREK: Body in bridge. On scene. Your kinda weird.

My breath hitched.

I reread it. Twice.

My fingers tightened around the phone.

A body?

My gaze flicked toward the shop door.

A chill — one that had nothing to do with Dot's fan blowing in my face — rippled down my spine.

The same familiar, nagging pull stirred in my gut.

The thing that had always led me to places I probably shouldn't go.

I set the phone down with a decisive click.

I didn't need to be an augur to know that my inner hound dog...

...he was about to howl.

READY TO UNCORK MORE MYSTERY & MAYHEM WITH MAISIE?

Get a sneak peek at The Body in the Bascule: A Read Between the Vines Mystery from Maisie Franklin!

Fireworks, Founding Fathers, and a body in the bridge. Welcome to Mystic, Connecticut. Population: Quirky. Murder count: Rising.

Zoe Romano thought running a bookshop-slash-wine-bar would be a quieter life after retiring her press badge — until Mystic's 4th of July weekend explodes with more than just fireworks.

The town's historic reenactment is Mystic's pride and joy. Cobblestone parades, powdered wigs, cannon fire, and men arguing over whose breeches are more "historically accurate." But this year, the festivities screech to a halt when the town's beloved (and obnoxiously theatrical) Benjamin Franklin impersonator winds up very, very dead — electrocuted on the iconic bascule bridge.

With a cryptic note in his waistcoat, a suspiciously pristine pair of bifocals, and a cast of rival reenactors with more drama than the Continental Congress, Zoe's once again thrust into the role of reluctant sleuth. Her partners in crime? Dot Richards, a seventy-something matchmaker with a penchant for gossip and puzzles, and

Addie, the pink-haired, over-caffeinated stock clerk who's convinced the killer is part of an underground Revolutionary cosplay cult.

As Chief Derek Cody works the official angle (and keeps giving Zoe *those* eyes), Zoe uncovers town secrets buried deeper than a time capsule—and realizes someone would kill to protect them.

Mystic's history is steeped in blood, wine, and secrets. And someone's rewriting it—one murder at a time.

Turn the page to read Chapter One!

THE BODY IN THE BASCULE

A Read Between the Vines Mystery

If there's one thing that ruins a perfectly good Riesling pairing, it's a corpse stuck in the bascule bridge.

I was still recovering from Dot hijacking the Manchego, Bernie hijacking Dot, and Addie's yurt ambitions when my phone buzzed. Not a wine order. Not Myrna reporting the sudden influx of Hessian garden gnomes in Arthur O'Leary's yard.

A text.

DEREK: Body in bridge. On scene. Your kinda weird.

Eight words. Zero fluff. Just enough concern — and just enough Cody — to make my stomach do a somersault. And not just because of the "body in bridge" part.

I didn't answer. I was already out the door.

*****

Mystic's Main Street was halfway to a Hallmark card that had been dropped in the saltwater and wrung out to dry. Cobblestones glistened from last night's storm, and the scent of brine and fresh bread from the corner bakery tangled with the distant hum of boat engines and seagulls with superiority complexes. Flower baskets drooped from every lamppost. The awning at Read Between the Vines fluttered like a gossiping skirt.

And just beyond, the bascule bridge rose like a steel spine above the river — normally charming, currently swarmed with cruisers, patrol cars, and one very unfortunate set of twinkling red-white-and-blue lights still blinking in grim celebration.

The first thing I saw was the crowd.

The second was the shoes.

They were colonial. Buckled. One was dangling from the steel joint like some kind of Revolutionary Roadkill.

Chief Derek Cody spotted me as I ducked under the crime scene tape. He didn't look surprised. "You made good time," he said.

"You texted me there was a body," I replied. "You didn't expect me to sit there and debate cheese pairings?"

"I was hoping," he said, "but not expecting."

His lips twitched at the corner. Just a flicker. Just for me.

I stepped up beside him. And there he was.

The man — or rather, the costume — was unmistakable.

Powdered wig, round spectacles, ruffled cravat, and what had to be the world's sweatiest woolen coat in July. If Ben Franklin had come back from the dead to haunt Mystic's Fourth of July celebration, he'd found the worst possible entrance.

"Please tell me this is some kind of bizarre, themed protest," I muttered.

"Nope," Derek said. "Real guy. Local reenactor. Name's Eugene Runcible. Lived off Pearl Street. Part of the Historical Society. Did the 'Ben Franklin Speaks' segments every year down at the park."

"Right," I said. "He's the one who did the kite demo with the key."

"Yeah," Derek said, "which makes the next part feel like irony punched us all in the face."

I followed his gaze. The man's wig was singed. His hands were blackened. The fingers on his right hand were still curled around something melted — part of a wire, maybe?

A string of red, white, and blue lights draped across the girder, where the reenactor had clearly tried to do some last-minute rigging.

"Electrocuted?" I asked.

"That's what it looks like."

"By patriotic string lights."

"Death by decorative exuberance," Derek said. "Only in Mystic."

People were starting to gather — locals craning necks, tourists pointing cell phones, and somewhere in the mix, I caught sight of Bernie Russo's telltale tweed coat flapping as he bustled toward the scene, his forensic kit swinging like a picnic basket.

Hm. I wonder how Dot's gonna feel about this first date.

I turned back to Derek. "Was he... well-liked?"

Derek blew out a breath. "Depends on who you ask."

"Anyone not thrilled to see him meet his end via holiday decor?"

"Plenty," he said. "Runcible had opinions. Loud ones. He'd petitioned the town council to ban LED lighting because it wasn't historically accurate. Called Archibald Crane a 'traitor' for using polyester thread to sew his buttons on his costume. Got kicked out of the Mystic River Chorale for trying to rewrite the Star-Spangled Banner in 18th-century meter."

"So… no shortage of people who might've wanted him out of the picture."

"That's putting it mildly."

I raised an eyebrow. "Any suspects?"

He checked his watch and gave me a dramatic look. "It's been twenty minutes."

"Just checking," I said, because that's what I do. Not officially. Not anymore. But some habits—and instincts—are harder to kill than a man in a wool coat on a steel bridge in July.

The sun broke through the clouds, and it hit the singed edge of Runcible's wig just so, casting a shadow on the riveted metal below.

Somewhere behind me, a kid asked his mom, "Is that the real Ben Franklin?"

I turned and started walking, Derek at my side.

"You did that piece for the Times on these die-hard reenactors, so I thought maybe you could give me some insight, but other than that promise me you're not getting involved," he said.

"Me? Absolutely not."

He gave me a sidelong look.

"I mean, unless someone asks."

He didn't answer. Just let out that low sigh I'd already come to know was code for this is going to be a problem. But he didn't stop me either.

And in Mystic, that practically counts as permission.

The Body in the Bascule: A Read Between the Vines Mystery

Coming June 15th
2025

Murder, mayhem, and Merlot guaranteed.

Want a front-row seat when the preorder drops (and maybe a few secrets Zoe hasn't shared with the Mystic gossip mill)?

Join the **Wine & Crime Club** — the VIP newsletter for Maisie Franklin's cozy mystery fans.

Scan the QR code to join now!

Or sign-up at
https://bit.ly/maisiefranklinauthor

ACKNOWLEDGEMENTS

Writing a mystery is a bit like untangling a necklace in the dark—you need patience, clever fingers, and the occasional flashlight from a good friend.

First and foremost, thank you to my readers. Whether you've been with me since page one or just wandered into *Read Between the Vines* for a glass of wine and a good story, I'm so glad you're here. Your support keeps the pages turning and the red flowing (red wine, that is— hopefully not the other kind).

To the real-life inspirations behind Zoe, Dot, and Addie—thank you for being smart, funny, fearless women who remind me every day that friendship is the best kind of mystery to solve.

And finally, to every indie bookstore and cozy corner wine bar I've ever wandered into: you planted the seed for *Read Between the Vines*. Here's to stories, sips, and second chances.

With all my appreciation,

ENJOYED THE MYSTERY?

If Zoe, Dot, and Addie kept you guessing—or snorting your Syrah—I'd be tickled grape-purple if you'd leave a quick review. Just a few words helps fellow cozy readers discover *The Augur's Assassin*—and keepss the corks popping for the next case!

You can leave your review on Amazon, Goodreads, BookBub, or wherever you love to talk about books. Every review means the world—and maybe even a refill.

Let's Keep in Touch!

Follow me for book updates, bonus content, and the occasional wine-soaked ramble:

Newsletter: https://bit.ly/maisiefranklinauthor
Instagram: @maisiefranklinauthor
Facebook: @maisiefranklinauthor
Website: www.maisiefranklinauthor.com

Grab a glass and come hang out—I'd love to hear what you're reading next!

ABOUT THE AUTHOR

Maisie Franklin believes life's best mysteries are solved with wit, wine, and just the right splash of snark. A firm believer that trouble pairs best with a full-bodied red, she's made it her mission to bring readers twisty plots, quirky sleuths, and the kind of small-town scandals that make gossip the town's second-favorite pastime (after murder, of course).

When she's not writing fast-paced, laugh-out-loud cozies, Maisie can be found outsmarting crossword puzzles, getting emotionally invested in British baking competitions, or insisting that "just one more chapter" is a valid excuse for staying up way too late. She's a lifelong mystery buff, an unapologetic pun enthusiast, and the kind of friend who would absolutely help you plot the perfect alibi (strictly hypothetically, of course).

Pour yourself a glass, grab a comfy chair, and dive in — because Maisie's got a case to crack, a few suspects to interrogate, and at least one exasperated detective to charm along the way.

www.ingramcontent.com/pod-product-compliance
Lightning Source LLC
Chambersburg PA
CBHW032157190626
46814CB00005BA/2001